Samantha Little is an Australian Criminal and Family Lawyer with her own law practice run by her and her partner, criminal lawyer Dane Keenes. She has a bachelor's in law, a diploma of legal practice and a background in psychological science.

After publishing her first non-fiction novel about mental health in September 2015, she received a glowing review by the 24th Annual *Writer's Digest* Self-Published Book Awards, and given an award for runner-up Young Victorian of the Year in 2016 and 2017 for her work in the mental health sphere, Samantha turned her attention to helping her clients in the legal field.

Based in the border town of Albury/Wodonga, on an afternoon when the sun is just starting to set, Samantha can be found typing furiously on her keyboard, enamoured by the next town and characters that she is carefully creating. *The Cure* marks her debut into the wonderful world of fiction publishing, with no doubt many more novels to come.

To all my readers, and to you who opened the cover of this book—to write for you is the greatest gift.

S N Little

THE CURE

To Find It, She Will Have to Lose Herself

AUSTIN MACAULEY PUBLISHERS
LONDON · CAMBRIDGE · NEW YORK · SHARJAH

Copyright © S N Little 2025

The right of S N Little to be identified as author of this work has been asserted by the author in accordance with sections 77 and 78 of the Copyright, Designs and Patents Act 1988.

All rights reserved. No part of this publication may be reproduced, stored in a retrieval system, or transmitted in any form or by any means, electronic, mechanical, photocopying, recording, or otherwise, without the prior permission of the publishers.

Any person who commits any unauthorised act in relation to this publication may be liable to criminal prosecution and civil claims for damages.

This is a work of fiction. Names, characters, businesses, places, events, locales, and incidents are either the products of the author's imagination or used in a fictitious manner. Any resemblance to actual persons, living or dead, or actual events is purely coincidental.

A CIP catalogue record for this title is available from the British Library.

ISBN 9781035878468 (Paperback)
ISBN 9781035878475 (Hardback)
ISBN 9781035878499 (ePub e-book)
ISBN 9781035878482 (Audiobook)

www.austinmacauley.com

First Published 2025
Austin Macauley Publishers Ltd®
1 Canada Square
Canary Wharf
London
E14 5AA

Thank you to my family—to my father for reading novels to me before I was old enough to read them for myself, to my mother for typing verbatim my words into our old (now obsolete) computer before I was old enough to spell, and to my sister for always being my biggest fan and the first to read anything that I write.

To Austin Macauley Publishers for believing in my work and for taking a chance on me. You allow me to live my dream and for that I will be forever grateful.

Chapter One

I would never forget the acidic taste of my father's blood. It was 4 July 2007, Independence Day—the irony of that haunted me for years. Sounds of death and drowning echoed through the hall. A thick, gargling sound, short ugly rasps of fractured air trying to squeeze through a closed vent. But this was much more sinister than that.

In seconds, I was lunging down the hallway. When I rounded the corner, I was met with a putrid spray of blood and bile. My ankle caught on the lip of Aunt Margaret's urine-stained rug as I lurched backwards, and clawed through the air for something to hold onto.

The hardwood floor slammed into my back, droplets of blood splattered across my cheeks. I tore at my face, feeling the blood smear across it like paint.

We'd said goodnight only minutes before, or had it been an hour? They'd just returned from dinner, their twenty-fifth wedding anniversary, of all days. It felt like only moments before that I'd heard him stack another three logs on the fire, enough to last the night.

"See you in the sunrise," he'd whispered, closing my door behind him. His mask was pulled tight across his face, but the smile reached the corners of his eyes.

Only three months had passed since his return from Africa, and yet, I could barely remember what he looked like without it. What I wouldn't have given to see his smile just one more time, to have fallen into his arms like a child, without any reservation, or fear. Had he felt the same?

He closed my bedroom door behind him, the thick creak a sign of its age, but I didn't mind it that way. Not when the wood still smelt like epoxy and varnish—my father's best attempt at home reno. I clung to that smell in the years after.

He was humming downstairs as I slid between my cotton sheets. The thick blankets hugged every inch of me and the candlelight flickered on my bedside table, dancing and weaving in the air. I marvelled at the beauty of it. After what felt like a minute but could have been hours, I woke to the sound of my mother's screams.

She was clutching my father's hand to her chest as she leaned over him, too close. The mask was like a noose around his neck, leaving his mouth frothing and fully exposed. She was too close to him. She needed to move, quickly.

"Charles," my mother whispered through curtains of tears. But he was as still as stone.

The dull orange lights of the ambulance pulsed faintly against the frozen window. Their presence barely registered. The patter of leaden steps grew louder as paramedics darted up the staircase in full PPE uniform from head to toe. One of them—the taller one—knelt over my father's body. Another ushered us out of the room, shoving a mask into my mother's trembling hands.

She collapsed to her knees in a crumpled mess beside me, her once white shirt now crimson with blood. A marker of death. She'd doomed us both. At that moment, I realised it might be our last.

They covered my father's face with a clear mask until it could have been anyone under the tubes and beeping machines. I wanted desperately to look away, to tear my eyes from the catastrophe unfolding before me.

The paramedics took turns kneeling over my father, pushing their palms into his chest. His bones crunched beneath their weight. My stomach retched and I fought to keep my dinner down.

As the flame in my father's soul flickered to nothing, my heart stopped with it. For forty minutes, the paramedics thundered against his chest until finally, they rolled back on their heels, exhausted.

A salute. A silent apology. A goodbye.

Chapter Two

Some wins are even greater than the lottery. Or maybe, just much less likely to happen. Despite there being over three hundred people in this excruciatingly overheated examination hall, Drew is seated to my front right, and that's a win for me—especially today.

I've been staring at him for the past thirty minutes, drinking in the view of his perfectly manufactured jawline, just far enough away that my pathetic lusting remains undetected, for now.

Boredom drags my attention to my left, where dozens of subtle glances are cast in Drew's direction. As expected, I'm not the only winner today. I grind my teeth, now well on my way to an hour of pitiful hankering, no better than the long batting lashes beside me. A slow breath drags between my lips.

Drew has been the football team's quarterback and captain for three years. With a steady gaze, washboard stomach and golden muscles that roll like soft mountains along his biceps, it's no surprise that the prom-king-turned-college-medical-student holds hearts like confetti in the palm of his hand.

Even I'm not immune to his carnal charm and easy style, but I keep my distance, mostly to avoid the heartbreak that would inevitably befall me if I were to ever lend my heart to someone like that. The repetitive tick of the digital clock face at the far end of the room unnerves me. Only a few minutes of this examination remain.

I look down at the scribble—hours of patient reviews and medical observations smudged in cursive and smeared across the page. To my right is my best friend, Jade. Feeling the weight of my gaze, she lifts her brown eyes to meet mine. I offer her a small smile. Her response is a tight grimace, a sentiment I share completely.

As she folds herself back over the writing booklet, strands of her long sand-coloured hair fall onto the page. Thick lines of light strawberry weave through it like a sunset, a stark contrast to the chocolate brown curtains that rest idly on my own shoulders. The only similarity between us is our long gangly legs and honey brown eyes.

Jade's perfect porcelain skin is flushed and fine, and no match for the fire behind her eyes. She shoots me a *kill me now* glare and continues to dig her pen angrily into the paper. I've had enough, so I slide my pen down gently onto the desk in front of me, careful not to disturb the others.

The oxygen in the room is a thick, stale crust on my tongue. But that's what you get when you mix closed windows, a blaring heater and borrowed air. I tug the black cotton sweater over my arms, tuck my white shirt back into the front of my denim jeans and slip out from behind the desk.

As I manoeuvre my way between the others, Drew and I lock eyes. Unlike the other students, who cast fleeting glances in my direction, when he turns to meet my gaze, he holds it and doesn't let go.

His mouth is set in a crooked half-smile, bordering on a smirk, but his eyes are warm and alive. I suck in a breath, determined to look away, but he's distracting and a little bit disarming.

Staggering good looks aside, unlike me, Drew's popularity is unparalleled—except for maybe by his own ego. He has to be one of the most pig-headed, arrogant, misogynistic people I've ever come across and yet, as he smiles at me, my heart flutters and I find myself smiling back, as giddy as a child. *Pathetic. Truly pathetic.*

Drew knows his way around women almost as well as he does a football field, or so Jade tells me. I presume he has sufficient practice at both on a regular basis. I may have only seen him play a couple of times for the college team, but—I'm loath to admit—the man knows what he's doing. As for his other skill set, sadly, I'll probably never know.

After what feels like a very long time, Drew smiles, winks at me, and then effortlessly shrugs his dark fringe off his forehead before returning to his exam paper. Somehow, by sheer willpower, I collect myself and exit the hall quickly, hoping no one else has noticed the red flower I feel blooming in my cheeks.

On my way down the hall, I pass a couple of straggling night owls who look as exhausted as I feel—students who disappear into the bowels of the library in the afternoon, and seem to crawl back out from it the next morning. Other than that, the hallways are as devoid of life as the blood-red bricks that line it.

It's usually humming with the sound of chattering teeth, the scratching of shoes on the wooden floorboards, the crash of armfuls of textbooks hitting the floor. I don't miss the sight of red eyes and feigned half-smiles. It's much better this way, and I find solace in the comfort of the eerie quiet.

There's a blank space against the brick by the doorway of an empty lecture theatre. The cool surface is a relief from the oven-grade heating slowly baking the insides of the buildings. My cheek moulds to the icy cold, letting the wall absorb my thoughts until everything stills for the first time in hours, and the angst finally begins to dissolve.

The minutes drag on like hours. It's all I can do not to carry my weary legs to the car park and curl up into the cocoon of Jade's passenger seat. If I only I'd remembered to grab her keys.

There's a cork board on the wall adjacent to me and I busy myself with the flyers overlapping each other, competing for attention. I sigh as my eyes wander lazily over each one in order. Ice-hockey, debating, indoor soccer, chess club openings.

Sports don't interest me, they never have. Unlike Jade, as far as I'm concerned, anything that flies through the air is an immediate threat. Birds, balls, it didn't matter; of every innocent bystander present, they all seemed to have a way of finding me.

Judging by the way the air is cutting at my skin, I know the ice-hockey season isn't too far away, which will please Jade at least.

My dishevelled reflection in the trophy cabinet across the hall catches my eye. I brush a few loose strands of brown hair back behind my ears, but it does nothing for my appearance. Tired, that's how I look. Exhausted maybe. Small bags carrying the weight of sleepless nights rest just under my eyes. They almost look hazel in the sleepy artificial light hanging from the ceiling above.

It's not much longer before a stream of students spill out into the hall. My sanctuary of silence is absorbed by a chorus of quiet chatter. I keep an eye out for Jade; her ruby hair should be easy to spot in this crowd of grey.

"Rae!"

Jade loops her arm through mine and pulls me into the stream of bodies flowing towards the car park.

"I'm so glad that's over," she groans. "I wanted to throw myself out of the window when that question about septal myectomy came up. They barely even covered that in class. God, I hope I pass—I can't go through those tutorials again. Pray for me, will you?"

Jade rambles without so much as a single breath until we are almost at the end of the hall. I prefer it this way because it's better than having to talk about myself. "Don't worry," I say, giving her shoulder a squeeze. "I'm sure you did better than you thought."

Jade laughs. "Easy for you to say—you're top of the class."

My cheeks burn, but before I can protest, I feel a warm arm slide across my back and come to rest over my shoulder. Even before the flutter of wings stir in my stomach, and even before the flash of blond hair catches in the corner of my eye, his warm, musky cologne fills my nostrils. Homely and familiar.

"Angus," Jade groans dramatically.

"Hello, Jade," he purrs, a wry smile spreading along his lips.

Angus Stone transferred from Florida, US, almost eighteen months ago. What started as a short northern exchange became another semester, and then another and another until his parents finally gave up and purchased a house here in Brunswick Shire. If I had to guess, I'd say it was the empty house, the all-too-frequent goodbyes that did it for them.

"Ace it, Rae darling?" Angus purrs.

"Doubt it," I mutter, aware of the weight of Angus's biceps still draped over my shoulder like a scarf.

There has never been anything romantic between Angus and me, unless you count the one time during a pharmaceutical tutorial about six months ago when he went to whisper something in my ear and I turned, almost meeting his lips. I shudder at the memory.

I couldn't look at him for about a month after that without my face burning bright red from the base of my neck right up to my hairline. He didn't seem to mind at all, which only made it all the more embarrassing.

We haven't spoken about it since. I knew for sure there could never be anything more between us. Not because my stomach doesn't whirl every time we lock eyes, and not because the purr of his words doesn't send a tender shiver up my spine. It's because he's one of my best friends, and truth be told, if he felt anything for me, he surely would have said something about it by now.

Even so, it's impossible to ignore the way my body seems to fit snugly into the crux of his chest when he drapes his arm around me, or the way his scent hypnotises me, wafting around in my memories even hours after he's gone.

I'm no romantic, and I'm certain I never will be. I've seen heartbreak first-hand, and even had my own broken a few times. It wasn't love, or anything remotely close to that, but it hurt just the same. Besides, I've seen the kind of love that ruined my mother's life. The kind that took more than it gave when my father died—the unhealthy, all-consuming kind that you can't live without, no matter how hard you try. Why would anyone want that? Not when it can be ripped from you in a moment.

"You're just being modest. She's just being modest, isn't she, Jade?" Angus says, and for a terrifying moment, I fear I've said my thoughts aloud.

Jade laughs. "Always."

I want to change the subject. "Anyway, what should we do to celebrate?"

"Well," Angus says, taking a quick step in front of me. I fumble to a stop, just in time to avoid plummeting into him. He grips my arms to steady me. It's only for a moment, but I know I'll still feel the tingling on my skin long after he's let go.

He's devastating from this angle, with blond waves and eyes so blue they could rival the ocean. Like Jade's, Angus's skin was crafted by angels. Imagine the pedigree between them. But they'd never stop bickering long enough to even notice each other—not like that anyway.

Angus's eyes glimmer with amusement. It's enough to make me dizzy.

"What?" I demand.

"I may or may not have invited everyone to my house for celebratory drinks." A smile dances across his lips, almost predatory.

The Stones have a six-bedroom home, almost triple the size of my parents' humble cottage. The property comes with an outdoor entertaining area, and enough space for a small festival. Okay—maybe not that big. But it feels like it compared to the older, more modest homes that line the streets of the Shire. Mr and Mrs Stone often travel for work, which means that Angus has the whole place to himself.

"Everyone?" If Angus has invited the entire cohort, that would mean… "Seventy people?" I gasp.

His mouth sweeps into a wicked grin. "Indeed."

"Your parents are going to kill you." I step around him and continue down the hall towards the exit. Jade falls into step beside me. The heat of trailing eyes is almost unbearable, and if it hadn't been happening for the past eighteen months, anyone might think I had grown a second head. Their thoughts are almost audible as Angus falls into line beside me.

"I can't wait," Jade croons. "Party of the year."

"One can only hope," Angus says. He looks at me, reaching out to touch my arm, but then his brow furrows in thoughtful silence and he's studying my face. "You'll be there, won't you, Rae darling?" He says, a hint of pleading in his heavy eyes.

I'll never grow used to the way his words caress my every muscle, sending burning flames crackling and dancing in my chest. He will never know how my heart aches for him. Is this how it feels to suffer cardiac arrest?

The look of genuine concern marring his cool features intrigues me. In a moment of selfish vanity, I let the angst linger between us and I bathe in the warmth of his attention. His eyes are like broad hands roaming my skin, and it takes me a minute to reorient myself when he finally looks away.

"I'll be there," I answer casually.

His mouth stretches into a grin and his eyes gleam in triumph. "See you at seven," he says, his attention turning to something, or someone, behind us. Giving my arm a squeeze, he walks off, heading along the corridor and back into the bowels of the building towards the examination hall.

As we walk towards the exit, I glance over my right shoulder, just in time to see a row of heads turn in his wake, their gazes trained to follow him like a compass needle homing in on north.

I don't blame them; for months, I've felt and fought his unerring pull. For months, I've buried my feelings. No one is immune to it.

"When the time's right." Jade pinches my shoulder.

I brush her off with a shrug. "I don't know what you're talking about."

"Ugh, whatever," she moans, looping her arm through mine. "Guys are the worst. Besides, we have more important things to think about."

"Like what?"

"Like what you're going to wear tonight."

I groan in protest and spend the rest of the walk from the lecture hall to the courtyard in silence while Jade prattles off a list of clothing items from tank tops to miniskirts. We both know there's not a snowball's chance in hell I'll be stepping so much as a toe into any of them.

The crisp winter air bites at my skin and I slip my black puffer jacket over my shoulders for extra warmth. The grey afternoon sky illuminates the thick coat of white stretching out before us from the tops of the buildings to our left, all the way along the gravel towards the car park.

We tread carefully, hopping over the slick, glistening patches of ice. Plough tracks are barely visible under the surface. Thankfully, there's no snow forecast for tonight, which is rare for a town that spends three quarters of the year under a crisp white blanket.

We stop in front of the yellow-stone clock tower that marks the centre of the campus as Jade forages through her handbag for the car keys. It's only four o'clock, but with the dark purple sky above us, it feels much later.

"You can come to mine to get ready. I've got snacks in the fridge but no juice."

Alcohol, she's talking about alcohol.

"We can stop by the grocery store on the way home and grab some." My breath turns to mist in the freezing air between us.

We continue our walk along the path towards the iron gates that mark the entrance to Brunswick University. Cars are streaming out of the parking lot. Just as I'm about to step forward, a faint crunch sounds underfoot, rustling against my shoes.

My knees groan as I crouch down to find a crumpled poster with a woman's face plastered across the front. It's the same one that's been pasted to every spare surface at the university for the past year, maybe even longer now. She's got short brown hair like mine, finishing just above a navy-blue turtleneck. Her eyes are narrow and a tad cold.

"She was top of her class before she went missing. It happened just before her final exam." Jade sighs. "Such a wasted talent."

"I remember," I say, recalling the wave of unease that swept through the halls in the weeks after her disappearance. The once tranquil Shire was suddenly infused with an air of tension. She had disappeared into thin air, with no trace, and with her, she'd taken the innocence of the town.

Naturally, people had their theories. Some believed that she had run away— that the pressure of medical school had overwhelmed her until she could no longer stand it. For this, I wouldn't blame her. Sometimes, the air feels so much thinner from the top of a dais.

But then it became clear through newspaper articles and television interviews that those closest to her had other ideas, more contemptuous ones, pointing perfectly manicured fingernails towards her rather long line of ex-lovers. I must admit, there were a few shady creatures on the list, but they were all cleared by the police, and eventually, the case went cold.

There's a familiarity in her dark eyes and hardened stare, an intensity that reminds me of my own. I feel a sense of relief in her gaze. If we'd met, who knows, we might have even been friends. Maybe then I'd know what happened to her.

"Her poor family," Jade ponders, peering over my shoulder.

"What do you think happened to her?" I ask.

"Well," she says in hushed tones, "I know someone who knows someone who knows one of the local sheriffs. They think she was kidnapped—or, woman-napped, I guess. But they can't prove it."

"Do they know who?" I gasp.

"Nope. They found some fingerprints on her phone that didn't belong to her, but whoever it is hasn't been in trouble before because there were no matches in their database."

"That's awful," I say, aware of the small groups of people walking by us. In the weeks following the disappearance, Mayor Watson made a public safety announcement mandating that everyone travel in pairs where possible. The hysteria has long died down, but even so, the Shire hasn't been the same since.

A few scowls are cast in my direction before I command myself to stop staring. I loop an arm through Jade's.

"Her name is Rose," I say, studying the name on the paper.

She takes the paper from my hand to inspect it. "Pretty name." She hands it back to me. "Okay, enough doom and gloom for one afternoon—we've got work to do," she announces, taking off across the car park at a steady pace.

I scrunch the soggy poster in my hand, drop the wet ball into the trash can, and dart across the car park to catch up with her. The silver Prado hums to life as I slide into the passenger seat and Jade, reaching for my hand, turns to face me.

"Promise me something?" She says, a concerned look in her eye.

"What?"

"That you'll never leave me, no matter what."

"Of course." I laugh, but it's a stark contrast to the gravity in her voice.

"Good," she says, releasing her grip. All traces of concern melt into the soft fabric of her grey car seats.

The tyres crunch on the gravel and ice beneath us as we pull out of the car park and onto the quiet main street.

Pockets of colour seep through the soft mantle of snow coating the storefronts that line the street ahead of us—one straight road of about a fifth of a mile lined with pines that match the forest landscape surrounding it, in stark contrast to the rustic pale pink of the trinket store, and the rich yellow ochre of the supermarket.

Smoke billows from the roof of the bakery to our right and a small cluster of people warm their hands by the barrel of open flames on the sidewalk, waiting for their hot cup of coffee.

I roll down the window. Quiet residential roads branch off from the main drag as we pass, the only sign of their inhabitants being the gentle notes of wind chimes and the tendrils of wood fire smoke that weave through the air.

Unlike the major cities encircling our Shire, you won't find Ralph's or Dunkin's here. No, here each shop or cafe is named after its owner, and has been for the past twenty-five years—or at least for as long as I can remember.

Past Mack and Finemores clothing boutique and Molly's Bargain Hunters, towards the end of the main street, a dense canopy of trees seems to swallow the eastern part of the town. Beyond it are the towering white-tipped pine trees and lush undergrowth of Brunswick Shire Forest. To the west of the town, the glassy, frozen Moorobin Lake.

"We can get some mixers from the general store. I think it will still be open," Jade says.

We pull into the parking bay and are meandering down the charming street, marvelling at the smell of freshly baked bread, when I'm suddenly hit with a feeling of unease. And just as I'm about to push through the heavy-set glass entrance of the general store, something tugs my attention back to the alleyway between Chris's Antiques and Dave's pie shop.

It's only for a brief moment, but I'm almost certain that the silhouette of a long-cloaked man ducks ominously into the shadows, just as I turn my head. The moment we step inside the store, the subtle sweet scent of baked bread melts me from the inside, and I forget all about the unease in my stomach.

Jade collects a six pack of pink Seltzer, a bottle of Grey Goose and some wine. I take a bottle of Pimms and a bagful of lemons. On my way through the register, I pluck a loaf of bread from the shelf and add it to the basket. For my mother, I tell myself as my stomach groans like the inside of an empty barrel.

***

"I'll be quick, keep the car running." I climb out of the passenger seat and onto my snow-covered driveway.

"Take your time," Jade says, reclining her seat and turning the radio up.

Inside, my mother is sitting in the old lounger with a blanket wrapped around her, sound asleep. Not even the groan of our front door induces so much as a stir from her.

The room is shrouded in darkness, and immediately, I'm met with a rush of cold air. I look up to find the kitchen windows swaying on their rusty hinges, almost as if they're welcoming the cold inside.

"Jesus, Momma," I curse, running over to catch the shutters. Snow particles rest delicately on the kitchen sink, unmoving.

I have clearly startled her because she wakes in a hurry, muttering—cursing probably—in Fijian, words that I can't understand.

"What time is it?" She asks in English through a yawn, after receiving no response to her mother tongue.

"It's five-thirty," I say, flicking on the light—I can barely see my hand in front of my face. The warm glow illuminates the lounge room and the kitchen, and my eyes take a moment to adjust.

Our home is average in every way a house can be. It's the standard height and size, a two-storey, three-bedroom home with a kitchen that runs seamlessly into the lounge room. The carpet in the bedrooms is old and worn, the wooden floorboards creak a little too loudly, and the drapes carry a pattern that society hasn't seen—or had to endure—since the sixties. It isn't much, but it's home and always has been.

I hold a glass of water in my right hand and two aspirins in my left.

My mother studies me carefully. "You're a life saver," she says.

She leans back, letting the two aspirin and water fall down her throat in one well-rehearsed gulp. She yawns again, slowly sitting up in her chair. "What's for dinner?" I can almost hear her bones creak like the frame of an old wooden house.

My mother is fifty-two years old, but she looks older, acts older. Six years ago, my father's death took many things from us. Sometimes, I wonder if I lost both of them that night.

Not long after the funeral, my mother started to take sick days. When those ran out, she took annual leave. Over time, she would spend more days at home than in the eye clinic, until one day, she just refused to leave the house at all.

I remember because we ate beans on toast for two months straight. Thankfully, we had enough grief lasagne to last us. That was until I worked up the courage to walk the four miles into town to buy us some groceries. But my mother didn't notice when I barged through the front door with four bags in hand and sweat pouring off my face. She didn't even look up.

There's a mountain of dishes piled high in the sink and a horde of dirty plates sitting on the rim of a used coffee mug—a delicate balancing act. It would only take a breath to topple the stack. I make a mental note to clean them when I get home.

"Momma, I told you I'm going out tonight. You said you would organise your own dinner, remember?"

"Mm hmm," she says, rolling over in her chair.

I turn back towards the lounge room, but she has already drifted off to sleep—into the familiar embrace of unconsciousness. A small white bottle perched on the coffee table catches my eye. Probably Lorazepam, my mother's preferred choice of sleeping pill.

She hasn't slept without it for years. The bottle is open, and I can tell by the way the light hits it that it's almost empty. I pray that this bottle will be the last, although I know better than to wish for hopeless things.

The frozen chicken korma is icy against my hands, so I quickly shove it into the microwave, setting the timer for fifteen minutes—it will surely be loud enough to wake my mother long after I'm gone.

I race upstairs to grab my denim jeans and a black strapless top to match. I choose a pair of short heels carefully, the most comfortable ones that I own and the only ones I can confidently walk in. Within five minutes, I'm back in the car with Jade, and we're watching the lights of my house dull to a faint glow in the rear-vision mirror.

"Ready?" She asks.

I think of the pile of dishes stacked like Jenga in our kitchen sink. I think of my mother and wonder whether she will eat tonight. There are parities between my mother and those dishes in the sink. Both seem to be made of porcelain, and at times, it feels like one wrong move, one slip-up, and the whole delicate castle might come crashing down, shattering into a million serrated pieces. For years, I know I'll cut my hands trying to pick up the pieces.

"Ready," I say, not really sure if I'll ever be.

Chapter Three

About seven years ago, I had the experience of eating a curry pizza at an Asian fusion restaurant with my father. It was like forcing two positive poles together; no matter how persistent you were, by virtue of their very nature, it just didn't work.

That's how I felt taking a careful step into Angus' world for the first time. As if his life and mine were just two incompatible forces. It was early in our friendship, about a month after we met, that he invited me into his home. Of course, it took a few months of encouragement and a little coercion before I finally agreed.

Knocking on the grand oak double doors for the first time, I felt like an ant standing in the shadow of this mansion. Stepping inside, it was like walking into a citadel. The walls could have swallowed me whole, and no one would have even noticed. I remember looking down at my stained white sneakers, ripped denim jeans and sweatshirt. I felt like an apple growing on a lemon tree.

The feeling smouldered away over time once I met Mr and Mrs Stone. Creatures of such wealth, I expected them to be entitled, arrogant even. To look down their long noses at me, disdain in their eyes. I should have known better than to prejudge the people that gave life to Angus. Moulded him. Angus, the most humble, generous and kind person that I know.

Somehow, the Stones and I bonded over roast beef and potatoes. They asked me about my family, and their eyes welled as I spoke about my father. I told them about my studies, and they gave me a montage of Angus' most embarrassing childhood moments. Angus laughed awkwardly through most of the stories, his mouth arched into a grimace at each word. I loved every second of it.

I became a regular addition to the Stone household, but only just long enough for the sun to set. I didn't like to leave my mother home alone for too long; it was too much to expect her to fend for herself. The Stones seemed to understand without any need for an explanation, their knowing smiles saying what their words couldn't. Each night, they sent me off with a bag of leftovers and a 'see you soon'.

Angus would walk me to the door, pulling me into an embrace that had me thinking twice about leaving. He never pressured me to stay, though, a fact I was grateful for. It was one of the things I liked most about him.

***

We shut the door behind us with a thud, and thank Jade's neighbour, Harry, for dropping us off. Jade stumbles beside me in her oversized heels as we walk up the footpath towards the front of Angus's home. Jade clings to my arm for support.

I save her a couple of times from plummeting into the hedges that line the footpath from the street to the front door. She's balancing a bottle of wine in her other hand, and I'm amazed that it arrives in one piece.

"My feet hurt already," she whines.

"I told you they were too high." I laugh.

She pokes me in the rib, nearly sending both of us into the snow.

"You can take them off once we get inside," I suggest.

Angus answers the doorbell a little too quickly. Was he waiting by the door? We're late—but that's not unusual where Jade is concerned. This time, I blame her four outfit changes. Over Angus's shoulder, the house is already teeming with people meandering about, drinks in hand, probably gawking at the grandness of it all. I can't help but feel a little jealous.

Angus's house is two storeys high, with rich brown timber flooring, perfectly white walls and marble everywhere.

"Hello, ladies." Angus grins. He looks at Jade. "Is that for me?" He asks. He's referring to the bottle of wine clutched close to Jade's chest. She's gripping the neck so tight I can almost hear it struggling to breathe beneath her fingers.

"My mother always says never come empty-handed," she mutters, prying the bottle from her own hands and shoving it against his chest.

"And here I thought you were raised by wolves," Angus teases.

"Whoever said I wasn't," she snaps back, wincing at her blistering feet. "Okay, that's it, I'm taking them off," she says, pulling the shoes from her feet. She sighs. "Ah, relief."

"You can leave them in my room," Angus says.

"Where?" Jade starts.

"Upstairs," Angus and I sing in chorus.

I feel my cheeks burn red, and I keep my eyes low, to the floor.

"Third door on the left," Angus adds with a smirk for good measure. Bless him.

Jade murmurs something under her breath, a sly grin sliding across her face. She gives us both a wink as she trots up the stairs.

"You, come with me," he orders, slinging an arm around my waist, pulling me further into the crowd of people now swarming the living room. "There's someone here who wants to meet you."

Angus marches me along the hallway, past the kitchen and dining area. He has put away all the valuable ornaments and vases and pushed the dining table towards the edge of the room, replacing it with a games table that I don't recognise.

"Got it online this afternoon," he announces as if he can read my mind. "I couldn't say no, it was an absolute steal."

I swallow hard. The only place that you would find a table like that in Brunswick Shire is at the travelling market that breezes through town every couple of months. If he really did find it there, it probably was a steal—the illegal kind.

He rushes me out towards the rear patio, where people are huddled in groups, mingling and drinking from red plastic cups. The waft of craft beer carries in the air towards us.

We should be half-frozen by now, being outside at this time of year, but the pockets of warm air radiating from the glowing bonfire in the centre of the yard keep me warm. There are a few people dancing, girls and boys, their bodies intertwined, swaying in time with the music, possessed by the rhythm and probably whatever substance they had taken before they got here.

Thousands of fairy lights are strung up in lines above us. They almost look like stars. "Wow," I say, stopping to gaze up at them twinkling against the dark sky.

"Cool, isn't it?" Angus says. I can still feel his arm behind me like a warm blanket. We have stopped walking, but he leaves his hand resting against the small of my back. Our breath billows from our lungs, white against the black canvas above us.

I barely notice that it's freezing out here because the only thought that blooms in my mind is how time seems to have slowed, and the music softened to a dull hum. The chattering of the guests quietens to a whisper. Angus' body is so close to mine that I can almost feel his heartbeat. I wish that the winter would freeze this moment forever, so that we can stay underneath these twinkling make-believe stars for eternity.

I'm thankful for the biting night air to remind me that I'm alive, and that this is not just another dream. Angus heaves me out of my trance and steers me down a set of stairs, past some people I barely recognise, towards a man I don't know.

"Alister," he shouts.

The man turns away from a small group of women clustered around him, his attention darting between Angus and me as we approach the cabana where they are standing.

The man's attention turns to me the moment Angus says my name. A heat washes over me, and I'm suffocating under his perfect stare, both intense and mesmerising.

"Finally," he says, taking a thin, long-fingered hand out of his pocket and holding it out to me. I take the offer, and as I do, my eyes are drawn to the wedding band sitting delicately on his finger. There's no hint of discoloration where the metal and skin meet. Newly married, I suppose.

You can tell a lot about a person from their hands. The eyes may be the window to the soul, but the hands—at least I believe, anyway—are for opening the doors.

"Nice to meet you." I smile awkwardly because that's what I do when I'm nervous.

Angus, maybe sensing my discomfort, begins to talk about an upcoming golf tournament. Blessing or not, I take the moment to reorient myself.

The man is about the same height as Angus, maybe a little taller, which means he's just over six foot two. A few strands of black hair escape their slicked hold and fall in front of his star-speckled eyes. He takes his long fingers and swipes the strands behind his ear in one graceful motion.

They're just long enough to tuck neatly in line. His gothic features visible once again, those amber-green eyes peer down at me from the darkness of his deep-set sockets.

My guess is early thirties because his hands are clean and not at all worn like my father's were. He is incredibly handsome, but that isn't the only reason I find myself staring. There is something about him that I can't place, an intensity that is both alluring and a tad off-putting.

A light pressure forms on the small of my back. Angus. The feel of him is ingrained into my memory. He has thick wrists and broad hands that could crush a larynx without any effort at all. And yet, they're soft, gentle. Perfect, just like every other part of him.

Maybe I've been caught up in my own thoughts for a moment too long, because at some point, the conversation has returned to me, and I have no idea what I'm supposed to say now. Angus and the man exchange a concerned glance at my expense.

"Rae, darling, Alister was just asking how your studies are going this year. I told him that you're the top of our class."

My cheeks burn.

"You should be extremely proud of yourself—there are some very bright students to choose from this year," the man adds.

"Thank you," I fumble gracelessly.

"Alister is a professor at the university," Angus says, "the youngest in the state's history to be given the position."

I take a sip from a red cup sitting on the table to my right, swallowing its contents without a second thought, grateful to find that it's just water, and not tequila as I had feared. With my dry throat no longer hoarse, and the professor staring at me expectantly with his deep, emerald eyes, I wonder if maybe my courage would have been better assisted by the latter.

"What do you teach?" I ask, understanding now the cluster of women that had gathered around him only moments before. They seem to have sauntered somewhere back into the darkness after we arrived.

"Angus is overselling me, as usual. I teach anatomy and physiology on a relief basis mostly, but I dabble in pathology as well."

"How old are you?" I blurt before I can stop myself.

The professor only grimaces and shifts his weight from his right to his left foot. In the corner of my eye, Angus does not bother to hide his amusement, his mouth pulled into a sly grin, a daring fire burning behind his eyes.

"Thirty-one," the professor says, taking a sip from his own cup.

Looking at him now, the mixture of lightness in his eyes and the shadow of a beard trekking across his jawline gives him away. Six years our senior and yet, his youthful appearance is accentuated by his dark features and black clothing.

"What are your plans post-study?" He asks.

"Medical research." I use the cup as a barrier between us. I just want this feeble small talk to end.

His eyes flicker with intrigue. "In a laboratory?" He asks. He puts his drink down on the table beside him, leans back, and crosses his arms. "Well, that really is a stroke of luck, isn't it?" He mumbles quietly. "I'm running an extracurricular medical research group, working to find a cure for a particular strain of *Mycobacterium pneuculosis*."

My throat tightens. "You're trying to cure a fatal lung disease that originated twenty thousand years ago? Respectfully, I think you're fighting a losing battle," I say rather abruptly. As if my words have loosened the thread of my patience, my hands clench into fists, the red cup folding between them.

Angus's hand is at my back before I can even register him moving. I place my cup on the table beside us. "I'm sorry, I have to go and find my friend. It was nice to meet you, Professor," I lie; truthfully, I'm not sure I've ever wanted to meet someone less.

"Likewise," says the professor. He takes a step towards me with an outstretched hand. It looks cold, almost reptilian. I end the handshake a little too prematurely, but he doesn't seem to notice.

Angus mutters something I don't quite hear, and we turn back towards the house, the pounding silence hanging stale in the air between us.

"Are you okay?" He asks.

"Of course." I shrug, but my voice betrays me.

We walk around the corner to find a quiet spot down the side of the house. It's much colder without the warmth of the bonfire, but after sweltering in the heat of the professor's stare, the cold is a welcome relief. We find a wooden bench and I lean my back against the cool bricks. Angus turns to me, but I don't feel like meeting his gaze. Not when my every thought is plastered across my face for him to read, like the headlines of a newspaper.

"I didn't know. He never mentioned the research team to me." Now Angus is avoiding eye contact. His head is bowed, and he kicks at some loose stones on the ground.

"It was a surprise," I admit, ordering the sting of tears to stay put.

"Rae, your dad—"

"Don't," I say, staring at my feet, a slight quiver in my voice.

I turn to face Angus, and I know that he can see my eyes welling now, but I don't care.

He gently takes both of my hands in his. "Would be so proud," he whispers, giving me a gentle smile. "Your dad would be so proud."

There's a small tug on my heart and I lean towards it—towards him. Angus closes his arms around me, tucking me in to him. Pressing my head against his chest, he absorbs me into the crux where his shoulder and neck meet.

Angus's scent overwhelms my senses, consuming my every thought as it drifts through me. Is it teakwood I can smell? Vanilla, maybe. My mind quietens until I can't hear anything except his heartbeat. The world around us seems to dissolve and still, just for a minute.

The feeling is a faint echo in my memory, long before the rug on the floor of my world was pulled out from under me. I was ten years old—much too old for nightmares. I'd cried out for my father as if he could somehow protect me from the monsters in my dreams.

He sat beside me, brushing the drenched strands of hair from my sweat-laden forehead, holding me while I sobbed inconsolably. I can almost see my father's face, so vivid are the wrinkles around his eyes, as if it were yesterday. He looks tired, worried, even now in the soft haze of my memory.

Nine years and two months later, my father returned from a humanitarian mission in Africa. He hadn't been home a week when he suffered what we first thought was a mild asthma attack. My mother immediately drove us to the hospital—as a precaution. They bickered the entire way there.

At the hospital, the doctors ran all kinds of tests. It wasn't until the following day that the floor fell out from beneath us. Six months later, he was dead. There is no cure for the strain of *Mycobacterium pneuculosis* that killed my father, or the chronic emptiness that I feel without him. The nights are the hardest, even now. At times, my mind wanders to the dark corners, the ones doused in shadows and sadness.

Please come back, I whispered into my pillow for months, through screens of tears, feeling every inch of my soul ache. There was nothing that could have been done to save him. There is no cure.

"Thank you," I whisper into Angus's shirt. It's damp where my tears have left a stain.

"Always," he whispers into my hair. I may be imagining it, and it might be a strawberry daiquiri head spin, but I swear his lips brush my forehead in such a way that another girl on a different night might have even called it 'a kiss'.

Chapter Four

My mother drives me to class in the morning with the windows rolled down. Snowflakes kiss my arms as my limbs flail in the wind. I'm wearing a singlet, my jumper tucked around my waist for later on the off chance that my flesh stops burning and my head stops spinning.

I was surprised when my mother offered to drive me today; she hasn't left the house in weeks. This fact alone says more about my hangover than I ever could, not without vomiting anyway.

"Can't you just have the day off?" She says. "You look so unwell."

I groan internally and shove my head out the window for dramatic effect, letting the cold air billow into my face.

"You're going to catch a cold," she warns.

I groan again, this time out loud. "I would rather a million colds than how I feel right now, Momma."

It's only a six-minute drive from my mother's house to the university, but I feel every agonising bump on the bitumen beneath us. The hum of the car reminds me of a boat out at sea, and for what feels like the hundredth time, I want to vomit into my lap.

"Nope," I announce. "I can't do this, take me home. I'm going to hurl." The seat absorbs me, offering a moment of peace while my head thrashes like a buoy in the ocean.

"I know just the thing," Momma says, pulling out of the gravel car park and back onto the bitumen. The yellow-stone buildings of the university blur to a faint shadow in the rear-view mirror as we head down the main street.

The pharmacy sits sterile in the middle of the main drag, a box-like building with a triangular roof. The exterior is a rich dark green colour to match the surrounding pines, and the shutters are a crisp white like the snow. I'm quite sure something similar came out of my stomach on Saturday morning as I retched into Angus' toilet bowl, hurling my dignity and three quarters of a bottle of tequila into it.

The pharmacy opens up like a giant mouth and swallows my mother as she disappears inside. I can just make out her silhouette through the large windows flanking the door. The streets are bare this morning; most of the shops are just yawning awake. We are the only occupants in a long string of empty car bays.

My head has been pulsing since early Saturday morning and I can still taste the sour burn of vodka in my throat. I was shocked—no, horrified—when my alarm went off this morning, and I learnt that it was Monday already.

From what I can remember of Friday night—which to be honest, isn't a great deal—it was a lot of fun. Angus and I talked for about an hour until Jade dragged us to the games table. After that, we spent the rest of the night dancing to rhythm 'n' blues.

Jade and I woke up at midday in Angus' bed, and Angus woke up on the back lawn by the smouldering fire, having used a protruding tree root as a pillow. His lips were near purple when I found him, his hands so cold they were like ice against my skin. I spent the rest of the weekend in his spare bedroom trying to sleep off the pounding headache and whitewash churning in my stomach.

The pharmacy spits my mother back out with a can of coke in one hand and a white grocery bag in the other. She dumps the bag in the back behind us and slides into the driver's seat with a grace I haven't seen from her in years. It would appear that when push comes to shove, not even grief can steal a mother's instincts from her.

"I got you a coke and some aspirin," she says. "If this doesn't get you through your classes, nothing will."

"How do you know?" I groan.

She scoffs. "Pft. You aren't the only one who partied at college. Who do you think invented the handstand keg?"

"No, stop!" I plead, but a smile tugs at the corner of my mouth. "Thank you." I sniff, taking the items stiffly from her hands. She'll never understand how much I still long to be taken care of.

The drive back to campus is mostly silent. We exchange a few comments about the weather, and she suggests some excuses to use for my tardiness. For a second, I'm eight years old in a fit of giggles, plotting my escape from primary school. But the nostalgia is ripped from me like a bandage when I hear the all too familiar clink of wine bottles in the back seat.

The rest of the drive is silent, and I spend it gazing out the window, trying to keep my eyes on the steady white mountains blocking the horizon. The town is picturesque in winter, the kind of subtle elegance that goes unnoticed when you've grown up in a place your whole life.

It wasn't until Angus pointed out the layers of beauty that I started to pay more attention. For three quarters of the year, the town is coated in a thin layer of fairy-tale snow. But it's the summer months that have always been my favourite, with streams flowing from the melting snow and the town basking in the warm glow of the sun.

With February now upon us, the trees that do so have all shed their leaves to be replaced by white branches and the town is engulfed in a never-ending shroud of fog. No doubt Angus would still find beauty in it, so I try to as well—even if it's my least favourite season.

We pull up in the parking lot of the college for the second time this morning. The aspirin is kicking in and my throbbing Travis Barker headache is dwindling to a dull heartbeat.

"Thanks, Momma," I say, giving her hand a squeeze. I crawl out of the car and grab my bag from the back seat. "I'll see you for dinner."

She smiles back at me, and for a moment, I don't recognise her. It's been so long since a genuine smile has passed her lips. Like a yawn, the contagion spreads and a warmth grows inside me. If only I could bottle some to keep forever.

With a sigh, I close the car door and meander down the stone path towards the Peter Hetchener building, one of the five single-storey buildings that make up the campus. The buildings are named after prominent medical professionals who have graduated from the university. I'm not sure exactly what each of them did, only that it contributed a great deal to medical science—or so they say.

The warm air of the classroom meets my skin in a rush, sending goose bumps soaring from my ankles to my wrists. A few classmates closest to the door scowl as I fumble in wearing nothing more than a singlet and jeans while the snow pours in from the open door behind me.

My lecturer—Dr Jean Madden—has her back to the class, writing a formula on the whiteboard. She doesn't notice me, and I quickly take a vacant seat at the back of the room and pull out my workbook. The lesson is about bedside manner and dealing with complex-needs patients. Having already read this chapter, I slump back into my seat, relieved.

Students with drawn faces sit behind their desks, flicking coldly through their textbooks. I don't recognise any of them. Never having been afraid to be alone, I prefer it this way. But it's not long before the boredom creeps in, the only downside to isolation. I sift through the wad of notifications on my phone. Most of them are photos plastered across the news feed. Thankfully, I can't see myself vomiting or passed out in any of them.

Angus' post is captioned 'Warming up'; he's referring to our graduation party at the end of the year. The thought draws out the nausea in my stomach and I will myself to breathe through my nose until the feeling passes.

When my stomach finally settles, I scroll through the photos one by one. The first is an action shot of Angus playing beer pong. His tight white t-shirt clings to sculpted muscles beneath; his blue eyes glimmer with a hint of mischief, and his blond hair is ruffled and ragged as if the photo was of a sixties model. My stomach twists into knots and a rush of heat floods my cheeks.

Everything about him is captivating, and I could stare at his image for hours and never grow tired of it. The second photo is a close-up of Angus and Diesel Wilson, one of Angus' closest friends. Diesel is a local school teacher who transferred interstate with Angus eighteen months ago.

Angus tells me that they attended preschool together, and for the most part that makes sense—they are totally inseparable. A lot like Jade and me, in many ways.

The third photo catches me off guard and I immediately feel a little light-headed. Heat spreads across my cheeks, neck, and ears. Angus' back is to the camera and he is carrying someone draped over his shoulder. It takes me a moment to recognise myself, but there I am, a grin plastered across my face so large that it almost spreads from ear to ear.

I'm laughing as Angus marches me away like a misbehaving child. My breath catches as I strain to locate the memory, wanting desperately to keep it forever. I envy the girl in that photograph, lost in an alcohol-induced bliss and not a care in the world.

When the lecture is over, I slide my notebook back into my bag and dress myself more appropriately for the weather outside. The lesson was a tedious waste of time, but at least I'm feeling better. My stomach growls—a reminder that it's been empty for too long.

As I walk along the eastern wall of the Peter Hetchener building, heading into the epicentre of the university—an outdoor food court—not an overly clever set-up for a place like Brunswick Shire. But the heaters are always running at full pelt, and despite the snow, not every day is cold, so it isn't as bad as it sounds.

The square is surrounded by buildings that house different cafes and stands with takeaway foods like tacos, smoothie bars and Potter's fried chicken. I meander around the edge of the square, keeping as close to the walls as possible to avoid the snowfall.

The queue for Chinese is long, but I join it anyway. Rubbing my arms does nothing against the bitter chill. Four people are waiting impatiently in the line ahead of me, struggling to keep warm. I recognise one of them from my lecture earlier this morning.

She has tight black curls that rise a good two inches above her head, giving her a taller appearance, though it doesn't help her much. Ghost white in her complexion, she would almost blend in with the snow. I don't know her name, and something about the way she scowled as I dashed into class this morning tells me that we may never be friends.

A shiver runs down my spine as I sense something behind me. Not *something*, but someone—tall and substantial. I turn my head slightly. Instantly, I wish I hadn't.

The professor stands out like black on white in the line of people now curling around the corner. He is much taller than I remember, and I have to look up to meet his piercing green eyes. His olive complexion and black outfit stand in stark contrast to the blistering winter behind him.

Again, that hot-cold feeling churns in my stomach—the heat of his gaze and the iciness of his eyes. Short, coarse hair gives him a rugged shadow across his upper lip and jawline. All the way up to where his slick back hair glides neatly behind his ears and tucks back down the nape of his neck.

"Aurelia, isn't it?" He asks.

"Yes, Professor," I say politely.

"How could I forget?" He smiles, and a heat courses through my body.

He is beautiful, handsome and terrifying—the ultimate paradox. I desperately want to run, and yet, I'm drawn to him like a lamb to the slaughter. There's a flower that acts in much the same way. The Rafflesia, I think it was called. It draws in prey through its beauty and scent, a perfectly designed predator.

His eyes home in, relentless, daring, and his features are mind-boggling, all the way from his perfectly symmetrical nose to his chiselled jawline. It makes me uneasy. "Please, call me Alister."

Finding the right words—any of them, actually—is impossible, so I offer a small smile and turn to face the direction of the queue. Despite there being three staff members behind the till, the woman at the front of the line has not been served. I clench my fists at my sides.

"Have you given any more thought to joining our study group?"

We finally take an even step towards the register. Half expecting this and half dreading it, I bite my lip and shake my head, hoping it's enough—hoping he won't attempt to engage with me again.

We wait in agonising silence for another five minutes until I finally collect my rice dish from the register, and we go our separate ways with a tight wave. Still feeling a heat on my back, I again glance over my shoulder.

The professor is standing at the mouth of the library, another small cluster of female students gathered around him. But while they are no doubt singing his praise, his gaze is poised in my direction, watching my every step as I walk out of the food court.

There's another fact about the Rafflesia plant that always fascinated me; after luring and feeding off its host, the flower blooms for five days, releasing a scent that reeks of rotting flesh in order to attract the flies it needs for pollination—a deadly cycle.

Imagine falling into such a trap. *That silly fly*, I think as I stride towards the Glenn Norland building for my second class of the day.

***

Later that afternoon, instead of walking to the car park, I head in the opposite direction to the corner of Shiffling and Plenty Road. From there, I hike the familiar mile and a half of Plenty Road, up the camelback hills of snow-coated Clayton Park until I'm standing at the wrought-iron gates of West Park cemetery, as I have done every Monday for the past six years.

It's late afternoon, and like green umbrellas, the great atlas cedars cast their shadows over the dainty field. The thin air has a crisp fresh sweet scent and I can't help but feel like a trespasser here, as if my father is part of a place where I'll never belong.

I take a deep breath and push my weight against the creaky hinges, wedging myself through the iron gate until there is nothing standing between me and the cemetery. For the most part, the grounds are completely vacant, save for a few people floating up and down the aisles like ghosts, stopping every few headstones to pay their respects.

I trudge down the hill towards the back-left corner of the cemetery. To my right—about twenty feet away—I can see a group of five or so all dressed in black, wailing around a newly erected headstone like a murder of crows floating amongst the white clouds.

My white sneakers sink half an inch as I walk and I wonder how many people must have mourned here, how many tears are stored in this damp, hollow ground. I descend past numerous flower bouquets, dotting the aisles like bright fluorescent fairy lights—a stark contrast to the sea of white and grey.

When I reach aisle 96 B, I turn, counting the headstones until I am standing in front of a light grey slab with the words 'Charles Kingston' carved into its chalky surface. Already, the letters are chipping at the edges, the stone browning.

Six years ago, after his return from an overseas secondment, my father told me about other cultures' mortuary rites, how in some cultures, the bodies of the living were painted tawny, like a sunset-kissed desert. About how smoke was used to drive away the spirit of the deceased, freeing them; about how their bodies were placed on a platform, covered in leaves.

My shoes slide another inch into the soggy soil. What my father didn't explain was what happened to a soul if there was no smoking ceremony, no platform for the body to rest on, no leaves to coat its surface. What happened to a soul that was locked in a wooden box trapped six feet beneath the surface, never to be seen again? Was there another way to free a soul, or did the spirit simply remain trapped there for eternity?

I pull a pink rose from my bag, fondling it in my hand. My favourite, not his—I never even had the chance to ask him. The fresh scent of dew warms me from the inside, pulling from so many angles that it could tear me apart. As the rose falls at the base of the headstone, some petals break loose, like splatters of blood against the white snow.

I think about my father's body underneath all those layers of dirt, entombed under there—quiet, eyes closed. In an endless sleep. He was claustrophobic; do things like that matter in the end?

Snow seeps through my jeans and smacks my skin as I fall to my knees and close my eyes. The memories fall like autumn leaves, a few here and there at first, and then all at once like a cascade of love and heartache.

It's unfathomable that while I'll age, while time will mould my face, while the years will weave creases onto my skin like winding rivers, while smile lines will trek the corners of my mouth, my father is trapped, frozen in time, never changing. I'll never know him as a grandfather. Never gaze at the wrinkles furrowing his forehead and wonder where the time has gone.

But while his body may remain here, he will never belong in this cemetery.

I lean back against the headstone. "I miss you, Papa," I whisper into the silence. Snow falls and melts through my clothes until I'm drenched.

Surrounded—literally—by hundreds of bodies, I've never felt so alone and so excruciatingly alive, two things that right now, I desperately do not want to be.

"Aurelia?" A voice calls.

I must have fallen asleep because it takes a moment to reorient myself to the world. The sun is only just scratching the top of the mountains in the distance and the sky is still eerily grey. I rub my eyes against the burning light.

Shifting myself upright, I brush off the thin layer of dirt that has grown over me in my sleep, and untangle a few pine needles that have lodged in my hair. God, anyone could be forgiven for thinking that I'd grown here with the other flora and fauna of this place. How the hell has anyone managed to spot me here?

I drag my legs underneath my body so that my back is resting against the headstone. Even though my father is literally no more than skin and bone beneath me, I still feel safer in his company.

To my left, along the row of gravestones, a man in all black wearing a ground-length trench coat is walking towards me. He is carrying a bouquet of sunflowers, and I have no idea how he's managed to get his hands on those this time of the year. They're certainly not from around here.

As the stranger nears, I think I recognise the mid-length black hair that glides over his scalp, ending in a flick at the nape of his neck. A wave of unease washes over me. No, not here.

"Are you okay?" He asks, his eyes roaming me for answers.

"Yes," I say, clambering to my feet. I dust off the snow from the front of my jeans. There are two wet patches on my knees where I was kneeling God knows how long ago. "What are you doing here?" I spit.

He laughs. "Are you asking me if I have followed you to a cemetery?" The smugness in his tone infuriates me.

"Well, what are you doing here then?" I demand.

His laugh turns to a frown and his eyes darken. "My wife has a tombstone right over there," he says, raising a pointed finger towards the northern end of the cemetery.

My stomach sinks. Have I lost my damn mind? I grimace. "Sorry, it's been a weird day."

"No need to apologise, death tends to bring out the worst in us." He smiles, but it doesn't reach his eyes.

"I didn't realise sunflowers were in season," I say.

His brow furrows. "Oh, these. I grew these in a greenhouse at my property. I can grow any flowers you want, all year round." He studies the bunch of flowers in his hand. "Sunflowers are my wife's favourite."

"*Were* her favourite," I mumble to myself.

"Do you want to sit?" He asks.

I nod. After how rude I've been, I owe him at least the courtesy of one conversation. We find a snowless patch of dirt underneath a thick-boned atlas cedar. Its branches act like an umbrella to protect us from the falling snow.

"When did you start teaching here?" I ask as we take a seat, our backs against the tree.

"I've been teaching on and off for around three years. I usually take some advanced biology and medicinal practice classes over the winter and then my wife and I would head back to Atlanta for the summer months," he says.

"When did she—?" The polite way to finish the sentence depends on the *how* of someone's death. People die in car accidents, but they 'pass away' in their beds at home. Thankfully, I don't have to ask.

He stares at me, a storm contained in the wash of his eyes—dark and daring. And in it, I find that familiar urge to run.

"She got sick around four years ago and deteriorated very quickly. The doctors couldn't do anything for her, so I took her home." He looks up into the clouds, releasing me, his mind somewhere else.

Passed away, for sure.

"What was—?"

"Pneuculosis," he says quickly.

My heart stammers, and in this moment of unrelenting shock, I realise just how unfair I've been. Is that the way it will be from now on? Will everything in the present draw out memories of the past like a cutting knife?

"My father," I stutter.

"I thought as much." He flashes me a knowing half-smile but his eyes remain cold, detached. "Angus confirmed my suspicions the day after the party. I thought you might have wanted to join the study group, but I realise now that I offended you. It really was never my intention."

"I should be the one to apologise." I sigh, my throat tight. "I was very rude."

The professor shrugs, and we sit in silence. It's not uncomfortable like I imagined it would be. I guess that's progress.

"Anyway," I say, "I'm not saying I will, but if I were to join the group, how many others are there?"

"About seven or so," he says, smiling slightly.

"And when do you meet?" I ask softly.

"Thursday afternoons, sometimes in the morning if some aren't available."

He climbs to his feet and peers down at me, offering his hand. His wicked green eyes are wide and glistening in the dull evening light. There's a fire behind them that I've not seen before. I can trace a line from the corner of his mouth to the sides of his nose, bending at his will. His eyes lock with mine as he pulls me to my feet.

"The door is always open if you change your mind."

I shift my weight from right to left, unable to explain the barrenness that grew into my heart the moment my father took his last breath. The kind that has stretched out before me like an abyss every day since. What would it take to learn of the very thing that harboured my soul? I just don't know if I can. So, I nod.

"Our next meeting is on Thursday at four," he says as he starts to walk towards the exit, back up the damp hill. "I'll see you there, Aurelia."

Then, he disappears into the fog like a ghost.

Chapter Five

I'm never late. Okay, maybe that's a bit of a stretch, but I do make a point of always being on time for Mr Caughlan's pharmacology classes, if not purely for the fact that his glare could turn stone to ash in an instant. But as I walk into the room this morning, the class has started, and I'm a generous twelve minutes late.

"Thank you for joining us, Ms Kingston," Mr Caughlan grumbles from the front of the room. He doesn't bother to glance at me, and I don't dare wait to see if he will. His slight, bony posterior is not half as intimidating as his grizzly cast-iron stare.

I hurry to find my seat next to Angus, who shifts his textbooks back to his own desk. The only other spare seat left in the tutorial room is next to Jasper Murphy, who seems to suffer from hay fever all year round.

Thank you, I mouth to Angus, and I mean it.

***

The lecture passes by in a blur. The scribble in front of me is more than I remember writing, that's for sure. Angus had me giggling like an idiot for most of the two hours we were seated next to each other, his leg grazing mine every so often, sending waves of electricity pulsing through my body. I can recall each time with frightening precision. It's enough to set my heart on fire.

He'd planted that spark eighteen months ago. We met over a dead body. A moment so traumatic, that despite my best efforts, it's forever been etched into the fabric of my memory like a tattoo. We'd been assigned as lab partners, and the purpose of the lesson was to dissect a human heart, searching for any obvious abnormalities like clotting, perforated arteries or cardiomegaly.

Angus had nicknamed the cadaver Steve, which made me want to hurl. We didn't talk much, save for a few pleasantries. I learnt his name, and that he had transferred from interstate. I was trying to concentrate on the lesson, but he was more interested in the third leg of a multi-bet that he and his friends had put money on.

I hate gambling, and so, when he asked me whether I thought he should 'cash out or risk it all', I made it very clear that I was less than interested, and I reminded him—rather bluntly—that passing this class was a hurdle requirement of our course.

The look of utter shock on Angus' face has me grinning even now, his eyes rounded like marbles. But it did the trick, because for the next half hour, at least, Angus focused so hard on the cadaver, I was worried his eyes might bleed. Only now do I wish he'd finished the multi-bet instead.

It was simple. I made an incision through the breastbone, which spread apart to allow me to access the heart. The ribs opened up like the petals of a flower, and the heart emerged from within it as stiff as the stale air of the laboratory. In reality, the heart would be temporarily stopped using medication, and a heart-lung machine would circulate the blood around the body while the procedure took place.

A coronary bypass surgery, for example, could take between three and six hours, depending on how many and how severe the blockages were. We were told that for the purpose of our lesson, our patient had suffered an aortic aneurysm, which meant we needed to make an incision in the descending thoracic aorta on the left side of the chest.

After that, we were to replace the weakened part with a graft. Simply, we needed to cut into the thing shaped like a fishhook, and patch it up. Angus leaned over my right shoulder as I made the first incision. While the lifeless heart lay dormant in front of us, Angus's was thrumming through his chest so loud I could barely concentrate.

"I think I'm going to be sick," he muttered, and as I turned to ask him what he meant by that, I felt the violent splatter of lukewarm vomit cover my shoes.

Angus chased me into the ladies' restroom, begging for my forgiveness—literally begging, on his hands and knees.

"Get up," I ordered, feeling the weight of his attention like a woollen blanket in the summertime. "You'll catch a disease."

By lunchtime, Angus had bought me a new pair of Converse, way more expensive than I could ever afford for myself. Every day for a month, he apologised for the incident, and from that day on, I couldn't seem to shake him.

Before I knew it, seeing this clumsy, weak-stomached larrikin had become as much a part of my daily routine as brushing my teeth.

***

Jade is leaning against the exit, waiting for us as we follow the current of students eagerly exiting the classroom. We walk to the hub side by side. Jade's excitement grows with our every step as she talks about the end-of-year vacation she's planned for us in Fiji.

I don't have the heart to tell her that there's no way I can afford to pay for the food on the aeroplane, let alone the actual flight. So, I go along with it and try my best to match her enthusiasm, all the while praying that by the time the school year ends, this idea will disappear with it.

Jade and I sit down at a table meant for two people because all the others are taken. Angus pulls a spare chair from a neighbouring couple and squishes in beside me, not a breath between us. I'd rather not, but I scoot over a little to make some more space for him.

"Do you want to come around to mine this afternoon?" Jade asks us. "It's Mexican night at Casa du Jade."

"I think that's French." Angus laughs.

I sigh. "I can't tonight. I've got study group."

"You signed up?" Angus raises an eyebrow.

"Yeah, he caught me again the other day in the food court while I was waiting in line for Chinese." Before he accosted me in the cemetery.

I haven't told them about my encounter with the professor at Plenty Road, mostly because I don't want to explain to my two best friends that this is where I skulk away to on a Monday afternoon.

"Oh, I remember him, he was a sub for one of my classes last year," Jade says. "I don't know a whole lot about him, but he's ridiculously handsome—in a creepy kind of way."

"What do you mean?" Angus asks, eyes widening, his brow furrowed with intrigue.

"I don't know, he's got that Christian Bale kind of look about him, but at the same time, I would be half-concerned that he might go all Fifty Shades on me, and then bury me in the backyard," Jade says with a shrug. "It could go either way."

"I know what you mean," I admit. "It's either *Batman* or *American Psycho*."

"You two just need to get to know him," Angus scoffs. "You won't find a more hardworking, dedicated man this side of the equator."

"Well, I hope you're right." I sigh again, mostly to avoid having to admit that I, too, find the professor's allure somewhat hypnotising.

I push back in my chair and swing my bag over my shoulder. "Speaking of, it's all the way on the other side of the campus, and I'm already late."

"I'll walk with you," Angus says.

"You don't have to do that," I say, despite the wings beating savagely in my chest merely at the idea of it.

"I left some books in the lab—it's on the way." His eyes are so sincere, and yet, I don't believe him at all.

"See you tomorrow." I wave to Jade as we head north.

It's about a fifteen-minute walk across campus, and to get there, we have to traverse the part of the forest that lines the eastern rim. It's a beautiful walk, and now that it's stopped snowing for a brief period, the view in front of us is brilliant, like the facets of a diamond.

The ground is coated in a gentle layer of powder, and the tree branches carry heavy white dust on their limbs, speckled amongst the deep green pine needles. My hands shoved deep in my pockets, I take a sharp breath through my nose and my lungs flood with crisp, pure air, and a hint of deep, resinous earth, so wholesome that it stings.

It's an effort not to stare at the ivory path stretching out before us, the squirrels that scramble up the rich brown trunks that flank us, the sleepy forest wakening with our every step.

We walk until the buildings behind us disappear in a cloud of mist and fog. I'm just about to ask Angus what time his parents' plane lands this afternoon when the path beneath us disappears and my legs flail from under me.

As I freefall towards the ground, Angus reaches out to catch me, but just as his arm circles my waist, we plummet with an almighty thud into a mountain of snow.

It takes a great deal of spluttering and a few gasping breaths to dislodge the snow jammed into my mouth. I managed to dodge the coarse gravel road—a small mercy. But the surface beneath me does not feel powdery or cold like flakes of ice. Horrified, I look down to find Angus grinning at me.

"Oh my god." I wince. "Are you okay?"

"Are you kidding? This is the best I've been in a long time." His blue eyes gleam.

"Shut up," I groan, relieved that I've not crushed him to death.

Pushing against Angus' chest, I lever myself off him. Muscle and more muscle ripple beneath my hands. It takes all my willpower not to rip his shirt right off his torso. Good breeding be damned—I'd have him right here on the ground.

We sit side by side, the ice seeping through our jeans, war-torn and bruised, and then Angus grins, his eyes glistening against the frost.

"Looks like you're going to be late for your first study group, Rae darling." His smile is wicked, tempting. "You look terrible."

I flick some loose snow at him, and we both laugh. "You look worse," I tell him, weeding a leaf from his blond waves.

Minutes pass like seconds, his smouldering gaze warming my cold heart, his gentle smile caressing my bones.

My soul aches as I clamber to my feet and offer Angus a hand. We almost fall again—and yet, I don't think Angus would mind, not one bit. But I'm almost twenty minutes late, and the thought of walking into another class, all eyes on me, has my stomach somersaulting.

"I should go," I say.

He sighs. "Always the responsible one, never any fun."

I shove him hard in the ribs and it nearly sends him toppling into the brush. "I can walk the rest of the way on my own, it's not that far now."

And just like the wooden fence marking the northern edge of the campus to our right, my own invisible wall again stands stark between us. Something I seem to do these days, without even trying. The half-smile-half-grimace doesn't reach his eyes. He studies the path ahead of us.

"Thanks for walking with me," I say, unsure what else I can offer him.

"Always," he says.

My stomach flutters and I hope he can't hear my heart thundering beneath my chest—another small mercy. He doesn't seem to notice the pink flush in my cheeks.

We part ways and I continue walking north towards the old Edward Felton building. Once I hit the clearing at the end of the path, I turn left where the wooden fence forms a T-intersection with the road. The room I'm looking for is only twenty yards ahead on the left—room EF-9. Lampposts hang overhead like tendrils spewing golden light onto the ice.

And like the evolving landscape before me, the loose gravel cured into hard concrete, the sky itself darkens, shrouding the world in a bleak fog. I walk purposefully now, under the cover of the building, past dribs and drabs of students finished for the day and heading home.

I hug the thick walls as I round the final corner, and the door to the laboratory opens up with a warm breath to swallow me whole.

The first thing I notice when I enter is the darkness of it. Not the lack of light per se, but the feel of it. Don't get me wrong, the sheer lack of windows didn't help. The second thing I notice is the seven or so students in the room clustered around benches, gazing into the long necks of microscopes.

A quick headcount confirms my figures. I don't recognise any of them from my classes, but I'm terrible with faces, so that much is not surprising.

The closest—a thin, strawberry-haired girl with large glasses that cover half her face, glances up at me as I stumble into the room. Our encounter is only brief as her spindly fingers hover about the spread of chemicals before her and she squeezes droplets of solution onto the glass square, replacing it under the microscope.

Her lab partner is a tall, dark-haired boy with shallow eyes and pale skin. He has a small brown mole in the centre of one of his cheeks that distinguishes him from the neighbouring gentleman, who has a similar appearance.

The remainder of the class are a mixture of males and females with varying shades of brown hair and brown eyes, all absolutely engrossed in whatever is planted under those microscopes.

"Aurelia, welcome," someone calls.

I lift my gaze just in time to see the professor beaming a mouthful of pearly white teeth in my direction, arms extended, his excitement as palpable as the scent of ammonia wafting through the lab. And contagious, it would seem, as seven pairs of eyes flicker in my direction, doing their best not to gawk at me.

"Sorry I'm late," I say quietly, shrugging my backpack off my shoulder and onto one of the stools closest to me.

"Not at all," he says. "I—*we* are just glad you could make it."

I keep my mouth shut and slide into place next to a short blonde girl with hip-length hair braided into two ponytails that drape down her front like curtains.

Her eyes are a candy blue, not royal like Angus', but much lighter. Her skin is ivory, as white as the snow no doubt piling up outside.

In a gentle and quiet voice, barely audible over the light chatter in the room, she tells me her name is Monique. We are going to get along just fine, I decide as she slides a heavy microscope across the bench towards me. We barely exchange a pronoun for the remainder of the class, and work away in comfortable silence.

Now that I'm seated, I take in the fullness of the blue-grey lab. Six benches in total, dotted two-wide along the narrow space. Ours is closest to the front, and closest to where the professor is rifling through pages of handwritten notes.

This is one of the smaller rooms I have been to on campus, and the severe lack of windows, and proximity of the other students gives it an elephant-in-a-closet kind of feel. It's something I'll have to get used to if I want to continue with this class, which—I have decided—may be useful when it comes to writing for future medical journals.

"We are looking at the cellular composition of phagocytes that have been infected by Mtb, specifically the role of streptomycin in altering the cellular composition," the professor says, and he does not take his eyes off me as he addresses the rest of the class. "Don't worry," he continues, "these samples are double glassed. As a precaution, I'd ask that you all put your masks and gloves on before touching the samples."

The medical-grade mask slides over my face with ease, my breath damp and warm against my chin, suffocatingly familiar. I try to concentrate on the professor's soothing voice instead of the memories gnawing away at the corners of my mind.

"You all know what it is, what it does. A sub-virus of tuberculosis, *Mycobacterium pneuculosis* was born in Africa, murdering its host within months of contracting it. Incurable—that's what they said, anyway." A smile tugs at the corners of his mouth, gone as quickly as it came.

"But we all know the history of the therapies from last week's readings. We have the pioneer discovery of streptomycin and para-amino salicylic acid in 1944. We have the triple threat therapy in 1952—streptomycin, para-amino salicylic acid and isoniazid, which presented an opportunity for a cure.

"It was eighteen months before we hit the 1970s and scientists recognised that isoniazid combined with rifampin could reduce treatment duration by half.

Finally, in the 1980s, they discovered that adding pyrazinamide might cure a patient with TB in as little as six months."

He pauses, his gaze roaming, absorbing the attention of the audience as eight pairs of eyes look at him with utter adoration and lust, hanging off his every word.

"Revolutionary," he says, and it raises the hairs on my arms.

My stomach churns, and I'm barely able to quash the urge to dash out of the room, the impulse to applaud, to fill the electric silence pulsing between us. Looking around the room, I might not be the only one.

"Why then, are we still looking for a cure for the evil twin? Why are there still fatalities in some parts of the world? And growing fatalities even here, in Canada."

"Drug-resistant strains." The words pour out, frigid and steady, fitting for the very thing that murdered my father in his sleep.

The heat blaring from the vent in the corner of the room has nothing on the eight pairs of eyes now focused on me, the sultriest being from my strawberry-haired friend, who I'm starting to think, based on her doe-eyed stare, has a particular fondness for our professor. One that may extend beyond his articulate knowledge of the sciences and fall somewhere below his no doubt brawny midriff.

I find solace in the pages of the textbook on the desk in front of me, anything to avoid her cast-iron glare. I once read an article about the importance of exposing the most vulnerable parts of the body to predators in order to avoid attack. Does that apply to lustful females too?

Fiddling with a test tube on my bench, I will myself into silence for the rest of the class. But her eyes burn against my skin, and I have my answer; in the animal world, baring one's soul may spare you from a fatal attack, but in real life, it only shows them where to strike first.

"Excellent." The professor's eyes linger as they fall on me. "And in order to develop and replace agents that have been lost to resistance, we need to go back and recognise how today's paradigms have been arrived at. Over the next three months, we will study and replicate the various models to learn their origins, development and uses. Who knows, we might even find a cure in the process." A wry smile for a cruel joke.

Soft, stifled sneers in perfect chorus echo about the room. Still, his gaze lingers on me. I feel its weight before I look up to meet his emerald eyes, and heat blooms in my cheeks. I desperately want to look away. But I can't. Trapped, like the mice in the cages around us.

The strawberry-haired girl summons the professor to her bench, breaking his trance, affording me a moment of relief. She asks for some assistance inserting the slides into the microscope, something she has no doubt done a thousand times before.

I snap one of the tuberculosis slides into place under the microscope. We're using a U2 digital microscope with a 5mp camera, seriously advanced technology that I didn't even know this campus had the budget for.

When the camera focuses at 40x magnification, milky, translucent, purple flourishes dotted like stars appear throughout the slide. In the centre, just to the right, an ominous dense purple patch. It's opaque and distinct from the other markings. At 100x magnification, the dense purple patch evolves into a wound-like shape with a distinct dark line down the centre, encircled by the same purple border.

At 400x—the microscope's maximum magnification—a worm-like shape appears with black markings dotting the interior. My hands ache from tensing, fingernails digging rivets into my skin.

A miracle—that's what the doctors had said through the thick plastic barrier between us and them—that my blood wasn't caked in the worm-shaped murderers after the direct exposure we'd had that night, the night my father died.

I wince once more as I look down the neck of the microscope. Never has death looked so sinister. I'd wager that it might never again. I imagine that *Mycobacterium pneuculosis*—the stronger, resilient and far more lethal twin sister—would look much, much worse.

The magnification returns to 40x, and the parasitic blobs return to purple squiggles. To the left of the screen is an option to enter the formula for different chemical compounds.

My mind traces the edges of my memory until I'm holding the textbook, searching for the formula. I type the compound $C_{42}H_{84}N_{14}O_{36}S_3$ into the search bar. The image transforms into a film with the shape of the bacteria shrinking and growing as it advances. I add the chemical compound for the para-amino salt of salicylic acid and again, the film evolves. This time, the bacteria decrease in a consistent pattern.

The purple worm disperses over a theoretical six, twelve, twenty-four, forty-eight weeks and six months until it's barely distinguishable from the non-infected cells.

The professor comes to stand opposite my bench, his tall slender figure casting invisible shadows over me. He stares with watchful eyes, much as he had done at the cemetery, as if he might be able to discern something else from my face—the truth, maybe. I smile tightly, trying to hide the discomfort I feel under his microscope.

He frowns. "You've done this before."

Not a question.

"I didn't even know the school had these microscopes," I say.

"They don't," he says. There's a short silence as the professor watches the cure manifest in the sample. His eyebrows crease. "But how did you—?"

"I read a manual for one of these microscopes in a magazine about a year ago," I say quickly. "I think this is the newer model though, because I don't recognise some of the settings."

I look up to meet his eyes. Up close, they're even more tantalizing. The emerald glass shifts and changes in the light. Flecks of green and gold flicker with pride. Truly mesmerising, the way they seem to dance and shine.

A faint smile—awe, maybe—ghosts in his eyes as he examines the empty bench between us.

"You already knew the formulas," he muses. "How?"

"I read of them in the *Registry of Toxic effects of chemical substances 1985–1986*," I say.

"When?" A green fire burns in those eyes. Terrifying, and yet, I can't look away.

"Six months ago."

"How?"

"I have a good memory," I say, feeling the burn in my cheeks.

It's a complete understatement, but I'd rather swelter under the heat of the mystery that now sits unanswered in the air between us than admit that my mind has more storage space than half the hard drives on Earth.

"I'll say," he says, "you're a walking textbook."

I can't tell if it's a compliment, or something else.

"They retired me when they invented Google." I smile weakly.

Relief, as the professor's face relaxes into a grin. He pivots, striding back towards the lectern at the front of the room with a lightness to his step, one that wasn't there before.

"You're a marvel," he says, loud enough for me to hear.

Chapter Six

Last night, I was hit square in the face by a flying hockey puck. Thank Christ it was just a dream, or I'd likely never smell another red rose in my life. Despite the thick hessian bags hanging beneath my eyes, by the time my alarm went off, I was already dressed—in my best navy-blue stockings, brown leather coat and black boots—packed, and ready to head out the door.

Now, nestled against the fence alone, a decent half hour earlier than I need to be, I wonder if I'll be facing the chill from the gloomy, storm-clouded sky alone for the next ninety minutes.

This arena is grand in every way imaginable. The icy field glistens, reflecting the lights hanging from the ceiling above it like a mirror, the ice completely untouched, not a single skate mark in its perfectly smooth surface.

The scoring nets sit in waiting at each end, a face-off separated by three horizontal lines trapped under the ice, one red in the middle and two blue flanking it on either side.

Blue and yellow grandstand seats line the field in a dome shape, stretching out above us. From where I'm standing along the front row, small groups of people are funnelling in through the entry gates behind me; all twelve stands start to fill, spaced evenly around the arena like the hours of a clock.

We are playing against our neighbouring college, Sandringham, situated around an hour's drive north of our campus. This game is somewhat of a local Saturday derby, or so Jade tells me. Behind me in the bleachers to my left, a small group of people huddle together under a blanket. I can just make out Zac by his fiery red hair.

I partnered with Zac in a laboratory class back in second year. We stayed in contact, but mostly, he just reaches out when he wants the answers to the weekly online quizzes.

Zac waves at me with both hands. When I'm satisfied that he can't be waving to anyone but me, I wave back, trying to match his enthusiasm—with great difficulty. At least I don't have to spend the next ninety minutes freezing on my own, I reason.

My frustratingly thin jacket does nothing to protect me from the chill sweeping in with the hundreds of spectators. I'm distracted by a loose thread when I feel a thick, woollen blanket drape over my shoulders.

"Hello, stranger." His smooth voice tickles my ear and I turn to find Angus, dressed in a tight white shirt practically glued to his muscles, dark denim jeans and a black college bomber jacket. His wavy blond hair is damp and messy and he smells of cologne and shampoo—a dizzying combination.

An explicit image pulses through my mind, sending heat soaring below the waistband of my stockings, and I pray that he doesn't notice my embarrassment as I struggle to compose myself.

My facial expression must be telling because Angus' mouth stretches into a wicked grin that seems to grow the longer he watches me. It's hard not to melt around him, despite how icy he's been to me this week.

The second week of study group was better than the first. We looked at streptomycin, para-amino salicylic acid and isoniazid, and the professor entertained himself by testing my memory of dictionary definitions and number plates.

Although slight and unnoticeable at first, his harsh features seemed to soften, his hard-lined mouth tempered by a smile that seemed to finally reach his eyes. I was starting to find comfort in his laughter and the soothing tones of his voice.

The strawberry-haired girl—who I now know as Susannah—even asked if she could borrow my calculator, and only glared at me twice, both times when the professor requested I assist her to adjust her microscope. It's not much, but it's progress.

Oh, and how could I forget the fortunate turn of events that was Drew—captain of the football team—asking me to be his partner for our pathology class? Whispers had spread around the campus like wildfire later that afternoon before I had even entered the hall. *Everyone* was talking about it.

Jade was the worst of them all, peppering me relentlessly with questions. Hysteria aside, I'm almost certain he just wanted to copy my notes.

Where warmth had radiated from Drew, only the opposite could be said of Angus, who failed miserably at small talk during most of our classes, his gaze falling anywhere but on me. As if he couldn't bring himself to look me in the eye. I put it down to the full moon and tried to forget about it. Men can be so complicated sometimes.

"I've missed you," Angus says.

"You saw me yesterday." I huff, mimicking some of the coldness he had channelled this week. He deserves as much.

He frowns. "You look cold."

"I should have brought a blanket." Cold, stiff, blunt. *You'd know all about being cold,* I want to say.

"Then I would have to find another excuse to come and talk to you, wouldn't I, Rae darling?" He purrs, and my cheeks flush. Is he seriously flirting with me now?

I spot Drew walking along the barrier to our right, a group of five or so staunch bodies in tow behind him like smoke to a flame. The other members of the football team, I guess. Our eyes meet and he gives me a thin-lipped smile—almost a smirk—accompanied by a quick wink. My response is a small, overenthusiastic wave. My cheeks burn and I busy myself with my woollen beanie. *Pathetic, totally pathetic.*

Angus scowls and rolls his eyes but, before he can say another word, the sound of the siren rings out across the stand, and dozens of people clutch their ears in unison.

"So," Angus yells above the noise. He tugs the blanket over my shoulder and shuffles closer, "Where's our girl?"

I turn, surprised to find the players already slicing across the field, the game well and truly underway.

"There, over there." I point towards the backline, where two players are shoving at each other.

"Might be a rough game by the looks of it. I've heard that Sandy can play dirty," Angus says as Jade's player lays another elbow into her ribs.

"It's so violent." I gulp.

"Golf is a much safer sport."

"Is that why you play?" I ask.

"No, I do it for the women." Again, that wicked grin.

I let out a long, theatrical groan. "Here I was thinking you were a half-decent guy."

Angus laughs, poking me in the side. And then his face grows solemn. "I wasn't sure decent guys were your type anymore," he says, nodding in the direction of aisle K, seven rows behind us. I follow his gaze to find Drew, surrounded—literally surrounded—by a cluster of women while he pulls himself up and down on a low-hanging water pipe in an effortless display of muscle and vanity.

"I hope that pipe is strong enough," I mumble.

Angus smirks. "But have you ever been swept off your feet by a golf buggy?"

"It can't be more dangerous than your swing," I tease, surprised to hear the flirtatious undertone threaded through my words.

"How dare you." Angus clutches his heart, and then his mouth stretches into a grin.

"Stop," I squeal as he tugs me under his arm, digging his fingers into my ribs.

He stops, but his arm remains draped over me, as toasty as any blanket.

"Angus!" Someone calls from behind us. Icy tendrils creep into our cocoon of warmth.

Angus' arm falls to his side and I shuffle awkwardly to my left, creating some space between us.

"Ella," Angus says, charming as ever. My stomach churns a little.

Ella McLeland. I recognise her immediately as she stalks towards us. I'd heard of her, mostly through conversations whispered in the library. With her long dark Tahitian hair floating behind her like a veil, her olive complexion and heart-melting hourglass figure, none of it surprises me; but her features are harsh, cold, as if she could turn you to stone with just a single glare.

Judging by the way her perfectly plucked eyebrows are furrowed at me, she doesn't like me. Probably because I've got prime real estate, right here next to Angus.

"Angus," Ella says with desperate glamour, "I knew I'd find you here. You promised you'd help me with my fundraiser today." She shoots Angus a devastating flash of white teeth—perfectly straight, of course. She's standing so close to him now that I feel like I'm imposing.

Angus takes a step back in line with me, casually rolling an arm around my back. "Sorry, Ella, I'd love to help, but I've already got plans with Rae," he says, flashing her a heart-melting half-smile, an apology that appears so sincere he might genuinely mean it.

Ella's gaze turns to me as if she hadn't registered my existence until now. "What plans?" She asks bluntly.

Angus' eyes widen slightly, a mirror of the stunned look that must now adorn my own face. He looks down at me in answer, his gaze lingering when his eyes lock with mine. He takes his time, and I'm very aware of his hand resting gently on my back. I could stare into those royal blue eyes for eternity.

After a long moment, Angus' mouth stretches into a reassuring smile as if a puzzle piece had slipped into place. He turns and answers her, breaking our connection to look her in the eye. "Mini golf," he says, pulling me a little closer.

"Ugh," she scoffs, "seriously?" Her disappointment is palpable. "Well, let me know when you're free, Angus."

"Sure," he says, giving her a tight wave. "Bye, Ella."

I can't quite wrap my head around what just happened, and yet, here he stands next to me. And Ella—well, she's probably licking her wounds a few rows back.

I turn to him. "Mini golf?"

Angus sighs. "She's been badgering me to do a photoshoot for a campaign fundraiser or something. I don't know, she wasn't really forthcoming with the details."

"What kind of photoshoot?" I ask.

Angus cringes. "Don't laugh."

"You know I can't promise that," I tease. "Tell me."

Angus rolls his eyes, and this time, his cheeks burn. "She designed some swimsuits she wanted me to try on."

I stare at him, no clue where to even begin my taunting.

He sighs. "Go on, get it over with."

He is visibly uncomfortable about the idea of having his perfectly carved body on display; if only he knew the number of women who already undress him with their eyes.

"What's the matter, Angus?" I quip with a smirk. "Afraid you might look too good in those swimsuits?"

"Yeah, well, at least I don't have to stuff my swimsuit with extra padding like someone I know." He sneers, nodding towards aisle K.

"No," I say, mouth gaping. "Really?"

Angus grins mischievously, giving me the impression that he might have just conjured this potential rumour. "Maybe."

I nudge him in the ribs. "Don't be jealous."

"I'm not going to do it," he says, focusing his attention on the field.

"You don't want to?" I ask.

"No. Not for her anyway," he says and my mind swims, wondering exactly what he might mean by that.

***

When the final siren blows, I can't believe it. Distracted by Angus for most of the match, I remember only bits and pieces of the game. Jade's team won by three—which means she will be out for the better part of the night celebrating.

Angus whistles loudly at the scoreboard. He high-fives a male to his right, and they cheer together as our college anthem booms through the speakers, as old and patriotic as the flags hanging from the ceiling. It's funny, I hadn't noticed the guy standing beside us until now.

Angus turns to me, his eyes gleaming. "Do you want to drive or should I?" He folds the blanket effortlessly into a perfect square.

"What are you talking about?"

"To mini golf," he says coolly.

"Oh," I fumble. "I can't."

I grimace. Unlike for Jade, sports of any kind are my Achilles heel, and Angus knows this—better than anyone. In fact, I've been the subject of his taunts at every possible opportunity for the past year.

"Please?" He pouts. "If you don't come with me, Ella will think I'm a liar."

I roll my eyes and groan. "And we couldn't possibly have that, could we?"

Angus swiftly drops down to his knee, taking my hands in his. I want to be mad, surprised even—but this is Angus, and I'm too mesmerised by his grace and the way he's looking at me to care.

"Angus," I hiss, "get up!"

He ignores me. "Will you, Aurelia Kingston," he's just being dramatic now, "do me the honour of attending mini golf this afternoon?"

"Say yes!" Someone croons on their way past.

I don't recognise the voice but, predictably, Angus yells back, "Thanks for the support, Matty," giving him a thumbs up. I forget sometimes how visible I am with Angus.

"Fine," I groan, "will you get up now?"

Angus smiles, doused in a triumphant glow. He jumps to his feet in one swift movement. "I'll drive."

***

Angus and I walk through the food court side by side. We pass the lecture hall buildings and trudge up the hill behind the campus through inches of snow. We find ourselves standing in front of a large dome-shaped building that is supposed to mimic a fluorescent pink golf ball, but looks more like an ulcer.

You can tell by looking at the building that it was designed and constructed by the architecture faculty of this college, a part of the school that seems to have more money than sense most of the time.

Last year, the medical board had requested an additional lecture theatre be added to the campus. Instead of outsourcing the build, the architecture students designed and funded the construction, which resulted in a lopsided stained-glass building that looks more like a church than a home for rats and test tubes.

In a centuries-old British-emigrant-settled Canadian town like Brunswick Shire, characterised by sandstone and aged concrete, the building stands out like blood on a white shirt. Needless to say, it did not comply with council standards, the newspaper labelled it a 'new-age atrocity', and the head of the faculty miraculously resigned a week before construction was due to finish.

I have other theories about his departure from the college, but none that matter. I tend to keep my opinion of college politics to myself. Though the offensive smell of fresh paint tells me that this is another new, and probably regrettable addition to the campus.

The interior is even more surprising, and much less offensive than the exterior. Almost impressive—almost. We enter through swinging glass doors so clean, I almost walk straight through them—and would have, had Angus not gripped my shoulders to redirect me.

To my right is an ocean of undulating green floor that reminds me of rolling hills. There are little sand bunkers and plants that line what I understand to be fairways.

The mini golf course is indoors, and yet, it feels as if the ground is still damp with morning dew. There's a slight breeze weaving through the room and I take some comfort from the long sleeves of my jacket.

A young female receptionist welcomes us into the building a little too enthusiastically. *Maybe it's her first day on the job,* I think, because I can't imagine anyone being overly excited to work in a place like this. Not the role itself, but the loneliness of it.

There's a first-year biology textbook lying open on the desk in front of her. I'd read it start to finish a week before classes started. This girl is probably a college student looking for some extra cash to get through the semester.

I can tell by the way her cheeks flush when Angus asks for two putters that she has not come across him before, which is odd because I'm quite sure that everyone who attends this college either knows or has heard of Angus.

He thanks the receptionist with his best heart-breaking smile. As expected, the poor girl's cheeks burn a fluorescent pink; she seems so overwhelmed by her own pathetic lusting that she excuses herself from the front desk and pretends to busy herself with tasks out the back.

We take our putters and score cards and make our way to the first hole of the course. The first fairway is a straight one, with the hole about five feet from where we are standing. Good, looks easy enough.

"Ladies first." Angus smiles, almost cunning.

He's standing off towards the left behind me, no doubt with amusement splayed across his face like paint. "You've never done this before, have you?"

"Yes, I have!" I spit, fumbling the putter in my hand. "Just give me a second."

I line the surface of the club against the ball, close my eyes and swing. Too hard. The ball ricochets off a nearby pot plant, and into the third hole fairway next to us.

"You distracted me," I grumble. When I look up, I'm surprised to see that Angus's face is drawn, painted with immeasurable concern.

"Okay, maybe I haven't done this before," I admit.

Angus just stares at me. A mixture of embarrassment and frustration builds, and I wrestle with the urge to tell Angus that he can shove his golf club up his—

But his laugh breaks the silence, his smile widening over perfect teeth. My frustration lifts like a cloud.

"What? Mr Quarterback never taught you how to play mini golf?" He teases.

I make a point of rolling my eyes and line up another golf ball with my club.

"Here, let me show you," he says, the smile carrying in his voice. He moves to stand behind me, his chest lining my back, arms coming to circle tenderly around mine. "For a start," he whispers, his breath tickling my ear, "you're holding the club backwards."

Thankfully, Angus cannot see the hideous warmth in my cheeks, my toes curling in my snow boots.

He manoeuvres the club in my hands, his cheek brushing my neck. It sends a race of goose bumps across my body. My heart flutters at his touch, but I will myself to breathe, to slow it back down. His scent is intoxicating, rich and warm, a mesh of teakwood and cologne. I beg myself not to pass out.

Then he places his hands over mine, taking control of the club. Together, with Angus' lead, we gently swing the club against the ball. Neither of us takes notice of where it ends up.

I glance up at him and am bemused to find his eyes locked on mine. Perhaps he's trying to read the lines at the corners of my eyes, the quiver of my lips. I turn slightly in his arms. He doesn't loosen his hold on me. Can he hear my heart ricocheting off the walls of my chest?

My breath catches in my throat. "What is it?"

He leans into me. "You need more mentoring." His lips brush my ear, sending a race of heat through my body. "Okay, I'll do it, stop begging me."

I laugh. "And what type of remuneration would you be seeking for your services?" I ask, surprised to hear a flirting lilt in my voice.

Using his thumb, he gently brushes a loose strand of hair from my forehead. Silently, save for the loud thumping of our hearts, Angus leans towards me until our lips are less than a breath apart.

"I'm sure we can work something out," he whispers, and then without so much as a pause, he presses his lips against mine with perfect tenderness.

I'm completely unprepared. I'd assumed that all the time spent with Angus over the past eighteen months—watching him talk, laugh, watching his lips bend and refract into myriad different smiles—would prepare me, but I was wrong. A burning flurry beats through my body as if I'm a million feathers, floating on air. He brushes the side of my face with his hand. My eyes open and close slowly, trying not to miss a single moment. When I don't pull away, he smiles against my mouth, pulling me closer than I thought possible, and a current flows between us, electrifying every inch of my body.

The golf club falls to the ground, rapidly vanishing beneath me. But Angus doesn't seem to notice. Out of instinct, or something else—I run my fingers through his blond hair.

"Rae," he moans, pulling back to look into my eyes. We remain that way for a while longer. "You have no idea how long I've wanted to do that."

His confession flickers between us like candlelight, and suddenly, I'm so elated that I think I might faint.

"Breathe," he orders, pulling back. He studies my vacant expression, a wave of concern passing over his eyes. "Rae, you look pale."

It isn't until my head starts to swim that I realise I've been holding my breath. Deep lungfuls of air clear my head momentarily until Angus brushes my cheek with the back of his hand and suddenly, I'm dizzy again.

"I need to sit down," I mumble, and Angus guides me swiftly to a nearby wooden bench. He seems to pull a glass of water from thin air, but I take it gratefully.

"Sorry," I moan.

"For what?" His lips crease into that familiar wicked grin.

"Honestly, I imagined that this could go a number of ways, but you fainting—well, maybe I should have known. You're only human after all."

"You planned this?" I demand.

He laughs. "Christ, no, but I'm always hopeful."

I groan, holding my head in my hands. "If your head gets any bigger, they'll have to crane you out of here."

Angus gently slides an arm around my back. "How are you feeling now?"

"Better." My heart sings as he gently tucks me into him, his warmth absorbing any tension left in my body. My cells seem to sigh with relief.

I let my eyes close, trying to focus on the places our bodies meet and not the room spinning around me. And then he's on his feet again in one swift, graceful step.

"I can't tell if I have terrible kissing skills, or you just have an aversion to mini golf," he says.

"Both," I grumble.

He pulls me to my feet in a gentle movement that has me feeling as light as air.

"Maybe I'm the one who needs mentoring," he says with a glimmer in his eyes.

It takes everything in my power not to lunge for him, throw myself against his lips once again. But I keep my composure. *Soon,* I promise myself. The look of utter starvation in his eyes as they roam my face tells me that I might not have to wait too long.

Chapter Seven

The moment I set foot in the house, I'm under interrogation.

"Why is there no dinner on the stove?" My mother staggers out of her armchair to lean against the arched doorway of the lounge room. Her silhouette is only one shade lighter than the darkness shrouding the house. I look down at my watch—it's nearly nine.

Even in the dark, it's clear she's unsteady on her feet, her long woollen dressing gown—the one with pastel pink flowers stitched into the fabric—swaying ever so slightly. It's fraying at the hems. I'll pick her up a new one from the market tomorrow.

There's a dizziness in her eyes that mimics the way I felt earlier today when I was with Angus; only the thick astringent scent of cask wine in the air, and the way she so easily shrugs the gown to the floor, exposing her bare shoulders, tells me that this couldn't be more different.

There's no love in her eyes, not tonight. I step gingerly towards her, my foot kicking something solid on the ground. The object skitters along the floorboards, ricocheting off the corner of the refrigerator. The light above us hesitates before it illuminates the room, as if it might be nervous to expose exactly what lay in the darkness. An empty wine bottle, and another two to my left.

The living room looks worse than Angus' did the night after our exams. There's a cold draught coursing through the house. In the far corner, the warm glow of the fire has reduced itself to ash.

"Oh, Momma." I sigh, feeling a tight cinch in my chest.

She takes a swig from the bottle of red wine in her hand, the bloody liquid staining her teeth. "Where have you been?" She hisses.

"I was out with Angus," I plead, bending down to collect the empty bottles. They clang as I drop them into the recycle bin. I pull the remote from the wall and with the push of a button, the old heating contraption in the corner of the lounge room groans to life. At least, this way, we won't freeze tonight.

"I could have starved to death," she spits, her words slurring.

Our eyes meet, but hers are cold and callous. Twenty-five years by her side and I barely recognise her. I never do when she's like this.

"Momma, there are leftovers in the fridge from last night, remember? I called you."

"Don't lie to me," she says. "You're just like your father—he was a fucking liar too."

"Come on, Momma." I take a step towards her, my arms outstretched.

"Get out," she says, her words as sharp as a serrated blade.

"I'm sorry." Tears sting at the corners of my eyes. "I'll make you something now. Are you hungry?"

"Get out," she seethes through clenched teeth.

"What do you feel like? I'll make it quickly." I cough, trying to dislodge the lump in my throat. But her eyes are too far from reason.

"Get out!" She screams, the sound riveting me to the spot.

I keep my mouth shut as I reach for the navy duffle bag hanging in the front entryway, and sling the long strap over my shoulder. It's still packed, waiting. I try not to slam the door behind me as I step out into the freezing night, alone again.

I might have allowed myself a moment to feel the sting of my mother's words, a moment to sob quietly in the comfort of isolation, had this not been a well-rehearsed dance between us. Had I not trekked this exact path, step by step, so many times before.

Keep it together, I will myself, blinking back tears. The dark sky is a welcome relief from the whitewash in my head. My eyes follow a trickle of light from the moonshine, all the way down the street ahead of me. What's the word? Ominous. That's it.

Heavy footsteps carry me to the corner of the block, stopping at the edge of the street. I turn into the frigid breeze carrying off the icy road to clear my head. My house is visible, even from here. Through a gap in the lounge room curtains, I can just make out my mother, darkness seeming to whirl up around her as she slumps back into her armchair, sipping straight from the neck of another bottle of wine.

A sigh escapes my lips, thick and weary as I pull out my phone. I type rigidly, my fingers frozen to stone, using our shorthand for 'fight with Mum'.

FWM. Can I stay at yours?

Seconds later, my phone buzzes. It's Jade.

Of course—you've got a key. I won't be home until late.

The gentle jingle of the lanyard in my jacket pocket eases the tension in my chest. I send Jade a quick message of thanks and shove my phone back into my bag.

Jade's apartment is about a half-mile walk from my house, heading south, in the opposite direction to the main street. The road is relatively straight, and I'll only need to make two lefts and a right turn to get there. The cold slows my racing mind, and damn nearly stops my heart at times, but I try to focus on the memory of Angus and me, his arms a cocoon of warmth. But it's too cold and I can't seem to concentrate, not even on him.

Streetlights flicker like candles as the snow falls gently to the ground. Thankfully, only light snowfall is scheduled for tonight so there's a chance I might make it to Jade's apartment without freezing to death.

By the time I arrive, my joints feel like they have been welded into place and my skin is a mixture of numbness and scorched flame. Her apartment is a small two-storey with two bedrooms, two bathrooms and a kitchen. She lives alone with her cat, Beatrice, which is how she prefers it—or so she says. It often occurred to me that she might keep the spare room vacant just for me, for times like this. I feel a flicker of guilt about that.

My key fits perfectly into the lock, and I shimmy through the front door. I hang my coat on the rack immediately to my left, throw my duffle bag through the door of the spare room to my right, and stomp upstairs to the kitchen. I pour myself a glass of water from the canister in the fridge.

The kitchen stretches into the living room, and immediately, my bones relax as I glance over the familiar decor—the sapphire velvet couch pressed against the wall, the matching royal blue rug lying underneath the glass coffee table, the bright green ferns dotted around the room and either side of the television. There's a picture of a pineapple hanging on the wall behind the sofa. The only plain thing about the room is the walls, painted a warm and cosy white.

The apartment is as painfully spotless as always. Jade's bedroom door is to my left, closed. I don't need to open it to know what lies behind. A laddered shelf stands in the living room next to the entrance, filled with books and photographs. I feature in most, if not all of them.

There's a snapshot of our trip to Whistler for the college break, Jade and I beaming, our teeth fully exposed. We're holding handfuls of snow, our backs to the stunning glass waters of Moraine Lake. It's as good a memory as any.

Another photo catches my attention. We are younger, our faces a little more rounded, oblivious to the years ahead of us. It feels like yesterday. Our first day of college, almost a year after my father passed away. It's there, clear as day—the subtle tinge of sadness behind my smile, one that I'd carry for the next six years, and maybe forever.

The spare bedroom downstairs is simple compared to the living room. A double bed backs on to the far wall. A desk and chair sit evenly in the corner of the room. When I'm not occupying it, Jade uses this room for her study.

I strip out of my soggy clothes and into some spare PJs that are packed in my duffle bag. The soft mattress envelopes me as I melt into it, closing my eyes for what feels like perpetuity.

Sleep escapes me, my aching eyes too swollen, unable to close. Images flash in the darkness, playing on a loop. Intolerable memories so vivid, it is as if my mother is standing before me, eyes dark and piercing like a crow, shouting at me to leave. It's unbearable, so I flick on the lamp next to my bed. The warm light is the proof I need that I'm alone, that I'm safe.

It isn't until around 3 am that my mind finally quietens and, completely exhausted, sleep absorbs me.

The night is quiet for the most part, but I wake sometime later to the remnants of a dream. Angus' arms are wrapped tightly around me like a blanket. Every part of my body tingles, tracing his touch like a tattoo carved into my skin forever. I stretch tautly, rubbing my blurry eyes.

Not a dream, but a memory.

***

Still in my PJs, I mope upstairs into the kitchen. Collecting some flour from the pantry, eggs and milk from the fridge, I mix them gently in a glass bowl that I found in a cupboard just under the sink. The olive oil sizzles over the heat of the stove. The spark reminds me of Angus.

The doughy puddle in front of me transforms into a thick blanket of air pockets, just in time for flipping. The golden sizzle of the oil has my stomach groaning. Jade whimpers from her bedroom, loud enough for me to hear through the closed door.

Her apartment forms part of a complex with about six others, exactly the same as this one. The paper-thin walls make for interesting listening. Standing in Jade's kitchen, I could just as easily be in her neighbour's living room. But the rent is low—which is why college students often take up residency here.

The whole apartment complex seems to shudder as subtle sounds of dubstep grow into a blaring cacophony, as if the walls themselves need sleep as much as I do.

I'm exhausted; I can feel it in the swelling under my eyes and the haze that seems to fall over them. There's a thin layer of condensation coating the windows by the time I flip the pancake onto my plate. It's barely light outside, which means it's going to be another frosty day.

"No," Jade moans, shaking a manicured finger towards the door. "Turn the light off." I step closer; her acrylic nails are dented, cracked, and some are completely missing. Her mascara has run down her perky cheekbones in black smudges. A wave of nausea hits me as she groans.

"I only opened the door," I say, sitting a plate on her bedside table. Jade's room is very similar to my own. The bed is tucked in the corner and the work desk is covered in peer-review papers. There are two platform shelves mounted on the walls, and a walk-in wardrobe that's half the size of the room.

Her decor is slightly different, of course—bright colours and random images of palm trees and beaches. Ice-hockey players and Victoria's Secret models are scattered across the walls in no apparent pattern. It's chaotic, and it mirrors her personality seamlessly.

I lie down beside her and sigh; her head is still buried in her pillow.

"What the hell happened last night?" She moans. "Am I dead?"

"Well, if you are, I am," I say, my lips tugging into a grin.

Jade lifts her head, and right when I'm sure she's going to puke, she shouts, "Oh my god!"

"What?"

"You and Angus."

I try and fail spectacularly to muffle a grin. After we left the mini golf, Angus and I had dinner at Marcelle's, the local diner. Angus protested when I suggested it, wanting to take me somewhere more exquisite for our first official date. But eventually, he gave in. Marcelle's is my favourite, after all.

Afterwards, he drove me to my house, my hand fitting perfectly in his giant paw. When he was satisfied that I could stand on my own, he kissed me again. This time, I didn't faint. This time, a burning desire coursed through my body.

I pushed harder against his mouth, pinching his bomber jacket sleeves tight between the fingers of my fists, pulling him closer, as ravenous as a wild animal. So much so that when he finally pulled away, I was engulfed by a hunger that ached through my bones. Actually ached.

Even now, I can feel the places where his hands touched me; the tingling sensation that he left over my skin, long after he was gone. He must have met up with some of the male hockey team after we reluctantly said good bye.

"Tell me what happened!" She demands.

"There's nothing to tell," I say, avoiding eye contact.

Her stony eyes narrow. "Interesting, that's not what Angus said." It both surprises and thrills me that Angus might have told someone, anyone else about our afternoon together. That for him, too, maybe the memory of our kiss had lingered long after we'd said goodnight.

"What did he say?" I probe, a spark igniting in my belly. I am powerless against the childish grin sliding its way across my mouth.

"You tell me," Jade says, peeking at me through the blackened slits in her eyes.

"We kissed." I shrug, trying to keep the burning of my cheeks at bay.

"I knew it!" She croons. "What was it like?"

"Sloppy and wet," I say, giving her a disapproving look.

Jade rips the pillow off her head faster than I can blink and looks me dead in the eye. Her expression is blank, stunned. "It was that bad?"

A laugh escapes my lips. "Of course not! It's Angus, everything he does is perfect."

She lets out a long, dramatic groan. "Gross."

We talk for a few minutes longer until Jade is satisfied that I've given her every intimate detail of my afternoon. We both lie there silently until I think she's fallen asleep again.

Every time I press play on the memory of yesterday, I feel like I'm going to evaporate, as if every particle of my being is baffled by its own existence. People like Angus don't exist outside of fairy tales and fantasies—and even if they do, they don't go around kissing people like me.

***

Laboratories may be full of life, but they're also some of the loneliest places in the world. When I potter about my day, making small talk to the microscopic cells, they don't ask me why dinner is not on the stove. When I divulge to the rats all the minor details about my afternoon with Angus, they don't tell me to get out.

Jade is probably still sleeping, exactly how I left her this morning. Angus, well, he's probably at the strippers. Of course, there are no strippers in the Shire, unless you count the college cheerleading team who are happy to take their clothes off for much less than money, or so the rumour goes.

But Angus does have a buck's party for a friend he went to high school with back in Florida. Much to my heart's discontent, I probably won't see him again until next week.

As the professor enters the room, it occurs to me to wonder if my sanctuary of silence will be ripped out from underneath me, and I'll be forced to return home. It's a Sunday after all, there are no classes today and the library—my other sanctuary, is closed.

The professor has bags that look like hessian sacks sitting just under his green eyes, so heavy I can't imagine how they haven't burst wide open with every rub.

"Did I sleep through the first half of the week?" He says, dumping a bag onto the bench.

It's all I can do not to gather my things and leave, pretend that I'm picking up a book. The only thing keeping me rooted to the spot is the solemn look in his eyes, all too familiar to me.

"I gave you a spare key so that you could use the lab between classes, get out of the cold even. Not to waste away your weekend in here mixing chemicals. Not that I don't admire your work ethic, Aurelia."

He studies my vacant expression, and I don't have the energy or the willpower to wax lyrical with him. I just sigh.

The silence softens his hardened mouth. "Unless," he says carefully, "is everything alright at home?"

He unwraps his satchel and places it on the workbench. It slumps, depleted.

"Home is fine," I lie, the sharp, crow-like eyes of my mother blinking into memory.

"That look in your eye. It reminds me of a feeling I used to get when my father came home from the pub," he says.

The professor unpacks, pulling out a display of foods, all the colours of a rainbow and much too expensive to have come from our local supermarket. Cheeses, the kinds you might see on the table of a king. An array of dried fruits all the colours of the sunset. There are boxes of sweet crackers and jam, a spread that could feed a party of ten, and much too luxurious for just one person.

"Are you expecting someone?" I ask, my stomach letting out a low growl.

His eyes furrow. I point towards the food he is unpacking from the mile-deep, never-ending satchel.

His face relaxes. "Oh no, Aurelia, these are leftovers."

From what? I wonder. A palace ball?

"Please," he says, motioning for me to sit on the bar stool opposite him. "As you can see, I may have over-catered. Nevertheless, there is plenty enough to share."

My stomach forces my legs to float me towards the banquet before my brain can protest. Not having eaten a bite since this morning, I clutch my stomach, praying that he can't hear the unearthly growl from within it.

The cracker is coarse and delicate in my hands and the professor hands me a spreading knife. It disappears into the oozing soft layer of molten cheese as I plunge it deeper and deeper. When the sharp tang hits my taste buds, my mouth waters like the monsoons of the Amazon.

"Oh my god." I groan.

He lets slip a high-pitched cackle.

"It tastes like heaven," I mumble, my mouth still full of cheese. I'm certain now that he did not pick up this spread at the local market, or any market within forty miles for that matter. No, he must have gone out of town. To Sandringham, maybe, or Kentoff County in the north.

The grocery store in town only stocks Miriam's Tasty Cheese, and even then, that shipment only arrives from the docks down south at certain times of the year when the roads are safe enough for the transport trucks to navigate. You could forget about serving anything like that to guests during the winter. And yet, here I am spreading another thick layer of a cheese that makes Miriam's seem like mouldy glue.

You had to get to the store early or it would sell out faster than toilet paper in an apocalypse, and even then, we could only afford one ounce.

Momma would ration the slices like nuggets of gold, Papa and I holding our hands cupped together like the holy grail; his were tough with long fingers, and nails as splintered as icicles, the flesh of his palms dotted with faded callouses. My soft pink paws, so plump and untouched, could have fitted into his fourfold.

"I remember one night, I don't know the year, and I think that's what your mind does when memories are too painful; anyway, my father came home late from the bar. The door slammed, and I woke up. I must have been only seventeen, maybe eighteen years old.

"I could smell the bourbon before I even saw the bottle in his hand. I'll never forget the look in his eyes—so round, and pupils as black as death. His words were slurred." He swallows hard. "I begged him to stop, but he grabbed me by the collar and pinned me against the wall. He was much bigger than I was, you see, so I knew there was no point fighting back."

He pulls a cracker from the tray and lathers a generous helping of cheese onto its hard surface. He won't meet my rounded eyes.

"'Defend yourself, you weak bastard, be a man', he said over and over as he punched me in the jaw. I begged him to stop, but after the fifth or maybe sixth punch, I just remember slumping to the floor, the thick blood spilling from my nose, my jaw hanging loose from my mouth."

"Why are you telling me this?" I gulp, putting the cracker back onto the plate.

"I don't know what you're going through," he says, "but I recognise that grey look in your eyes. I want you to know that whatever it is, there will always be someone who will listen to you. Someone who might even understand."

My eyes fall to my lap, and even though I'm not looking at him, I can feel him looking at me, searching my face for any kind of answer, the truth.

"Are you familiar with the work of Viktor E Frankl?" He asks after I don't respond.

Finally, I lift my eyes to meet his.

"Between stimulus and response, there is space. In that space is our power to choose. No matter how long and vigorous you shake a bottle of water, when you open it up, it will still be calm, crystal clear, stable and covered with a layer of serenity.

"This is different from soda, you see? I don't have to tell you what happens when you shake a can of soda. I mean, we were all children once." He pauses. "My father was a can of soda, and alcohol would shake him to the core."

"Which one are you?" I ask.

His eyes narrow as he ponders for a moment, mulling over the question like a fine wine, as if it were the first time he'd ever asked it of himself. A dozen emotions dance across his face.

"Both," he says evenly, after a short pause, "but that all depends on who's doing the shaking."

The air falls still and silent between us. Intrigued, I watch him. His eyes glaze over like frosted glass shutting me out, as if his memories have taken him some place I cannot follow. I wonder about his father, about what happened to him. Did he ever muster the courage to fight back? The callousness that's crept into his eyes tells me enough to wonder if I might not like the answers.

"The real question," he says, breaking his trance and taking another cracker, he laces it with a slab of schmaltzy Saint Andre, "is which one are you?"

***

By the time I plod up the pavement to the chipped wooden door, the afternoon light has all but been absorbed into the mountains, leaving the sky in a damp darkness that seems to swallow everything into a black hole. Everything except the nervous ache in the pit of my stomach.

I peer through the window that flanks the front entryway. It's frosted but there's a dull orange glow filtering through the home like a dragon's breath. Shadows bounce off the walls, dancing slowly to the rhythm of my mother's rich hum.

The acidic sweetness of tomato, fresh basil and pepper wafts around the house. I'd know that smell if I were ten blocks away, blindfolded. Even as a young child, I'd forego the pizza, fluffy pastries and pancakes just to get a lick of the spatula as Momma laid down the sheets of pasta in perfect order, just as she had done a thousand times before. Lasagne has always been my favourite, reserved for birthdays, special occasions and apologies.

I inhale deeply and push through the front door into the open lounge room. Momma is standing at the stove, pushing a thick liquid slowly around a large pot. Caramel sauce, maybe? Every now and then, it gurgles as if it too is taking a deep breath.

She's wearing an old dressing gown, cream in colour with light green stripes, so faded they're almost invisible. Maybe it's the warmth of the house, or maybe I'm just too exhausted to care, but despite all my worries, I can't help but be grateful she's wearing something different, and clean.

"I've made lasagne," she says without so much as a glance in my direction. It's as close to an apology as I'll ever get from her.

"Smells good," I say. I hang my overnight bag back on the coat stand. I don't unpack, because while there's hope in my heart, I was not raised to be ignorant.

A hint of stale air hovers between us, as if we're in a cave slowly running out of oxygen. But this is a familiar place, and a few deep breaths won't kill us, not straight away.

"Come," she orders, waving a plate over the benchtop.

If I slump a little, my mother and I are about the same height. We share many things, but it's not the richness of our skin tone, our youthfulness or the shade of our eyes that makes us so alike, it's the sadness caught in them, trapped in an endless fog.

Years, it's been, since laughter carried in the hallways of our home. Rather, a darkness seemed to befall us when my father passed. Always cold, always empty. Doomed for destitution—my mother's words, not mine. Although on quiet nights like this, it's not hard to believe it.

Gratefully, I take the steaming plate from her hands, and we both take our places at the dining table—a place we rarely eat, with the silence screaming between us, neither willing to rock the boat lest it capsize what's left of us.

I want to talk to her about what happened. I want to beg her to take the steering wheel of her life and hold on to it like a raft, not to be swayed or tempted again, not to turn to the band aid of red wine and spirits. Instead, to focus on the road ahead of us, to be a family again. But these calm waters, like a millpond, are rare. I know that neither of us could withstand a ripple, let alone a wave.

She adjusts the wooden frame beneath her and digs in. The faint pitter-patter of her slippers against the floorboards is the only sound. For a moment, there's a flash of something brighter in her eyes, and then, just like a shooting star, it vanishes, replaced by tendrils of darkness and shadows.

I pray that this is the last time. Despite the cheesy goodness that drags me back to better days, I could go without it if I had to. My aching bones and depleted heart can't handle another cold winter in this house.

For the last time, I hope as I dig my fork into the steaming dish.

Chapter Eight

I didn't see Angus on Tuesday, or the day after that, or the day after that. In fact, I haven't seen anyone for the past two weeks. I spend the days as close to sleep as possible without actually drifting off, as stiff and frozen as the blizzard now standing between us.

Angus' flight has been cancelled, twice. No doubt he was frolicking amongst the summery streets of Florida, a vision that made my heart ache even more. He's due to arrive in town tomorrow, but hope is as melancholic as the winter snow outside.

Grey eyes stare at me in the reflection of the windows to the left. My skin is now a few shades lighter, almost pale. It's incredible how much can change in just a few days.

A few things haven't changed over this past week, one of which is the way I feel about Angus. The flutter in my stomach, the spring in my step. The kiss he gave me at my doorstep the day he left.

I thought I knew how it would feel—to fall in love with someone. I'd seen it with my own eyes. The way my father would lift my mother off the ground during an embrace, her toes barely grazing the floor beneath them. The way her face would light up at the sound of his truck pulling up outside. The way she practically stopped living when he died. Terrifying, isn't it? To love someone so much that the absence of them could shatter you into a thousand pieces.

Alister is setting up the lab when I stumble into the room with the grace of a pelican, tripping on the ice-coated door ledge, my arms thrashing, trying to steady myself. A few bemused smirks as they pretend to busy themselves with their microscopes.

But Alister's face is cold, harsh. "Careful," he growls, low enough that only I can hear. He steps towards me, ready to catch my flailing body at any moment.

"Sorry," I mutter.

My muscles groan as I slide quickly onto the stool closest to me. Mortification is the reason I'm sitting three back from the front today. With a bit of luck, I won't cause any more injuries to myself—or anyone else—for the next two hours.

Alister shrugs, the tension draining from his body with every step. He turns to address the rest of the class, his voice light as air, soft like velvet. As if responding to a silent command, my shoulders relax, his silky words lulling my attention gently towards him, the hairs on my arm catching fire.

The rest of the students trickle in lazily, pulled, coaxed obediently by the siren song. I'm starting to recognise their faces after all this time. It's no surprise, given that the kidney sprouts dotting the eastern wall are nearly eight weeks taller than they were when I first set foot in this laboratory. But I'll take the small victory; I need it today.

Ron, Andy, Suzanne, Beatrice, Harold, Kia, Usung. I count them one by one as they take their stools. Quiet chatter weaves like mist between the test tubes.

The weather is expected to start warming up in the next few weeks with the start of May nearly upon us, the snow melting into the soil like a sponge, absorbing the bitter winter. It won't disappear completely, but after the last few weeks, I'll be glad for the extra degrees.

Of course, the flu will run rampant for the initial months as bodies struggle to transition through the change in atmosphere. Change is always hard, no matter how slight, whether it's the seasons, or the plaguing absence of a person. I know all about that probably better than most. The four empty seats to my right tell me that today, at least, I might not be the only one still adjusting.

"Alright, now that you have all defrosted a bit, time to get into it. Take out your textbooks and turn to page two hundred and thirty-nine," Alister says.

I don't even bother to try and recall the name of the chapter; I'm too distracted by the dainty squeal of laughter threading though the corridor.

Juliette and Eamon. They're floating past the open door of our classroom, his hand tucked neatly into the back pocket of her navy denim jeans. She's clutching a third-year textbook to her chest. Eamon is big, like a serious bodybuilder with golden eyes and dark hair.

They're similar like that, so similar, in fact, they could be related. Juliette is beautiful too, with legs that stretch on for days, bright eyes and a warm smile. Together, they seem to float rather than walk—just that little bit taller than everyone else, as if it's a dance they've been practising for years.

Will people look at Angus and me the same way? Like two souls entwined by destiny. Or will they look on me with disdain, wondering just how someone as flawed as me managed to charm someone as goddamn perfect as him?

"I'm leaving."

The words are like stones, shattering the image of a shirtless Angus, dragging my lusting mind back to the class. Leaving?

Cool indifference plays on his face, but he shifts slightly from one foot to the other. "I will be returning to South Carolina for the fall, so this will be our last class."

And just like that, the world seems to darken again. And maybe it's my aching heart talking, the one pathetically longing for Angus, or maybe it's the forty-hour study weeks, but I will myself to breathe normally, to slow the blood thumping like a drum behind my ears. I choke back the lump in my throat, caught there by a web of emotions I can't even begin to untangle.

The room erupts into a chorus of groans and hushed whispers. He thanks us for having him this term, and his mouth spreads into a twisted half-smile, but it hits differently this time. Darker even—if that is possible. As usual it doesn't reach his deep-set eyes, which are homed in on me like a pair of headlights, unwavering and lifeless.

"Honestly, it never does get easier, even after all these years," he concedes. "But I never leave, not really."

My breath catches and I will myself to look away but I can't, like a deer in the glare of the hunter's flashlight.

"When will you be back?" Susannah asks. She's sitting somewhere behind me.

Alister blinks, his pointed stare finally breaking. My shoulders sag with relief.

"When the trees turn white, and the lake freezes over." He offers her a crooked smile, and I have no doubt that it alone is enough to have melted her heart like butter. She shifts awkwardly in her chair, trying to avoid eye contact as her pale cheeks bloom.

I busy myself with the pages of the textbook in front of me but, like the heat of an open flame, I feel it the moment his gaze settles on me again.

"Don't worry," he says to no one in particular, "I know I'll be seeing you very soon."

***

I must be dreaming. Listening to the soft thump of Angus' heartbeat, my ear pressed against his naked, muscled chest, the tips of his calloused fingers trailing the equally exposed skin along the side of my body, I wouldn't even care if I was.

With each stroke of his hand, a line of fireworks trail close behind, pulling me deeper into the crux of his warm embrace. I'm totally absorbed in the rustic, sweet, teakwood smell of him, the gentle grey light sneaking through the gaps in his curtains.

He'd slipped an arm over my shoulders, tucking me close to his body as we walked between classes on Friday. Every unbearable moment spent craving his touch, every agonising, pathetic, insecure thought evaporated the moment he pulled into the parking lot.

He had laced his fingers through mine as we walked from building to building, showered me in soft kisses as we parted ways at the door of our classrooms.

Jade had made a string of hurling gestures towards us. Others passed us in the halls, gawking, their hearts bleeding as Angus adjusted the jacket over my bare shoulders, as he delicately tucked a stray hair behind my ear.

Some had even hovered by their cars a few moments longer than necessary, just to catch a glimpse of our final embrace. But it wasn't, not really. Angus—as chivalrous as ever—unhinged the door of his Chevrolet, and I climbed into the passenger seat. We'd spent the afternoon so entwined in each other that our bodies were a mess of unidentifiable limbs, at times, impossible to distinguish.

This morning, I'd awoken in much the same way, with chaffed lips and a bulging heart. Angus's eyes are closed but his mouth curls into a devilish smile as I press a longing kiss to his chest. "You stayed."

"I did," I mutter, relishing the soft press of our skin as his arms wrap tighter around me, the warmth of him absorbing the chill of guilt churning in my stomach and the wrath that is sure to follow my return home tonight.

"How did I get so lucky?" Angus whispers, pressing a cool kiss to my forehead, my cheek, my lips, lower and lower. My stomach flutters with every brush of him. What beauty and elegance he beholds in me, I may never understand.

"Fuck," Angus curses, throwing back the covers. He frantically searches the floor for his jeans. "I didn't realise it was so late."

"When will you be back?" I ask, dragging myself to a sitting position. We hadn't really spoken about his golf tournament. Quite frankly, apart from the brief groan between kisses, we'd barely spoken much at all.

Angus pauses, his brow furrowed, his white t-shirt halfway over his arms. "Oh."

"Oh?"

"Well, I'd assumed we would be going together. But I suppose that might have been a bit presumptuous of me. You probably have other plans."

Angus lowers his eyes and my heart thunders. I fight the urge to drag him back into bed and have him ravish me all over again.

"I'd love to." I grin.

***

"What is it?" I turn my head to see Angus' eyes locked on mine instead of the miles and miles of road ahead of us. The tyres drearily hiss over the rain-washed highway and the air that creeps though the filters is sweet like pine.

One side of his mouth pulls up into an uneven grin. He laughs. "Nothing."

My brows furrow. "Tell me."

"I like watching you think," he says. "You look so serious." He wrinkles his nose into a silly frown, straining to fight off the laughter brewing behind his eyes.

I groan, and Angus' face softens into a satisfied grin. "What were you thinking about anyway?"

I sigh. "Well, if you must know, I was thinking about Alister and the lab. I was actually starting to enjoy it."

Angus squeezes my hand, a knowing look in his eye. "He'll come back, he always does."

"How do you know him so well?" I ask, remembering their familiarity at the after-party earlier this year.

"I met him at Elkwin University in South Carolina."

"Is that—?"

Angus nods. "The university he goes back to each fall."

"But isn't that—?"

"My old school? Yes. He taught me during my first two years at Elkwin. I used to miss him when he left to go north, but you get used to his comings and goings over time."

There's nothing but unfiltered admiration in Angus's eyes. They sparkle with every reference to their past together. I don't dare to hope that he might carry that same awe in his undertones when talking about how we met. I will have to ask Jade about that tomorrow. Angus steals glances at me for the next twenty minutes.

"Watch the road," I order, "or neither of us will make it to Whistler in one piece."

Angus frowns. "But I'm a good driver."

Angus is playing in a one-day amateur golfing tournament in Whistler, a neighbouring town about four hours from the Shire. I barely notice so much as the bumps on the road because Angus' hand has been curled around mine the entire time, and we are only one hour away from our destination.

"Are you nervous?" I fiddle with the heater. Icicles spread along the windscreen like mould.

"A bit," he says coolly, "but I haven't noticed, I've been distracted."

His fingers glide lightly up my arm, leaving a trail of fireworks in their wake. When they graze my collarbone, my heart catches fire. I cup his hand in mine as he moves up towards my face. He brushes loose hair gently behind my ears and the familiar rush of fervour courses through me.

"Oh?"

I loosen the seatbelt at my waist and lean over the centre console until my lips are brushing his neck, just as delicately as he had only moments ago. Reaching across him, I slip my fingers under the fringe of his shirt. His skin is molten and soft beneath my hands, muscles tensing ever so slightly with my touch.

The ribbed washboard of his stomach ripples, rising and falling with his razored breath. The waft of sweet teakwood and vanilla is dizzying and it takes a moment for me to compose myself. Starting at the base of his neck, I let his cologne overwhelm me, silencing my racing mind. My lips move up and up, pausing just behind the soft part of his ear.

"How distracted?" I whisper onto his skin.

A starved growl is his only answer. And then a ragged scream.

No, not a scream—but a screech from somewhere beneath us. Tyres spin on invisible axles, sliding from side to side across the icy road. My stomach lurches as the air is ripped from my lungs like a vacuum. As the car spins, spins, spins, everything slows.

It doesn't happen like they say it will—where memories flash past like a slideshow. It all happens at once, the memories—a thousand years' worth of existences shoved into one moment. The pain of my father's death, his last breath, my mother's soul leaving her body as she screams out for him, as he lay dying in her arms.

My father's love—like a warm embrace. Angus' longing, his patience, his jealousy. Alister's helplessness—Lucinda's life hanging in the balance and him refusing to let go. It was like stepping through a window into their souls, one by one, reliving their darkest moments.

"Rae?" The voice is panicked, drawing me back to the present. It's close, maybe inches away, but I can't see anything through the flecks of light and thick black blotches clouding my vision. "Rae?" So familiar, so warm. My heart aches for the sound and I'm reaching for it through the darkness. Always reaching for it.

A steady hand traverses my waist to unbuckle my seat belt. "Aurelia, can you hear me?"

"What happened?" I groan, clutching my aching forehead.

My stomach drops as the car seat disappears from beneath me, eyes flying open in shock. Warm, solid arms carry me as if I'm no heavier than the cold air now flooding into my lungs.

I'm lowered gently onto a fallen tree trunk underneath the umbrella of some large pine trees. It's the only spot for miles not coated in white. He kneels before me, taking my hands. Behind him is the unblemished skin of the Corvette.

"Are you hurt, Rae?" Angus asks; his eyes wild, searching my face for answers.

I grimace, lifting my shirt to search for the source of the sharp burning pain reaching across my stomach and chest.

Angus's eyes are wide. "Are they broken?"

I trace the thick purple bruise snaking from my left hip bone to my right shoulder. Where the seatbelt constricted around me, I suppose. I shudder to think what would have happened had it not.

"I don't think so."

"Let me see." He crouches before me, his eyes focused in careful consideration, years of placement in the ED taking over. With his thumb, he gently caresses my skin, starting at my hip and tracing the bruise up the flat surface of my stomach to the lip of my sports bra.

His eyes furrow. "Does it hurt, Rae?"

I shake my head, the chill of his fingers offset by the warmth in his eyes.

"I don't think they're broken," he surmises, "just bruised. Paracetamol and ibuprofen will take the sting and swelling out of it."

I nod, because it's all I can manage, totally overawed by his cool professionalism.

"I'm so sorry, Rae," he whispers after a moment of silence. "The deer, it just came out of nowhere. I'll take you home."

I look down into his wide eyes, rounded like moons. If only he knew what power, he wielded in them. "It's not your fault," I whisper, cupping his face in my hands. His eyes close against the touch of my skin.

A few strands of his golden hair fall over his eyes, but I brush them away in one swift movement and pull him closer, hungry for him. Starving. "I'm fine, I don't want to go home."

He leans in, his face now no more than an inch from mine. His breath, sweet like honey. Aching, teeth chattering, I smile against his mouth.

He leans into me, kissing me hard and fast. I bite back a yelp as he pulls back, just in time to leave me utterly ravenous for the feeling of his body pressed on mine, our limbs tangled like a web. I tug him closer, wincing against the burning over my chest. He kisses me again. It's one of those earth-shattering kisses I'm certain I'll feel long after he pulls away.

"I love you," he whispers against my mouth, leaning his forehead against my own, so quiet and gentle I'm convinced it was nothing more than the whistle of the wind through the trees around us. And the searing pain across my chest does not matter, nor the trucks careering past us as he kisses me again.

A lovers' kiss, two souls once cleaved apart, now coming home. My throat tightens at the longing in his eyes, as if merely being in each other's presence would never be enough, not anymore.

"I love you too," I whisper as I kiss him back.

***

The weather is slightly warmer in Whistler, but only by a couple of degrees. But what comfort is offered by the slight increase in temperature is offset by the conditions now facing me at the golf course. The stubbly grass looks more like a lake, and there's no clubhouse for spectators.

At least, the rain is a welcome vacation from the ten inches of snow back home, although I wouldn't be surprised if that too began falling from the sky any minute.

Angus meanders after his ball with cool indifference plastered over his face, the picture of calm. It's one of the reasons he'll make a brilliant surgeon one day. Diesel's brown hair is plastered to his pale round face as he jogs towards me. He shakes his head on arrival, sending water droplets flying.

His soft brown eyes gleam wickedly through the curtain of his soggy fringe. He towers over me at around six foot, and he's built from head to toe, weighing in at just over two hundred pounds.

"I used to think I was his good luck charm," he says, sauntering over.

"Well, if that's the case, do you think you could do something about this rain?" I laugh.

He peers down at me, eyes plagued with a mixture of awe and concern. "Hi, Rae."

"Hi, Diesel," I say, letting him fold me into his arms. My abdomen pinches and I wince against the pain.

"Sorry," he says, releasing me. "Gus told me about this morning. Are you okay?"

"I'm fine." I wave him off. "Just a bruise."

"How do you think he's going?" Diesel asks, holding his umbrella over my head.

"It's hard to tell with all this rain. Not that I would know even if I could see," I admit. "How do you think he's going?"

"Pretty well, he's happy enough. But then again, that part hasn't really been a problem since he found out you were coming to watch."

My throat tightens, cheeks burning. Almost two years, and I'm still as overawed by Angus as the day we met—even if it did involve scrubbing his vomit off my shoe.

"You two are adorable," he drawls, scuffing up my hair.

I laugh, shoving him away. "Stop it—anyway, aren't you supposed to be keeping him dry?"

"Oh, I would, but I was given strict orders to come over here and make sure his number one fan was not going to freeze to death. And you know," he shrugs, "he's the boss, so I gotta do what he says."

I look over to where Angus is lining up against the ball. In one smooth stroke, it vanishes into the small hole in the earth.

"Honestly, I think he might actually win," Diesel says. "He's loving the wet weather."

"Well, his spectators aren't." Around us, only one or two wandering bodies dot the fairway now.

"You're the only person he wanted here today, you know. I was under strict instruction to keep my big mouth shut about the tournament." He rolls his eyes.

He's right—if Angus had told anyone else, the course would be lined with people, rain, hail or shine. The pressure would be enormous.

"Well, that's my cue," Diesel says. "I'll catch you later, Rae. Try to stay dry. I think I've got a spare blanket in my truck if you need it."

I lunge to catch the keys as he tosses them in the air.

"Thank you," I pant, my breath carrying. "Tell him I said good luck."

"I will." Diesel winks, jogging back across the fairway.

***

After the ceremony, Angus carefully loads his golf bag and trophy onto the back seat of the Chev and slides gracefully behind the wheel. His damp white shirt hugs his chest. I can't help but gawk at the ripple of muscle now transparent through the fabric. It takes all my effort not to reach out and touch him. To have him right here, on the back seat of this car.

I secure the blanket around my shoulders—the one pulled from the back of Diesel's truck—and wait for the heater to defrost my frozen limbs. Angus turns to me, one hand draped over the steering wheel.

"Before we go, I have something for you." He unfurls a cloth-wrapped box from his pocket and holds it out to me, his hand steady and firm.

"For me?" I gasp.

His eyes glimmer. "Of course."

Angus places the delicate little box onto my palm. It's light, hardly the weight of a feather. Angus busies himself with his dashboard, wiping away dust particles and adjusting the time. Basically, everything he can not to look straight at me as I tug at the longest part of the pink ribbon.

The delicate silk slides loose, as soft as Angus' hands against my skin, against the parts of my body that only he can find, the parts I'd hardly known existed until they electrified at his touch.

The lid of the box opens to reveal a bevelled golden heart with the letters 'A' and 'A' engraved on its smooth surface. Its thick golden body hangs from a delicate golden chain. I suck in a breath.

"Angus." I stop, my bristly voice threatening to scratch this perfect moment. "It's beautiful," I whisper.

He smiles then, and reaching his hands gently around my waist, he tugs me across the centre console until I'm straddling his lap, our bodies again entwined.

The pain across my ribs ramps up all the way to searing, faster than I can blink. And then, just when I can no longer stand it, Angus' hands start to roam under my shirt, and suddenly, the burning feeling dissolves like mist under his numbing touch. My hair falls between us like a curtain.

"Tell me again how much you love me," he whispers, a brazen grin dancing on his lips. I haven't known him to be so brash. It does nothing to douse the heat between my legs.

"I don't remember telling you that the first time," I say, surprised by my boldness. As the words roll casually from my tongue, I recall the moment on the roadside clearly.

He frowns. Fear? Is that what now clouds his perfectly rounded eyes? A sort of cackle sound comes from somewhere deep in my stomach. My mouth stretches into a grin, and I watch as Angus' face softens.

The sight of his mouth curling into a smile has me biting my lip. Has there ever been a face more perfect than the one before me?

I pretend not to notice the way the others look at him—the women who worship him like a god. I wonder how long his love for me will stave them off. Like wolves to a carcass, they hover their careful distance around us. How long will it be before a better version takes my place?

I'm sure when the day comes, I'll be scraping up the fragments of my pride as they lie broken on the floor, left to rot in the sunken fields of heartbreak. Love is no contract, after all.

I brush the fringe from his eyes, tracing his face with my fingers as if seeing him for the first time, trying to memorise it all—just in case. Will it be the first argument that capsizes us? Or the second?

"I think you do remember," Angus probes. "You're just too proud to admit it."

"Oh? Is that so?" I tease.

"Well, I think that necklace pretty much speaks for itself as far as my feelings are concerned."

I take the pendant in my hands, finding the place where our initials are carved.

"Here." Angus takes my hands in his, tilting the heart into the light until it catches the surface. The shiny face transforms as three words appear on its skin like a tattoo.

I love you.

My breath catches. Angus holds my gaze. I have never seen him this vulnerable, the bravado slipping away through the cracks. I lean in, letting our lips meet tenderly. Maybe some boats are stronger than others.

"I will always love you," I whisper against his mouth, the walls of the world melting around us, just as they have always done.

Chapter Nine

Thunderous claps hammer against the all-too-fragile shell of my skull, my mouth as dry as sandpaper, every breath as jagged and strained as shards of glass. My head is stuck in some sort of box. Rags with a metallic reek have been pulled tight against my mouth, leaving only my nose to save me from suffocating completely. I tear open my dry eyes, allowing the inside of this malevolent contraption to take shape. Carpet or foam of some sort rubs hard against my nose.

Tight rough walls that smell like pine press flush against my face. A thick rope is tightening around my neck and sharp splinters dig in. The subtle groan and rich scent remind me of leather. Hot, frantic breaths coat my sweaty chin and upper lip. Compared to the cool air that pricks my arms and legs, it's unbearable.

I try to keep my breathing steady, but while my heart jackhammers against my chest, panic thrums through my throat and lungs, choking me from the inside.

Snippets of light flicker somewhere in the corner of the room, visible only through two small penny-sized holes cut into the panel in front of me. The rest of the world is an incoherent blur, and it takes immense strain to make sense of anything.

Soft satin sheets brush against my bare ankles and feet, caressing the back of my bound hands. Not a coffin then—it's only my head that's stuck in this box. But there's no relief in my discovery and nothing to soothe my aching and brittle bones. Where am I?

Thick wiry ropes dig into my skin, and with each agonising movement, there's another bolt of pain. A dusty scent crawls up my nostrils and the crackling of grey static fills my ears. I wriggle my limbs loosely against the mattress, but my head remains trapped, the belt-like device around my neck tightening with every tug.

Panic sets in as I try to scream, but only muffled sobs echo in the silence. I arch my neck enough to recognise crimson sheets beneath me. Thick, blood-red blankets draped over the sides of the single mattress. If I don't get some fresh air soon, I'll surely suffocate to death.

The more I slow my breathing, the easier it is to make out some of the other shapes around me. The four walls are rough and grey, like stone or concrete. What bothers me more is what I can't see. There's no desk shoved tightly in the corner of the room, no kaleidoscope lamp that has sat beside my bed since I was five, no frayed carpet and tattered curtains.

No soul-chilling breeze blowing through the room. The lack of windows makes it impossible to tell what time of the day or night it might be. Every creak and groan of the wooden box around my head echoes like a sinister lullaby.

A dull crackle of voices carries from the corner of the room. I gently manoeuvre my aching neck towards the sound just enough to make out the silhouette of an old-fashioned box television with an aerial sitting atop it like chopsticks. Sweat trickles into my eyes, blurring the view, but it's as if I've fallen down a wormhole and come out in a completely different era.

Bucking, kicking and arching my back a few times, I manage to roll off the bed with a hard thump. A loud crack and a surge of pain from my shoulder causes me to cry out, but I bite down harder against the fabric between my teeth until I'm practically crawling towards the television screen.

It's not much bigger than a cereal box. The old floorboards are hard against my exposed knees, but I barely notice while I wait to catch glimpses of information through the static. I can see just enough to make out the evening's breaking news headline: *Brunswick Shire medical student still missing.*

My head swims, body trembling despite the suffocating heat. If this were a dream, I would have woken the moment I hit the ground. The moment my bones started to throb. But I'd discarded that old soggy flyer in the bin weeks ago. Rose has been missing for over fourteen months—why would this be today's news headline?

"Hello?"

I whirl towards the sound. To my right, no more than four feet away, towers a high wooden door with a small clear window cut into it that appears to be shuttered on the outside, maybe permanently, because I can't see through it.

A draught is snaking its way under the impossibly small space between the floor and the lip of timber, hardly big enough to fit a fingernail. With barely anywhere else to go, the heat of my breath coats my face.

"Hello?" The voice is angelic and feminine, one I don't recognise.

"Who's there?" I groan.

No answer. I reach inwards, trying to cling to fleeting memories, to discern how or when I got here. My eyes hurriedly roam the smooth wooden surface—there has to be a handle or lever of some kind. Nothing.

Nothing but the smooth, wooden surface of the door. Locked from the outside, bolted shut maybe. My stomach plummets, dread washing over me. My ears thrum with panic and the impatient *drip, drip* of water somewhere beyond the door.

"Hello?" I cry, another surge crashing through me like a tidal wave, my eyes stinging with tears. "Let me out!"

"Shhh," a voice hisses, deeper and gruffer than the first, "he'll hear you."

I ignore the warning, ignore the veiled threat coating the words, and scream louder, my body shaking violently with every plea. I haul myself to my knees and throw my body weight and every available bound limb against the door. But a stone battering ram wouldn't rock it. It would have to be made of paper for me to do any damage in this state. My heart throbs, fists balling against the binds, preparing to fight whatever might lie on the other side.

"Let me out!"

A soft *hiss* echoes from somewhere behind me like a leaky glass cylinder. I stop thrashing for a moment, the acidic new air seeping through the wooden box, filling my lungs with every panting breath. The translucent mist falls weightlessly into my open palms, dissolving on impact. As I take another breath, a wave of calm washes over me, through me, its tender fingers reaching deep enough to cradle my thrumming heart.

The mist pours down from the ceiling duct above the single bed. I can only just make it out through the peep holes. Darkness sweeps in, wrapping its arms around me like an old friend. I fight the lure of sleep, willing my eyes to stay open, but the weight of oblivion closes in around me, and I am powerless to resist it.

As I lie helpless and exposed against the hard wooden floor, it's not the endless dark that I'm afraid of, it's what I might find in the light.

***

The next morning, anger roars through my body so hot, I wonder how long it will be before I combust into flames. It's more than my weakened and frail body can handle.

This time, when I finally came to, the wooden box had been removed from my head, and there was a light burning sensation over my ankles as the air kissed the burn marks where the rope had cut too deep. My hands remained bound behind my back, this time by a pair of metal handcuffs. My mouth is still gagged, but at least I can see. Never again will I take the cool kiss of air for granted.

I know it's morning because the television set is playing *The Breakfast Show*, but the little date stamp in the corner is days older than the last time I remember being home. Scraps of memory have been floating in and out all morning, and now finally, I've managed to glimpse the full picture.

It was around 10 am on Thursday when I received a text message from Alister inviting me to the lab. The details are sketchy, mostly due to the dull, glamoured veil coating my memories, and my throbbing head.

I arrived half an hour late because Angus had insisted on driving me, to allow us to sleep in. But his car tyre was flat, and rather than wait for him to change it, I opted to walk. I figured the crisp air would help me cool off after spending the morning tangled in him.

Alister was pairing crackers and gooey cheeses on a board when I arrived.

"Am I early?" I asked, noticing that the lab was empty.

"Just in time." Alister ushered me into the room. His eyes were darting, throwing glances at the door. "Coffee?" He offered.

By the time I'd answered, he had already poured a steaming mug of the brown liquid and was sliding it across the bench towards me. He stared at me expectantly.

"Thank you," I said, taking a monitored sip.

He smiled wickedly, triumph in his deep-set eyes. Then he released me from his stare and hurriedly shoved items into his briefcase—empty jars, syringes, loose pieces of paper—and then wiped down the benches and door handles.

"You will have to forgive me, Aurelia, your invitation is slightly different to that of the other students," he said, still fluffing about with his items.

He was moving so quickly, I struggled to keep him in focus. Rubbing my eyes didn't help much.

"I have asked you to come a little earlier. I was hoping for the chance to speak to you privately."

I could hear his words clearly, but they echoed on a loop in my head. I took another sip of the coffee, hoping that might clear the lump forming in my throat.

"You're very important, Aurelia, your knowledge, your talents. They cannot be wasted in a place like this."

"Thank you," I tried to say, but my voice was nothing more than an echo.

I'd thought maybe I was having a stroke. I tried to concentrate on my breath, but my head was swimming. It reminded me a little of how I felt with Angus right before I fainted. But this was different, unpleasant.

A sense of dread washed over me. Nauseous and disorientated, I could hear Alister, but it sounded as if he were miles away. As if I were at the other end of a tunnel, trying to call out for help.

"The outside world and all its distractions, illusions and stimulus prevent us from reaching our full potential. There's so much we could achieve if we had more focus, better motivations. Strict routines. You understand that, don't you, Aurelia?"

"I don't feel—" I stuttered.

My legs started to tremble and I scrambled to grab hold of the bench, but it dissolved in my hands like air. I was flailing towards the hard laminate floor. Closing my eyes, I braced for impact, but right before I hit, something—an arm, maybe—wrapped around me like a net, and the floor disappeared from beneath.

A dark, cube-shaped box was placed over my head, covering my face completely, stripping the world of light and air. And then, everything dissolved into darkness and I woke up here, on a bed in this little room with no windows, and a bolted door.

A cage.

Chapter Ten

Thump.
Wince.
Thump. Thump.
Wince.

The wood is cool against my forehead and teardrops stain the floorboards below. My shoulders are blue and bloody, but I ram the door as hard as I can. I've been at this for hours with no progress. No one has come to find me. Is there even anyone out there to hear my muffled cries?

"Let me out!" Sandpaper laces my throat; my voice is hoarse and broken.

"Baby, it's no use, no one can hear you," a soft, ethereal voice whispers through the walls.

"You don't know that," I groan, "you're not real!"

The voice sighs. "What's your name, sweetie?"

It's a sort of drawl, the way her words come out.

No. Don't engage, I tell myself, *it's not real.*

"Forget it, Patrice, this one's deranged—she thinks she's hallucinating," the deeper voice says, louder and harsher than the first. *Female,* I think.

"She's adjusting. We all struggled in the beginning." The first voice again.

"Not like this," the second groans, "what's it now, day five?"

Five? No, it couldn't be.

"Enough, Rose," the first hisses. Mid-twenties, I guess.

The second voice grunts. "Just shut her up, Patrice, I'm trying to sleep."

I press my ear against the door to hear them more clearly. I still don't know if they're real, or at what point I've let go of the tether tying me to reality.

"Where am I?" I ask through the door.

"You're safe, baby, that's all that matters for now."

Patrice that must be her name. A gentle and kind voice, almost motherly. Baby. The word has a soothing quality to it. Affectionate. She reminds me of my mother—or at least, the kind of person she used to be.

"Safe." The second laughs. *Rose.* Patrice had called her Rose.

"Rosemary!" Patrice growls, almost in confirmation.

Rosemary. I roll the name around in my mind. The harsh one.

"Why am I here?" I mumble.

"We're lab rats," Rosemary snaps.

"Rose—" Patrice tries to interrupt.

Rosemary ignores her. "Look around you. You've got four walls, a bed and a toilet. It's a cage. If you behave, you get fed. When you're adjusted enough, he'll let you out into his little lab and you'll be put to work. *Ergo*, lab rat. For the greater good." The last part was riddled with sarcasm and resentment.

Patrice sighs. "You've always had a way with words, Rosemary."

"I have to get out of here," I mutter, more to myself than the others.

"Good luck." Rosemary laughs. "This place is like Alcatraz."

"Prisoners escaped from Alcatraz," I growl in reply, the anger still muffled by rags.

"And died," she taunts.

My stomach lurches, anger rising through my chest like a flood in a storm drain. Patrice's voice is gentle, but it does nothing for the gut-wrenching fear coursing through every inch of my body.

"Baby, what Rosemary is trying to say is that you need some rest—it's almost midnight and you've been at it for hours. You can try again in the morning."

I slump to the floor, defeated, back flush against the door. My shoulders ache, and I'd just about give anything to be able to hug myself. Instead, my body throbs like a heartbeat. Broken, maybe, just like the rest of me. It's an effort to drag my weary body onto the soft mattress. It's hopeless, but I still pray that I might wake up from this nightmare.

"I'm not going to give up," I murmur against the gag, "there has to be a way out."

I roll onto my side, eyes wide, mind racing.

"How can you possibly sleep in here?" I ask. "We're rats in a cage."

"Told you," Rose jeers.

"Close your eyes," Patrice says, "pretend you're someplace else. Use your memories."

My eyes well up, and I'm utterly powerless to stop them.

Rosemary sighs. "I think about my mum, getting ice cream in the park together when I was five."

"I think about my partner, Jack, our first date by the lake. South Carolina has the most beautiful lakes," Patrice adds.

Rolling on to my side, eyes squeezed tight, I promise I'll try again in the morning. That I'll find a way out of here no matter what it takes. That I'll never give up.

My aching bones will have a better chance if they're rested, so I try to conjure one of my earlier memories of the university, not long after Angus and I met. It was during the warmer months, which makes it harder to visualise in this cold, dark room.

At first, it's hard to concentrate; the picture keeps dropping out, almost as if I'm so far from my previous life that there's no signal. Eventually, the solid walls of my mind soften, and I give myself fully until I can smell the liquor-stained air and I'm in the tavern once again.

***

It was ten-thirty on a Friday night and already, the Eagle Tavern was overflowing with intoxicated first-year students. The sticky-sweet scent of raspberry vodkas and Jager bombs coated the air. Even from outside, I could practically taste it.

Once we finally made it past the security guards, Jade shoved us in the direction of the bar. While the people around us reeled off the names of various rums, liqueurs and spirits, none of which I'd ever heard of, I leaned back on the bar and took in the sheer size of the room. There were about four hundred college residents and yet, somehow, still room to dance.

To our right, the brown oak bar stretched out about ten metres, rounding the corner and out of sight, disappearing into a room with red-surfaced pool tables, a wall of green shrubbery, and a mass of people clustered around them. To our left, the bar dropped off, and a great big stretch of tar-like black dance floor marked the space between us and the rest of the patrons smoking and drinking outside.

Across the dance floor, through the gaps between the dancing bodies, all moving in waves, a group of girls in waist-high shorts and strips of fabric that would barely cover an eye gathered in a star-shaped cluster.

It could have been the jet-black polo, stark against his olive skin, his blue eyes the only speck of colour amongst a sea of black bomber jackets, but I recognised Angus immediately.

There he was, leaning against a brick wall, legs crossed at his denim ankles just above his Converse sneakers as if plucked straight from the screen of an eighties movie. I watched him carefully, his movements soft and rhythmic. His eyes flashed from sky to royal blue when he smiled.

Meeting him, I felt something wake in me that had been dormant for a long time. Granted, it was a rough start, but the more he pestered me, the more I seemed to want him to. It sickened me to think that this was what I'd become, no better than one of those groupies gathered around him.

It had been a decent four weeks since the incident in the laboratory. Any lingering sense of obligation to me had well and truly dissipated, and over time, I saw less and less of him. In fact, this was the first I'd seen of him in weeks.

"Here, take this," Jade said, stealing me from my pathetic lusting. She handed me a drink. "Is that the guy?" She asked, following my gaze outside. "The one from class that you were telling me about?"

"Yeah, he vomited on my shoe." I sighed.

"Looks like you might have some competition," Jade said, nodding towards the cluster that surrounded him like a shield.

"Indeed." I sighed again. I looked at the drink in my hand, grateful for the distraction. It looked like a mixture of Halloween pumpkin and a vial of blood.

"It's a Captain Morgan," Jade explained. "Try it, I promise you'll like it."

I took a swig—my first mistake. It was like fire and ice at once; as the drink touched my lips, I could taste vanilla, which was quickly overawed by the sour taste of molasses, leaving a bitumen path tracking down my throat. The second sip was no better, so I held my breath and let the contents of the glass bypass my taste buds.

"That's the way," Jade crooned, "want another one?"

"No," I gasped, willing my gut to stop churning. "I'm going to get some air," I yelled above the noise. It was impossible to hear anything over the thundering of the music.

I strode across the dark dance floor, past the DJ and headed towards the beer garden. It was about six degrees colder than inside, but the night air was the only thing keeping me from hurling.

I found a bare patch near some wooden tables where I could stand with my back towards the north wall of the bar. The place was less garden and more beer, if you asked me. The turf underfoot was faux grass, but like a balding, middle-aged man, most of it was bare and grey as if it had been rubbed with sandpaper. There were a couple of green bushes dotted amongst the picnic-style tables, but the only purpose they seemed to serve was as ashtrays.

The wide expanse of the night nipped at my face as I closed my eyes. For a moment, I let myself forget about Angus, about the women hanging off his every word. About the gnawing ache I felt in my stomach whenever I thought about him, about the overwhelming tug pulling me towards him.

Then, he tapped me on the shoulder.

"Hi, Rae," he said, his voice as smooth as silk.

Oh no. As I turned, my attention caught on the piercing blue of his eyes.

"Hi, hey," I fumbled.

He laughed. "I don't know if you remember me," he said.

I couldn't help it. A gust of laughter burst from me, spilling into the air between us. "You vomited on my shoe and then followed me around for weeks afterwards. How could I not remember you?"

"Well, at least I got your attention." His mouth twisted into a wry smile and it was so perfect, it made me dizzy.

"Do you want to sit down?" Angus asked. "You look pale."

I nodded, sitting down on one of the wooden benches. Angus sat beside me. His knee brushed mine, leaving a trail of sparks like a fault line stretching all the way down my leg.

We were only a few metres from the suspicious glances being cast our way, the jealous peeks from the girls that had crowded around Angus only moments ago, but my mind was a world away. They all seemed to fade into irrelevance.

"Don't worry," he said, clocking my nervous glance. "I can stomach liquor better than I can stomach cadavers."

"I hope so," I said. "I happen to like these shoes."

"Go on. Ask me," he said, rolling his eyes. "Everyone else does."

I frowned. "Ask what?"

"How do I plan on becoming a doctor if I can't stand the sight of human organs?" He drawled rhetorically.

"Well?" I asked.

He grinned. "I don't know, I'm still trying to figure that out."

I laughed, cradling the empty glass to my chest. The more Angus talked, the more I felt like I already knew him. When his blue eyes caught the light, I couldn't will myself to look away. He was stunning with his olive skin and chiselled jawline. Even his wavy blond hair was perfectly ragged that night.

His eyes furrowed. "Are you cold?"

He peeled his bomber jacket off his shoulders as if it were a second skin, and wrapped it around my back. The smell of him was intoxicating. The musky sweet scent was now flooding my nostrils. It caught fire somewhere deep inside me.

"May I?" He asked, slowly sliding his arm around my waist, pulling me closer. Giving me time to pull away if I wanted to.

But I didn't; my body was transfixed by his touch as though a match had been struck against it. I folded perfectly into him.

"Better?" He asked.

Angus didn't seem to notice the dozens of people staring at us as he played affectionately with the ring on my finger.

"Is it real?"

Are you? I wondered.

He looked at me expectantly. "Your ring," he said, taking my hand in his.

Some people needed to wait to see the fog lift before they knew whether what they had was a diamond, I thought, *or just a rock in disguise.* Not Angus. To him, all things carried beauty.

***

Now, terrified and totally alone, a tear breaks free from the corner of my eye and rolls angrily down my cheek, splashing silently on the too-soft mattress beneath me.

"I will find my way back to you," I whisper through the lump in my throat and into the darkness.

***

"Okay, hit me. What's for breakfast? I'm starving," Rosemary croons.

My salt-crusted eyes crack open slowly. It still feels like midnight without windows and morning light, but to my surprise, the gag across my mouth has vanished. Searing pain surges from my bruised shoulders, still tightly pulled behind my back. But it's a small win; I must be doing something right.

In the hushed dimness of my room, shadows play games with my tired mind. A black dog with ethereal green eyes and feathered fur lurks in the corner of the room like a predator.

"No, no." I scramble backwards until my back and bound hands are pressed against the solid wall. Just as it launches towards me, I turn my head and close my eyes. The impact never comes. The razored teeth never make their mark. Gone. As if it had never existed at all. Am I going mad?

I manoeuvre myself quickly so that my back is to the lamp on the table beside the bed. I wince through the pain as I finally manage to flick the switch, casting a warm glow over the room. Empty. I breathe a sigh of relief.

"How about eggs Benedict?" Patrice laughs.

"Or a strawberry soufflé?" Rosemary says.

I open and close my mouth repeatedly, getting reacquainted with the feeling, grateful for the distraction.

"A bacon and egg roll."

"A fruit panna cotta with strawberry syrup."

"Pancakes," Rosemary says.

Next, I lace my cracked lips with spit, using my tongue to smear it around. It's not a lot, but it will do for now.

Patrice giggles. "Toasted granola with yoghurt and—"

Rose pauses. "No, Patrice, really, there's pancakes, look."

Immediately, I recognise the sticky-sweet smell of maple syrup wafting in the air.

"You're kidding me," she gasps. "I can't remember the last time I—"

"Hey, new girl, lift the lever to the left of your door," Rosemary says, chewing.

Warily, I take two paces towards the door. Just as Rose said, a small metal lever sits to the left. I hadn't noticed it before.

Again, the searing pain shoots through my shoulders as I turn to tug on the metal bar. A small compartment in the wall opens up like a mouth. Inside it is a square container, about the size of a shoebox. I manage to manoeuvre the item to the bed. The smell is intoxicating and my stomach howls.

The lid slides off and I'm met with an array of steamy colours—blueberries, raspberries, strawberries, banana, kiwi—and beneath it, a stack of three fluffy, perfectly round pancakes. The syrup glistens in the artificial light of the lantern above me. My mouth floods with six full days' worth of saliva.

But an uneasy dread fills my stomach. Starving and frail, the survivor in me tells me to feed the ache in my belly. But when I woke this morning, the laceration on my shoulders had left behind a green stain on the sheets, a clear indicator of a brooding infection.

There's a small white folded card in the corner, but before I can convince myself otherwise, the card is on the table beside me and I'm using my face to inhale the fruit, barely swallowing before the next mouthful passes my lips. I eat so fast, my head starts to spin.

"Don't eat too quickly or you'll give yourself a belly ache," Patrice warns in a motherly tone.

I don't listen, instead stuffing torn pieces of pancake into my mouth. Even if I wanted to, I can't stop. The syrup is so rich and sweet, I could drink it. The pancakes are equal parts light and full. When there's only crumbs left in the bottom of the box, I cast it aside, lying back against my pillow, which seems to completely absorb me.

"Too late," I groan, more to myself than the others.

Patrice laughs, and it makes me laugh too, and suddenly, the three of us are cackling like fools. For the briefest of moments, I almost forget where I am. Almost.

"You must be special," Patrice says, "we never get pancakes."

"Did you get a little love note with it?" Rosemary snickers.

The note, I'd forgotten about it. I unfold the bright white card carefully.

Welcome, Aurelia, it reads, *I'm so glad that you are here with us.*

And just like that, the delirium passes and my stomach lurches. I shove the card into the bedside drawer and close it quickly, locking him inside in case this room might feel like a safe place for a fleeting second. As if his presence suddenly feels close, he might be standing just outside the door, listening. Waiting. Like a warm breath on the back of my neck.

I let the air fill the deepest parts of my lungs, steadying myself.

I need to get out of here.

***

I wrestle back the covers and hustle out of bed, my mind still and focused. After days of stomach-aching hunger, I must be pale and gaunt by now.

With the glamour and haze now lifted from my sight, it occurs to me that the room is slightly larger than I'd first thought. If I'm standing in the middle of it facing the door, about three paces to my left, the television is tucked in the corner. Next to it is a wide expanse of bare wall where I imagine that, in a normal house, there would be a window, with golden sunrise views out onto a garden full of cottage flowers. To my right—the bed.

Behind me is an archway into the bathroom. There's no door, just a basin and a stainless steel lavatory. A shower head jolts out from the wall with no screen or proper drainage—just a small hole in the concrete floor about the size of a coin.

The bathroom looks relatively new, but the grime in the bottom of the toilet bowl and the overwhelming scent of Clorox tell me that it has been used before. The plumbing works, as far as I can tell. So that's a positive—though I don't intend on being here long enough to make use of it more than absolutely necessary.

Next to the archway, there's a built-in wardrobe, barely an arm's length deep. In it, is about seven days' worth of old clothes ranging from size eight to size eighteen, including an oversized black trench coat with a moth-eaten hem hanging from a plastic hanger; folded jeans in my size are folded in the cupboard.

There are also plain t-shirts in varying shades of white, a packet of brand new underwear, pyjamas, and a faded charcoal-coloured hooded sweat-shirt that reminds me of something Jade used to wear.

The inside of my black t-shirt reeks of night sweats and fear. Maybe I can afford to delay my escape for an extra five minutes for the sake of some basic human hygiene.

I shed all the clothes that I can, including shoes, socks, pants and underwear. I can't pull the shirt over my head, so I don't. Instead, I leave it on, bra and all. The shower splutters to life, the sound of the running water soothing me, the steam flush against my crusty face.

Warmth tumbles over my body like a waterfall. I close my eyes, letting the sting of it seep through my shirt, pouring over my aching bones. Pure relief washes over me.

Cold air bites at the bare parts of my skin and I huddle under the narrow stream to keep warm. The water pressure is a dribble compared to the showers at Angus' house, but more akin to the ones I grew up with. It's homely.

The water is tasteless, and quite possibly the purest water to ever pass my lips. It can mean only one thing.

The town's water supply is laced with chlorine, so much so that you can smell it on your skin for hours after each bath. This water is pure, untouched, and not from Brunswick Shire. A couple of years back, I was waitressing a table at La Mercer when I glimpsed a map of Brunswick Shire's sewerage system as I was delivering the local counsellors their cappuccinos. Every house in Brunswick Shire was connected by the water pipes, all sharing the same dusty, chlorine-infused liquid.

This place is somewhere else entirely. The television is all but a total whitewash most of the time with flickering snippets of the local news. While we might not be in Brunswick Shire, we are close enough to be in range of the satellites.

We might even be just on the outskirts of town, near the mountains. This would make sense given the plummeting temperatures. In what direction, though, I have no idea.

The concrete floor is cold against my feet as I fumble with the old towel by the sink. It barely covers me, but I'm grateful for the dryness of it against my soaked t-shirt.

I trudge out to the wardrobe, turning my back to run the soft, worn fabrics through my calloused and bloody hands. If I can't get this shirt dry soon, I might give myself pneumonia—or worse. I manoeuvre the oversized sweat shirt from its hanger. Warm and oddly familiar.

It can't be. Sure enough, blurred into the velvet tag by her mother's black permanent marker, are the initials JB—Jade Berigan.

A stifled cry escapes my lips as I slump to the floor and use my knees to bury my face into the fabric, the remnants of her rosy perfume lingering in my nostrils. The last time I saw it, Jade had been stuffing it through the lid of the thrift shop donation bin. God, it must have been almost a year ago now.

At least I can manage some dry underwear, albeit with great difficulty. I step into a fresh pair and lie down on the cold floor. With some wriggling and straining, I manage to pull them up to my waist. That will do, I decide, trying to relax my throbbing shoulders.

I'm coming, Jade, I whisper, remembering our promise.

Chapter Eleven

After an hour of thorough searching, I know only one thing for certain; there's no way out of this room. Not alive, anyway. The concrete walls feel about a metre thick and rock solid, totally impenetrable. A grenade may not even shake this building. Maybe it's an army barracks. An old one based on the rust-stained walls.

The wooden floorboards are easy enough to lift when you pull at the nails, but underneath them, more concrete, every bit as thick as the walls. The door itself is made of oak; it would take several years at least to scratch through, and that's assuming there was a blade of some kind to use, which I don't have.

There is some sort of plastic-glass hybrid communication window cut into the middle of the wooden door, accessible only from the outside.

The vents, one above the bed and the other in the bathroom, are no bigger than a shoebox, and much too small to crawl into. Even if they were big enough for me to fit through, they don't even lead outside. I know this because when I push my face against them, there's not one breath of air, just a smoky sulphur scent I can't quite place.

A cage, that's what Rosemary had called it. A cage.

I'm locked in. There's no way out.
There's no way out.
I'm locked in.
It's a cage.

Panic rises through me, from my stomach, through my chest, lodging in my throat. The oxygen in the room seems to dissolve like salt. I throw my shoulder against the door repeatedly, creating a thumping sound. The pain is excruciating, like shards of glass splintering down my arms.

"Let me out of here!" I scream.

My heart thunders through my chest like a drum, raspy breaths absorbing the scraps of air in my lungs.

I can't breathe, I can't breathe, I can't breathe.

"I can't breathe!" I cry.

"Shhh, he'll hear you," Rosemary hisses.

"I can't breathe," I shout.

The walls are moving in, encircling me like a tunnel. I try to suck in gulps of air, but my chest is heaving too quickly and it never reaches my lungs. My head whirls, my stomach clenching and surging, clenching and surging.

"Listen to me," Rosemary warns, "you are going to be okay. You need to slow your breathing."

"Help!" I wince, falling to my knees.

"Take both of your hands and cup them over your nose and mouth like a mask."

"I can't," I sob, my head so light, it's swimming.

"Use your pillow," Rosemary growls. "Or you're going to pass out."

I do as she says, fighting the panic still rising in my chest, thoughts of the wooden head box, the thinning of the air around me, fighting the ache in my arms and legs. I push my head against the pillow. The air is warm against my cheeks.

"Deep breaths," she says.

After what feels like an eternity of deep breathing, my head stops spinning and my muscles soften like wax. The carbon dioxide numbs me from the inside. My cuffed arms fall leaden against the floor as I lie still on the ground, the damp of my shirt a welcome relief from the heat of my skin. I lift my knees tight to my chest, trying to disappear. Evaporate. Even if I could, I doubt there'd be anywhere for me to go.

"Are you okay?" Patrice whispers.

Of course I'm not.

"What's your name, new girl?" Rosemary asks.

I roll onto my side, staring blankly at the wall. If I squint a little, the chinks in the stone almost look like stars. I used to love the stars. Will I ever see them again? It's such a simple question, and yet, I struggle to find the words. How long would it take to completely lose myself? To forget who I am entirely?

"Aurelia," I say. Not really sure if it's true anymore.

***

I leap to my feet at the sound of metal grinding on metal. The double-glazed glass-plastic hybrid-screen-window thing slides open, and a pair of dark, soulless eyes stare at me.

The aerial is knocked clean off the television set as I lurch backwards, tripping over myself. There's the green-eyed beast that appears in the corner of the room every now and then, and now this, which is much worse.

Alister.

But it can't be, this isn't real!

His eyes are as intensely green as they've ever been. It's hard to imagine how I'd once found comfort in the anticipation of his stare. Now, his gaze is fixed on me, the blood in my veins turns to ice. His once gentle eyes are dark and ominous, much wider than I've seen them before.

"Don't be afraid," he says plainly, "you're safe here."

"I want to go home," I say, trying to mask the quiver of fear in my voice.

"Of course, I will take you home." He smiles, but it's cold, reptilian. Wicked. A lie as thick as the walls around us.

"Why am I here?" I spit.

"Aurelia," he sighs, "you're not a prisoner. If you follow the rules, we are all going to get along just fine. Together, we can find the cure."

His lips are obscured by the bars between us, but his eyes gleam as he talks, a dangerous passion locked inside them. I make a point of looking around me. Everything is locked, bolted, indestructible. The very definition of a prison cell. I'm the mouse that fell for the cheese.

"What cure?" I spit.

"The first rule," he says, ignoring me, "is that you must refer to me as 'sir' at all times. The least we can do for each other is show a little respect, wouldn't you agree? Particularly considering how much time we are going to be spending together."

"You're deranged." Anger flares up inside me. "Let me out of here, you psychopath!" I scream.

He purses his lips and scratches his forehead. Something like concern plagues his dark features. "Not a great start, but you'll learn. Rule number two, you must do as you are told at all times. If you follow my direction and play by my rules, you'll be given all your meals. If you don't, you'll be punished. I don't want to punish anyone, Aurelia, especially not you."

His eyes soften as he says my name.

I take a step towards the door with more confidence than sense. "Then let me go," I seethe through clenched teeth. "Let me go, now."

His green eyes widen as he takes half a step back into the shadows. The silhouette of his face is now in full view. His brows furrow and his mouth moves as if to say something else, but instead, he takes a step forward into the light until I'm close enough to see the darkening irises of his eyes. The full depth of them. He smiles, cruelly.

"I'm not worried," he says after a minute, "you'll come around. You just need some motivation, some time, maybe. Thankfully, we have plenty of that."

I shiver in disgust, and with cold fear pressing in on me, I buckle under the icy chill of his gaze. Before common sense and self-preservation can prevail, I turn my back, lift my hands towards the window, and flip him off. The grind of metal bars fills my ears in response, and he's gone, replaced by the familiar flat surface of the brown oak door.

"No!" I scream, lunging forward.

Moments later, I slump to the floor, defeated, blistered and broken. His vacant expression and intense stare burn in my memory. Even in the bleak silence, his words strike me with fear, over and over.

Huddled against the big oak door, I cling to Jade's jumper. "Don't leave me in here like this."

How long had it taken anyone to notice I was gone? Who had been the first? Was it Jade, when I didn't reply to one of her text messages? How many had she sent before she finally decided to go to my house, only to find I had not been home?

How long would my mother take to realise? How many curses would she mutter about me until she gave up and decided to heat her own dinner in the microwave? Whether it be through sheer contempt or starvation, in my heart, I know that one way or another, she would survive. Angus would ensure it.

Maybe it was Angus who noticed first. Maybe he'd thrown lover's stones gently against my window. Maybe he'd invited me for dinner. Italian this time? The new Chinese restaurant downtown? I would have loved both of those things.

What was the last thing I'd said to him? My mind aches with the strain of the memory, but it's too fragile to cling to. I let it go, fearing that if I hold on too tight, it might fracture completely.

***

Two hours later—or maybe longer, I'm not sure exactly—I wake to the sound of gentle tapping. My ears strain to focus on it over the hissing of the air vent above me. The sound is coming from one of the rooms next door. I can't decipher which one.

"Hello?"

"Oh good, you're still alive," Rosemary says, "you had us worried there for a minute."

I sit up, rubbing the thick kink that has formed in my neck. My shoulders ache so much that I wonder if they're broken, but my hands are finally free. My shirt is still damp, so I can't have been asleep for too long. Only, I don't recall falling asleep at all.

"I thought you might have bumped yourself off after all that." She laughs.

"Are you okay?" Patrice asks, a soft caress in her every word, as gentle as the beating wings of a butterfly.

"What time is it?" I yawn, fighting the urge to pass out.

"Almost dinner," Rosemary says, "which is timely because I'm starving."

"You're always starving," Patrice says, her eye roll almost visible through the walls. "I wonder what feast we will be having tonight?" She sings. "Thanks to the newcomer."

Right on cue, the familiar grind of metal on metal, and a clanking that sounds like a tray being slid along a solid surface. I tug on the metal leaver and the box opens like a mouth. As I slowly retrieve the tray, my eyes roam the small cavity for any chink in the armour, a loose screw, a hint of a way out.

"Lasagne!" Rosemary croons.

"Fresh tomato, too, I think," Patrice adds. "From the garden."

Are my eyes playing tricks on me? My brain tries to somehow connect Rosemary's excitement with what sits on the tray before me. But no matter how many times I rub my eyes, the food does not transform into a steaming plate of lasagne. Instead, the half-boiled, now cold potato rolls around my plastic plate like a boulder, squashing the small pile of brown rice in its tracks. I grimace.

An ambrosial corky scent fills the room, and my stomach yearns for what must be slapped in a pile of molten cheese on my cellmates' plates, just beyond reach.

The gamey smell of potato reaches my nose before it brushes my taste buds; dirt wedges between my teeth, scratchy and grainy. The outer layer of the potato is soft, but just below the surface, the layers turn floury and hard, like chalk.

I shovel the rice into my mouth quickly, drowning it with a gulp of water. How long can a person last without eating before they wither away to their bones? How quickly would it kill me if I refused to eat another bite? Is that his plan? To starve me into submission?

Placing the half-eaten tray of food on the bedside table, I climb onto the bed, pressing my back against the cold, rough surface of the wall. It digs in just below my shoulder blades, but I don't mind.

"How long have you been in here?" I call into the silence.

I can hear Rosemary chewing violently. "Too long," she says, her mouth still full, "but not as long as Patrice."

"Patrice?" I ask.

There's a short silence.

"A little over four years," she says quietly.

My stomach plummets, the kind of drop you feel when you go feet first down the vertical face of a roller-coaster. Only, a roller-coaster has an end when you unbuckle your seatbelt and climb out, planting your feet firmly on solid ground. Here, the freefall is endless.

Rosemary whistles. "It'd nearly be your anniversary, Pat. Darn it, I forgot to get you a cake."

I swallow hard. "Has it always been just the two of you?"

This time, Rosemary speaks first. "Promise you won't freak out?"

"Rose, don't," Patrice growls.

Not sure if that is a promise capable of being kept, I stay quiet, and let them have it out between themselves.

"I can't speak for Patrice, but since I've been here, two girls have come and gone."

"He let them out?" I sit taller, pressing an ear to the wall.

"I guess you could say that." Rosemary laughs grimly.

I'm confused. I replay the professor's words in my head. He definitely said *the* cure, not *a* cure. I could go home once we found *the* cure. Why would he let two others leave when they haven't found the—?

But then my stomach lurches, and I clasp a hand over my mouth to stifle my cry.

"Did they—?"

"Leave in body bags?" Rosemary answers.

"Rosemary!" Patrice hisses.

"Hiding it from her doesn't make it go away," Rosemary argues. "If we have to live with it, so can she."

"Did he murder them?" I gasp.

"Not exactly," Rosemary says.

"That's enough!" Patrice growls. I picture her standing at the door of her cell, scowling, wishing she could reach through the wall and shove a hand across Rosemary's big mouth. I imagine Rosemary lying on her bed, belly full and a defiant grin stretched across her face. I can't decide which of them I like better.

"One girl hung herself with her sheets," Rosemary goes on.

"We don't know that," Patrice says.

"Yes, I do, she told me she was going to do it," Rosemary says.

"I never heard her say that."

"It must have been while you were out in the garden."

I pause, almost certain I've misheard. "The garden? He let you go outside?"

But they ignore me, still arguing back and forth amongst themselves. Throwing insults like stones.

I sigh, resigning myself to the fact that it's probably just another one of Rosemary's cruel jokes. It's hard to tell the difference when you aren't standing in front of the person. Maybe the eyes really were the window to the soul, after all. *Eyes.*

I can't help but remember Alister's dark, green ones, focused on me like a hawk. I shudder. Hope is like a toxin in this wretched place. It keeps you sick enough to weaken you, but doesn't do you the courtesy of finishing you off. Not like a poison would, anyway.

The half-eaten potato sits still as stone on my plate, beckoning. At first, I assumed the professor was crazy—there is no doubt left in my mind now—but a murderer? Though, when you take one step towards insanity, what difference does a few more make? I shrug out of the wet shirt and peel a dry one over my head.

Sometime later, I wake to the sensation of hundreds of tiny spiders crawling over my body. Their filthy, delicate little steps are like whispers against my skin. I buck and kick against the sheets, desperate to free myself from their hairy legs. I sit upright, frantically searching, only to find myself swatting and swiping at thin air. Nothing.

Eyes closed, I try to calm my panting breaths. First that beast with the green eyes, and now this. I shrivel back under the covers and squeeze my eyes closed tight, as if the warm blankets might be able to protect me from the things that only I can see, and the haunting sounds that only I seem to hear.

I focus on the soft hiss of the air vent and the gentle mist filling the room. I let it consume me, lulling me to sleep.

"It's not real," I whisper to myself, not knowing what to believe anymore.

***

I tumble in and out of a sleep so leaden that I can't decipher what parts are dreams, memories, and what parts are real. Night terrors feature wooden boxes being lowered over my head and gags being strung over my mouth until I can't breathe. Every twitch causes a searing pain to shoot through my body.

At some point, I wake to the scent of lavender wafting from my bedside table. When I awake fully, sun streams through the windows. No, not sun, cold white light shedding down from the ceiling. I squint towards the television in the corner of the room, the stone walls lurking all too close.

Sweat pools in the curve of my back, over all the places that don't feel like mine anymore. Nothing feels like mine anymore.

Lunging for the bathroom, bile hiking up the labyrinth of my throat, I retch into the bowl of the toilet. I retch at the realisation of where I am. I retch at the bleak abyss of the professor's eyes, focused on me. I retch at the nightmares seeping into my sanctuary of sleep, the ones that lurk in the darkness, waiting. Of those reptilian hands crawling over my skin.

When the television flickers images of the Sunday breakfast show, my stomach finally stops churning. I stay in bed for the rest of the day, my blankets cocooned around me like a shield, blocking out the sounds of bickering between the cells next to me.

No place is safe; no one can be trusted, not even me.

Not anymore.

Chapter Twelve

The door in the room next to mine opens again, the metal bolts clanging against each other, springing free from their locks.

Free. Something I haven't been for over two months now. Or at least I think it's been two months, based on the number of meals I've eaten. It might even be my birthday, but I haven't got a calendar, and I don't feel like celebrating.

But the clang I can hear is the doors outside opening, not the meal lever, so it must be twelve o'clock—yard time.

"See you soon," Rose whispers.

"See you soon," I mumble, pressing my ear to the door.

I catch a whisper of the birds chirping for the briefest moment; it's like music to my ears. Patrice's turn in the garden is at two o'clock, so I might hear them again if I'm lucky.

Lucky.

A word reserved for lotto winners, lovers and people who find loose change on the sidewalk. Not me. Nothing about my life has felt lucky—that is until I met Angus. And now, the absence of his voice, his warmth, the touch of his hands has sunk into my marrow like a cancer.

The news stations haven't reported on my disappearance for the last five days, so I've got no idea how close I am to being found, or—more accurately—if anyone's even still looking.

Today, they're covering a story about a man who made an application to the court for a restraining order. The reason it's plastered as a headline on the front page of every newspaper in the state today is that the applicant suffers split personality disorder and the respondent is one of five personalities residing in his mind.

I'll give it to him, this guy managed to silence even the most outspoken of judges this morning in Alberta District Court. I might even laugh if I wasn't so exhausted.

The television flickers in and out of the same channel, and at midday every day, it drops out of reception completely. Even so, it's my only connection to whatever lay beyond my door, and the means for me to hold on to the remnants of my sanity.

Sometimes, it's as if I'm sitting in my lounge room with my mother, flicking through the channels. I talk to her sometimes, turning my head, half expecting to see her sleeping in the armchair beside me. They don't say anything, but I know the others can hear me. Maybe it's because sometimes I catch them mumbling into the abyss too.

There are no hard feelings. There's only so many places you can look for someone. By now, they've probably stored the file on a dusty shelf in a locked room. Another case gone ice cold. In a few years' time, they'll dredge the lake, looking for my body. Who knows, by that time I might even be there for them to find.

I don't bother stripping down to my skin. I just turn the tap, sending a sauna of heat around the room. It reminds me of the shower head in my bathroom back home, the one that sometimes runs cold for fifteen minutes straight. I miss it, more than my heart can bear.

My body aches with grief and my chest cinches like a corset around my lungs. It's as much a part of my daily routine as the clanky plastic tray that arrives at 8 am, 12.30 pm and 6 pm.

I wait until the steam envelops the room like a cocoon around me. There's a blank space above the sink where the mirror in any other bathroom would sit. What must I look like now? Starving and empty, my skin like pale rice paper, much too thin to hold my brittle bones.

Two paces and I'm under the boiling stream, the water sinking through my t-shirt and jeans, scalding my body until it's as cold as ice. The water pounds against me like thousands of ants biting at my skin as I sink to the floor.

I relish in the utter agony of it. The way it silences my racing mind. The way it halts the memories of Angus, Jade, and my mother. The way it distracts from the aching hollow of my stomach.

It hurts so much it steals the breath from my lungs. If only it were that easy. If only it would all just stop. Hopelessness carries in the weight of my drenched clothes, pulling me down, down, down towards the floor, pinning me in place. The water cascades over my arms, tracing the parts where Angus' hands used to roam.

The burning stream winds over the sides of my stomach like fingers grazing my skin. Like they had once before. The water purposefully manoeuvres its way across my body, following the contours of a river, over both my cheeks, sliding down from the sleeves of my arms to the small of my back.

A familiar rush of heat burns through me again—a heat I had come to expect in the moments before Angus would kiss me. When I woke to find him lying next to me, lips curled into a devilish smile, watching me as I slept. But as my eyes open, the feeling dissipates. Vanishes like hope down the drain, leaving me scalded and burnt on the bathroom floor.

Desperation has me pulling a soggy square card from the pocket of my jeans, one of the three that arrive each day with my meals. This one, bearing Alister's handwritten plea, implored me to change my mind about joining him in the lab. I unfold the card; the smear of my blood splayed across its surface is still visible from an hour before.

A shudder scurries down my spine as I fold the parchment tightly, stuffing it through the small slit in the drain. Maybe this time would be different. Maybe, this time, someone would trace the bloodstained plea for sanctuary back to me. To us.

Or maybe, like me, it will sink to the bottom of whatever well they're all trapped in, never to be found.

"Why me?" I cry, watching the white mist carry my words as if they're a message in transit.

They linger without challenge, without recourse. Like me, they've nowhere to go.

***

When I'm done feeling sorry for myself, I muster the energy to climb out of the shower, pat my skin dry and slip into some clean tracksuit pants and Jade's hoodie. The smell has mostly faded, but it's still there—just. I dread the day that it is taken from me too.

My stomach groans at the familiar *clang* and *grind* of the meal box. I meander over to the lever and tug it open. It's heavier and heavier each day, despite the dwindling rations.

"Hmm, bacon and eggs," I mumble wishfully. Closing my eyes, I shovel the food into my mouth, barely swallowing fast enough to protect my taste buds from the familiar foul-smelling starch and rice. The tray clatters against the wooden desk as I cast it aside and crawl back into my bed.

The sticky-sweet smell of maple bacon and cheese wafts from the room next to mine. What I wouldn't give for just one taste, one lick of salt.

"Why do you keep doing this to yourself? It isn't helping anything," Patrice whispers gently.

I roll onto my back and stare at the ceiling in brooding silence.

"The longer we delay finding the cure, the longer we'll be stuck here," she adds.

"There is no cure," I say, with more bite than intended, "we are never getting out of here."

"You'll starve to death if this goes on any longer."

"I can only hope so," I say, rolling over to face the wall.

The small holes in the stone hold my attention until my eyes are tired enough to close on their own. Until I can be in my own bed, in my own house.

A tear breaks loose and rolls angrily down my cheek. I clear my throat, willing my heart to plug the leaking dam. Patrice is right; I can't keep this stubborn facade up for much longer. I'm still getting used to blackouts, the rush of blood, the flaky skin and muscle aches. The pulse in my wrist is but a faint whisper, and perhaps, for more reasons than one, my heart is dying.

Not long now, I promise myself. *It will all be over soon.*

***

The vent hisses softly above me, and I can almost taste its sweet scent as it funnels deep into my lungs. I'm so hungry, even the air seems to have flavour.

"Did you miss me?" A voice sings outside the door. It trails off and then grows quieter as the chains rattle and the bolt clinks, locking her back inside the cell, two across from mine. The fading echo of footsteps tells me that Patrice has just left for yard time.

Yard time—like the damn prisoners we are. What I wouldn't give right now to see the sky, to cut a hole in the dense roof above me. I'd crawl to it like a vine, grow towards it, no matter how small or narrow the slit. I often lose myself in the fantasy of it, let my mind wander towards the light, only to open my eyes to the darkness. To the realisation that the cost of freedom carries too high a price.

I groan quietly and slide out of my bed; I must have fallen asleep.

"What's new?" I rub my eyes, pressing my ear to the door until her voice is clear, or at least audible.

"The circus is in town," Rosemary says.

"Oh yeah? How much are tickets?" I ask.

"My shout," she says, "you can get the popcorn."

Wincing, I clutch my stomach as a sharp pain sears through me. Just another feature of my rapid physical decline. Fantastic.

"Sorry," Rose says, sensing the change of pace, "sometimes I forget you're starving."

"What's it like?" I ask, slumping to the floor.

"You've never been to the circus?"

"No, not that," I say. "Outside, what's it like?"

"Better than in here." Rose sighs. "And worth mixing a few chemicals for."

"Don't you start too," I groan.

"I just don't get why you are doing this to yourself."

"It's none of your business, Rose," I manage to huff through the pain.

"Whoa, take it easy," she says defensively, probably with her hands raised.

I glare at the wall between us, but against my greater urges, I take a breath that's all too shallow, steadying my racing heart. Fine. She can have her fun. After all, I have no intention of starting something with her—she might well be the only friend I have left.

"Sorry," I whisper, "it's the hunger talking."

"What school d'you go to anyway?" Rose asks, and the normalcy of the question makes my chest ache.

"Brunswick Shire Med," I say, jerking my chin a little higher, like a fool. School pride really is a disease.

"Lame," she groans.

"My school is one of the most prestigious in the state," I protest, my cheeks burning hot.

"All I'm saying is if we had been less worried about prestige, we might have gone to Sunder College out in Preston. But then again, we would never have been given the real-life experience of being drugged, locked in a prison and fed through a wall, and that would've been a real shame."

Now that I know her a little better, I'd say Rose's abrasive humour is almost appealing.

"Wait, you went to Brunswick Shire too?"

"Doctrina Perpetua," she recites, answering my question.

Doctrina Perpetua or *Forever Learning* is Brunswick Shire's motto, printed in black ink on the school crest. For some, it serves as inspiration; for me, it's a reminder that I will never quite know enough.

"Why didn't you tell me?" I ask.

"Didn't think it was important," she says, but a sinking feeling in my stomach reminds me why it is.

"Oh my god." I swallow, remembering the brown-haired woman in the soggy poster stuck to the bottom of my shoe all those months ago. How long had Rose said she had been here? "I think I know you."

"And after only two months, sweetheart, that's a record."

"No, your face, Rose! I saw it on a missing person's poster just the other day!" Only now do I regret tossing the soggy poster into the trash. How many people have mindlessly discarded me the same way since I've been here?

"You did?" Rose asks quietly, the humour in her voice now nothing but a quiet undertone.

Footsteps carry her closer, to the door maybe. "They're still looking for me?"

"Of course they are!" I cry. "They never stopped."

Rose sniffles. She goes to say something but stops, silence falling between us like curtains. I want to reach out to her, comfort her, but the walls that separate us are much too thick. I place my hand on the wooden door. I imagine her doing the same, though she probably isn't.

"I know," I whisper, somewhat savouring this almost human version of Rose.

Over the past two months, I've become so used to the hardened, dark humour and taunting that I was sure there was nothing softer lurking beneath the surface. Turns out her shell is made of glass, much like the rest of us.

I slide my back down the face of the door until I'm sitting on the wooden floorboards. We don't speak, but the silence is shrill and defiant. Restless with wonder.

An hour goes by, and I must have dozed off at some point because I wake to the screech of iron hinges, and the quiet shuffle of Patrice's footsteps as she returns from yard time.

"Hey!" I clamber to my feet. "Can I talk to you?"

Before I can mutter another vowel, the metal window slides open and, through dust-ridden Plexiglas, a pair of deep-set emerald eyes stare back at me. I lurch backwards on shaky legs, bumping into the bedside table. Goddamn it.

"I give up," I declare, steadying myself.

He steps towards the glass, his cold features swimming into view. Brows furrowed, he hums. "What did you say?"

"I'll do it, I'll help you find the cure, sir."

His eyes glisten with desire as he rocks back onto his heels. "I knew you would come around."

I grimace, but the ache creeping through my chest keeps me strong.

Here. We. Go.

"I'll be back for you tomorrow, just after breakfast," he says, slamming the window shut. The patter of rubber boots grows quieter until it disappears completely. I count twelve steps until I hear a wooden door creak and close with a heavy bang.

"Um, what just happened?" Rose demands, a lightness to her voice.

"Finally," Patrice breathes.

They can't know the truth, not yet anyway. "I'm just sick of potato and rice." I shrug.

The bed barely clocks my weight as I slump back against the pillow. I scan the room one last time to take in the view, to remember how so many things looked on the eve that everything was about to change.

***

I doze on and off all night. It's hard to sleep with the stomach cramps, but it's not the kind of ache I have become accustomed to. It would seem that Alister's hasty departure yesterday was not without good reason. Last night, much to my surprise, when I opened the metal lever, the wafts of rich gravy and roast beef hit me with the force of a freight train.

I should have been more careful, taken each bite slowly, but I couldn't. Instead, so accustomed to the plain, blanched flavours of starch, I shovelled the food into my mouth faster than I could chew, just as I had done with the pancakes; God, that feels like a lifetime ago now.

My jeans, now two sizes too big, slide easily over my bare legs. I roll the legs three times over, exposing my ankles, so that I don't trip over. Jade's jumper is like a blanket over me now, but it's enough to fight the cold that awaits outside. The only thing that apparently hasn't shrunk in the wash of starvation is my feet, cramped against the walls of my joggers. It's not perfect, but it should do the trick.

I wait with bated breath for Alister to open my cell door for the first time in over two months. My stomach is alive with beating wings. I have never been more ready than this.

***

Twenty seconds. That's how long it takes for him to unlock the metal bolts on my door and drop the keys with a jingle in a pile on the floor. Ten seconds. That's how long it takes him to jimmy open the big oak slab just wide enough for a body to pass through. One second. That's how long it takes me to run.

No one has ever seen me run, not since primary school. I'm fast, well, faster than the other girls were anyway, although nearly everyone could beat me in a distance race. What I lacked in coordination, I made up for in stride length. The only difference is that back then, I sort of knew where I was going.

My feet shuffle for a moment, confused by the direction that my brain wants to take. I run down a short, stony hallway and lunge up a set of twenty or so stairs. Thankfully, the trapdoor is unlocked when I reach the top, and I push up as hard as I can, bursting out into the daylight.

I climb out quickly, taking a few uneasy steps forward as my eyes fight to adjust to the light. I can hear Alister's dazed footsteps behind me and all my fear condenses into pure terror.

Adrenaline powers through me and suddenly, I can see just clearly enough to make out the foliage under my feet. Bark, moss, leaves. But there's no time to relish these small pleasures.

Branches scratch and claw at me as I run full pelt through the shrubbery and trees. The vegetation is thick and suffocating. Great big trees cast shadows like umbrellas, blocking the sky above. Atlas cedars, just like the ones in the cemetery. We must be in some sort of forest. It evolves as I thrash forward.

The cedars are intermixed with a variety of other trees, some I recognise, and some I don't. If it's the forest to the south of the Shire, I only have to head north until I reach the highway. But if it's the forest to the north, I'll be forced to cross the frozen lake. A fleeting glance at the moss coating the trees has me pivoting sharp right, heading north.

Twigs crack and crunch behind me and instinctively, I run harder, panic flaring, hurtling forward, and weaving through the thick-trunked trees.

When the footsteps quieten, I dare a quick glance behind me and my foot catches a protruding tree root, plummeting me towards the ground. Arms and legs flailing beside me, I land with a thud on my stomach. The hard ground steals the air from my lungs. I clutch my middle, gasping.

There, no more than an inch from my face, is a solid grey stone wall. Had I been an inch taller, I would surely be dead, my skull split in two.

I quickly get to my feet, studying the wall. It's rough but flat, stretching up into the sky about thirty feet with barbed wire curled like a ribbon along the rim. To my left, the medieval bricks stretch out as far as I can see, bending around a corner of trees and out of sight. To my right, the same. It's impossible to tell from where I'm standing how long it is, or if there's any way around it.

My knees sting through my jeans, my chest heaves, and my right ankle throbs, but I force myself to keep running at a pace I think I can maintain, at least for a little while longer. I look back only to check if I'm being followed, but there's nothing behind me but dense foliage and thick tree trunks. I've lost him, for now.

I keep the wall on my right as I run the perimeter, staying as close to the tree line as possible so as not to be seen. The soft pine needles layered over the ground conceal my footsteps, making it harder for anyone to track me. I'm invisible, and that's a good thing, for now.

It feels like hours have passed when I make a third ninety-degree turn. My heart catches in my chest, the realisation sinking in. One more turn, that's all it would take to break me. One more turn would confirm all my fears.

Keep moving, I urge my aching bones, but my legs are trembling and weak. My chest prickles with each gasp for air. Using a fallen trunk to take my weight, I duck behind a dense green bush. Surely, one moment's rest can be spared. A couple of woodpeckers tucked into a nearby pine tree startle at my arrival. They flap and flutter into the sky, gliding gracefully over the wall.

My heart sinks, all traces of hope disintegrating with every beat of their wings. It was foolish and reckless to try and escape so soon. I was foolish not to heed the subtle warnings of my comrades in the cells next to mine This place is no different than one of those tiny pieces in the bowels of a Matryoshka doll. A tomb.

A rush of cold air hits my face, as if the forest itself is giving me a warning. I'd be a fool not to listen.

The thicket beyond is a myriad of bosque greens and browns and crystalline whites. The trees are dense and old, the brown earth dotted by stones, pine needles and moss. Not a footprint to be seen on the damp forest floor. None but my own, trailing behind me as I run, ducking under low-lying branches, my pale breath stolen by the passing wind.

I slow to a walk at the edge of the clearing, a dry burning in the back of my throat. The stone wall to my front. To my right, more wall. My legs sting with cuts from the underbrush and my ankle is swollen, stretching my already tight shoe.

"Help!" I scream, bashing my fists against the concrete wall. It's futile, and sure to give away my position, but I can't help it. Compelled by fear and dwindling hope, I begin to weep.

When the twigs behind me crack underfoot, there's no time to respond. Animated by renewed terror, I dash frantically along the western wall, or maybe it's the north. With the wall to my right, I dart left, staggering back into the tree line, away from the sound of pounding feet behind me. The sense that someone is closing in, hunting me like an animal keeps me pelting forward against the uneven ground clawing at my ankles.

"Aurelia, this is childish, you're bleeding," he calls, much too close.

I'm strong, all things considered; maybe I could hold my own for a bit, but I don't like my chances. I continue, changing my course towards a clearing in the trees ahead where the ground flattens out deeper into the forest. If I can just get past it, there might be a way out.

The ground softens with each tentative step, and beneath me is loose dirt, much darker than the light brown forest floor. I slow to a walk, glancing behind to make sure I'm not being followed. Ahead, three distinct arches protrude from the soil, dotted across the clearing. Not arches, headstones.

***

I shouldn't have been surprised. Not when I'd spent so long gaping, trying to quell the surge of vomit tracking up my throat. A twig snaps behind me, and in one motion, I turn, only to be met by the eerily cold, dark eyes of my kidnapper.

Alister.

He's slowly edging towards me from the tree line, one hand held up in surrender, the other obscured behind his back. Only ten feet away, and closing. Alister angles his head as I take a step backwards, and another, towards the headstones. Towards my end.

Would he hack me to death right here in the cemetery? Had he already carved my name into the weathered stone?

"Don't come any closer," I order.

"Things are not what they seem, Aurelia," he says.

But I can't see how that's possible. A graveyard. A graveyard!

"You're a murderer," I spit, edging backwards.

"Let me explain, let me show you," he says, offering an outstretched hand.

"You're a monster," I growl with borrowed courage.

There's a way out of this place, there has to be. I glance at the tree line behind Alister, the well-manicured pines and shrubbery, broad enough to shield whatever lies beneath them. Invisible from the skies. The barbed wire, the wall. Much too high to climb, and even if it wasn't, I would surely fall to my death on the other side. And suddenly, it dawns on me.

A prison, this place is a prison.

"Just let me go, please. Sir. Let me go home." My voice breaks as I beg for my life, certain that this moment is my last.

"Soon." He cocks his head, close enough now that I can see his wild round eyes. "They couldn't see the bigger picture, but you can."

My stomach churns with dread.

"Please," I beg, my knees giving way. "If you're going to kill me, just get it over with."

Alister clicks his tongue as I cower before him like a lamb to the slaughter. Distaste mars his dark features. I keep my eyes low as black suede shoes stop inches from my face. He draws the wooden box dangling from a leather strap and a thick serrated knife from behind his back. My executioner. This is how I'll go.

My teeth hammering against each other, I will myself to be still. To die with some semblance of dignity. One swing—that's all it would take. After all, I don't have a thick neck and it's certainly no more plump thanks to my recent diet of potato and rice.

My mind wanders to my mother. To Angus, Jade. Would they ever stop looking? Can they feel how close we are? Just out of reach, just out of earshot, trapped in a prison on the outskirts of town, only minutes from the house I grew up in.

Would they hear my screams in their nightmares? Does a mother feel when part of her leaves this earth? The thought of never seeing them again is unbearable, so much so that when Alister raises the knife against the trees above us, my only hope is to die quickly.

But before the blade thrusts towards me, he pauses, letting it fall once again to his side. And there's that familiar tilt of his head, the click of his tongue as he studies me disapprovingly. But I'm not dead. The searing pain in my knees tells me that I'm still very much alive. Not even death could be this painful.

Alister crouches in front of me, his hand outstretched, the light bouncing off his emerald eyes like a mirror. Soft now, gentle. No hint of the cold, callous man from only moments ago. Incredible, how something so incandescently beautiful can be so terrifying. I let out a sob in earnest. Relief, maybe, as air refills my lungs. I hadn't even realised I'd been holding my breath.

Something deeply primal tells me not to run. That to run would mean certain death. He'd chosen to spare me amongst this graveyard. I haven't the faintest idea why.

"Will you give this place a chance, Aurelia?" He asks, studying my face. "No one else has to suffer."

When I don't respond, he grips my arms in front of me, latching them once again with leather binds. Next, he secures the head box firmly over my face, threading the leather strap around my neck. It's claustrophobic and uncomfortable, but I don't dare protest as he hauls me to my feet. At least twice as strong as he looks. I'd have stood no chance against him one on one.

He takes a gentle step back, creating some distance between us. His hand falls once again to his side, the knife hanging limp beside his trouser leg.

Perhaps it's the sight of me gagged and bound by my hands, but a thought brings a fresh wave of sympathy to his voice, and when he speaks it's as if he hadn't just held me at knifepoint.

"I know you miss your family. I'd be an arrogant fool to ignore your cries for them, to pretend," he says. "I wanted to give this to you earlier." He cocks his head and grimaces.

My weight shifts nervously between my feet, nearly sending me tumbling headfirst into the dirt.

"Don't worry," he says casually, sensing my unease, "there are things in this world to fear, Aurelia, but I can assure you I am not one of them."

If only I believed him.

I can vaguely make out the silhouette of a gold chain with a bevelled heart, as he pulls it from his pocket. My own heart lunges towards it, but my feet remain planted as still as stone. The fear and the fight seep out of me all at once. The pain searing every inch of my body dissipates for a moment. I move to wipe my nose with my fists, but I'm met by a wall of hard wood.

"My necklace." My voice wavers as I fight to keep it steady, desperation leaching through like poison. "Can I—" I cough, "can I have it?"

The professor's face tightens, eyes narrowing as he unfurls his fingers, releasing the delicate chain into my filthy, bound palms. Still as shiny and perfect as the day Angus had given it to me. Only I'd changed, maybe beyond reckoning, bloody and covered in dirt and pine needles, hardly worthy of such a beautiful thing. I clutch it to my chest.

"Thank you." I'm suddenly grateful for the wooden box shielding my face.

Alister takes a silent step closer, and before I have time to register, darkness swarms. The sharp prick in my thigh, already a dull ache fading into the bleak abyss, dragging me down, down, down with it. I clutch the heart to my chest as the forest around me disappears into a void, swallowed whole.

***

The faint pitter-patter of rain gently lulls me awake. Eyes closed, I will myself to go back to sleep. The thick sheets make it easier, heavy and soft, absorbing my body into the fabric like a cloud. If I keep my eyes closed, I can almost pretend there isn't a wooden box fastened tightly around my head, that I'm not suffocating to death inside it.

My mother's loving voice calls out to me from downstairs, a gentle caress over my brittle and aching bones. But the closer I am to wakefulness, the further away she seems. "Momma?" I whimper into the darkness.

And then suddenly, the voice takes shape, clears. *Patrice.*

I'm sitting bolt upright in seconds, the box travelling with me. For a heartbeat, the room around me looks unfamiliar through the tiny coin-sized holes. The blood-red blankets draped across my legs are too soft, too warm. Where is the creaky windowpane? The hum of cars as they pass by on their way to wherever they're going?

A pile of fresh clothes lies at my feet, folded in hard lines. My throat tightens with tears, hoarse from exhaustion and understanding. It all starts to funnel back to me, along with a pounding headache.

The mud-stained clothes hit the ground with a thud as I strip down to the oversized underwear hanging loose at my waist. I can only pull my shirt off as far as my bound hands, but I manage to tear the old fabric with some ease. He couldn't know that I've dropped two sizes since being here.

That my skin feels like sandpaper again. I crawl back into the bed, tucking the covers tight around me like a cocoon. The sheets feel all wrong, but there's some comfort in the familiarity of them.

"Why didn't you tell me?" I whisper; I must be barely audible to them with all the shrapnel over my head. The hiss of the air vent dilutes my quiet sob, sending me off to sleep again.

Patrice sighs, maybe relieved that I'm awake. But her voice is sombre; she knows all too well what I've seen, they both do.

"Baby, sometimes hope is the only thing that keeps us alive," she says.

Chapter Thirteen

"Tell me about your family," I say after writhing for an hour half naked, desperate to keep my mind anywhere but on the aching barrel of my stomach and the stench of my rotting breath as it heats my face repeatedly. It's been weeks of this—five, maybe six.

I forget how many times I've dragged that metal lever open, only to find an empty tray waiting for me. Not that I can eat anything anyway. How many times have I prayed that he will return and remove this medieval torture box from my head? I would do anything for it.

"I don't have one, baby," Patrice says, matter of fact. "It's always been just me and my daughter."

"I didn't know you had a daughter," I say, my heart lurching through the concrete walls. "Is she with her father?"

"It's a long story, baby, it'll probably bore you."

"I've got plenty of time," I plead. I'm not normally one to involve myself in other people's affairs, but stories are as good a currency as any in here. And with those vibrant, piercing green eyes burned into the fabric of my mind like a stain, I'm desperate for the distraction.

"I was sixteen when I fell pregnant with Arna. I thought they'd handed me the wrong baby—she was too perfect to have been mine. It felt impossible, and by some deception of fate, I was allowed to take her home. Picture porcelain skin so white it rivalled the snow.

"Plump rosy cheeks, the softest brown curls hanging just below her ears. The biggest brown eyes with long dark lashes beating gently over them. She was an old soul in that tiny little body, you could tell it just by the way she looked at you."

"Thankfully, she's not with her father. He used to beat me," her voice wavers and then settles again. "So one day, I grabbed Arna and we took off. We caught a bus and skipped two towns. We had no food, no money. Just the clothes on our backs."

"I think I only had one diaper left by the fifth day. An elderly couple found us camped on the footpath in South Carolina and took us into their home. I worked casually at the laundromat to pay our dues, but they never took any money from us. They took us in as if we were their own. Treated Arna as if she was their granddaughter."

"I'm so sorry, Patrice, I—"

"You know what's funny, baby?" She says. "We had everything when her father and I lived under the same roof. Physically, at least. Shelter, money to pay the bills, food in our stomachs—and yet, it was unbearable. Then we had nothing, and it was the happiest we'd ever been, just the two of us. Even if we were running for our lives." There's a smile in her voice.

"The last time I saw her," she says, "I had an afternoon class at the after-hours college. A bridging course to get back into medicine. Arna and I went to the park at around lunchtime. It was warm and Arna wanted to play on the swing. She was about to turn five."

"I pushed her on that swing for hours, until the afternoon light started to fade, and it was time to go. She was so disappointed, I can remember her little nose all scrunched up, arms crossed. We had an appointment with the second-hand shop to pick out some clothes for her first day of school."

"I'd been saving for months to afford even the shoes. I'll never forget the look on her face when she saw herself in that oversized t-shirt and shorts, her floppy hat pulled tight to her head, with the drawstring done all the way up under her chin." She sniffs back tears.

"I never even got to take her to her first day of school. Never found out if she made a friend, if the other kids were nice to her. If someone was there to tie her shoelaces, pack her lunchbox, cut her sandwiches into triangles instead of squares."

Rage simmers in my veins like hot oil. Patrice's words are blood-clotting liquid lead. I recall Jade telling me a similar story about her own mother and biological father. They'd left when she was around the same age, sleeping on the streets for months before a family took them in.

We're both silent for the rest of the afternoon, finding solace in the mere presence of each other. The heaviness of our burdens sitting stale in the air between us.

Hours pass as my mind wanders through old memories, of my father, of Jade, of a better time, willing myself to move, to shower, to do anything but lie here like this and suffocate. As usual, it's the thought of Angus that disrupts me from my stupor.

One person's grief is enough of a cataclysm, but to live with the grief of a mother encumbered by memories of her daughter was a different sort of weight entirely.

Just try to sleep; I coax my weary eyes, though my mind is restless and roused with desperate wanting, with restraint. But as darkness envelops the room, my sniffs turn to bone-shuddering sobs, the sound of which, I have no doubt, carries through the slits in the box, under the wooden door and out into the eerie hollow passage.

***

I managed to sleep, but it was fitful, haunted by dreams and nightmares of coffins, cages and dark, damp tunnels.

Alister appears at my door just after daybreak. This time, as the bolts clang and the door grinds against its hinges, I don't bother to run. What a frivolous and pointless exercise it would be, and without an ounce of energy to spare, I'd end up right back where I started, which may have been all strategy on his part, now I think about it.

If I just do as I'm told for once, he might spare me another day of wearing this satanic box on my head. It seemed to work the last time, but that was before I'd thrown the delicate bond of trust at the ground and smashed it like glass.

Ginger footsteps drag me to my feet as his shadowy figure fills the room. "Christ," he says as I try to scratch an itch on my nose but am again stopped by the wooden box. Something like concern flickers in his eyes as he examines the loose clothing draped over my body in generous folds.

My bound arms haven't fit through the sleeves of any shirts or sweaters for months, so I've taken to using sheets like a tunic over my midriff. The expression on his face vanishes, replaced by cold distaste.

"There's food in the house," he mumbles, almost in answer. "Let's go."

I don't bother to ask where we're going as he places a dark covering over my head. It's a pointless addition considering I can barely see anything as it is. Only, now I really feel like the air has thinned to nothing, like his hands are around my throat.

He secures my hands with an additional sharp, thin tether, almost like a cable tie. Every tug on those binds is like taking a knife edge to rice paper as he drags me along the tunnel, up the stairs and through the wooden trapdoor. Where we go after that, I haven't the slightest idea.

***

It's silent as we walk, save for my extremely shallow breaths and the crunch of wood and stones and pine needles beneath our feet. Faint sounds of rain splatter against his trench coat, making it harder to listen for clues about where we're going. As we walk, the scent of week-old bile dissipates ever so slightly, giving me a moment of relief.

I try to count my shuffling steps, every twig and pothole underfoot, draw a map of our track in my mind, but it's useless. I'm stumbling through the darkness, completely blind, nearly falling flat on my face so many times, I've lost count. By the sixth turn, my map is a mangled mess of criss-crossing lines. We must be travelling in circles.

After a while, the sweet trill of bird song fades away, and we step out into a clearing of sorts. It feels like the forest is a wall of trees behind us. The flat, solid ground beneath, and the soft hum of electricity confirms my theory.

"Wait here." He releases his stony grip on my arm and takes a step forward, leaving a frigid chill in his wake. It winds up the loose fabric of my tunic, digging its cold claws into my bones.

We step through an entry way, and the clang of bolts sound behind us as a heavy door slams shut. The static air and solid ground confirm all my fears—another cage.

But there's no dank odour, no musty mildew feel about this place. It's somehow clean. The faint smell of lavender comes first, and then a rush of warm air crawls up my neck. It must be pungent to have penetrated the headwear. Alister pulls the covering from my head and, after spending weeks suffocating, he finally unbuckles the wooden headdress.

At first, the light is piercing, so much so that it feels as if I'm staring directly at the sun. My head throbs in agony, but at the same time, I'm relieved to feel the fresh air caressing my brittle skin. Never has it smelt so incredibly sweet, like mildew and vanilla bean.

I drink it in like liquid chocolate until my lungs burn. If I never tasted another meal, at least I'd have this. He leaves my hands bound by the, yes, as I guessed, cable ties. I can't see him loosening those anytime soon.

The hallway stretches out before us, dimly lit by candlelight. My eyes are slowly adjusting. Light floorboards barely creak as I take a careful step forward. To my right, the white wall gives way to an arched entryway. Through it is a modern but modest kitchen with porcelain-white cabinets and a grey stone benchtop with peach accents in the centre. There's every kind of appliance and condiment you would want in a kitchen, except there's not a granule of coffee in sight.

On the benchtop sits a plethora of food, enough to feed an army and then some. The waft of blue cheese and fresh bread knots my stomach, and like a siren song, I'm being drawn towards it.

"Please, eat," Alister says, trailing me inside. He motions for me to sit on one of the wooden stools lining the bench. But I ignore the invitation, instead lunging for the thick slices of bread, grappling fistfuls of it in my bound hands, shovelling it into my mouth.

I've barely finished chewing before I'm biting into the block of cheese like an apple. The lack of cutlery or china doesn't faze me, and I lick the remnants from my fingers, savouring every smear, every soggy crumb.

Berries, cured meats, muffins, the more I eat, the more frenzied I become until there's nothing but scraps splayed across the benchtop. I press a hand to my bulging stomach. I'll pay for the lack of self-control later, but for now, I relish the lack of hunger for the first time in months.

"Thank you, sir," I breathe as Alister moves to stand across from me. Tears pool in the corner of my eyes, threatening to spill over. *Just do as you're told.* I will myself to be compliant. The thick wooden box sits at the edge of my memories, taunting me. I'd do anything not to have to wear it again.

"Come on." He gestures back towards the hall. "There's so much more to show you."

***

Alister hadn't been exaggerating when he said there was more.

Open doorways on either side dot the remainder of the hall. One leads to a mahogany-themed dining area. Others to lush opulent bedrooms and a paper-filled study. We pass one door on our right without stopping. I don't ask why or what might lie behind it. I won't give him the satisfaction of appearing to care.

We carry on down the hall until we reach the final door. The pervasive smell of chemicals hits me first, and then the fluorescent lighting. Three grey laminate benches line the wall on the right. Shelves and refrigerators occupy the left.

At the far end of the room, a wall of clear glass frames the thick pine forest beyond. Some trees are so tall, only their trunks are visible. If it weren't for the faint coating of dust, I might have tried to leap out through it.

The rain seems to have eased, and tiny water droplets sit brightly on the leaves. I can almost smell the dew. I'd give anything to feel the fresh air fill my lungs, just one more time.

"I want to show you something," says Alister.

He inclines his head, motioning for me to join him at the bench closest to us, a line of blood samples in hand.

I reluctantly join him, if only to learn more about the cure that might grant us our freedom from this wretched place. I'll be damned if I have to spend another minute in that sodding bunker, starving. It's hard to concentrate. The thought of returning to that dark place beneath the ground is enough for my blood to thicken and the air to grow thin around my lungs.

"The immune response to infection with *Mycobacterium pneuculosis* is arbitrated mostly through T-cell activation," Alister says. "As part of this response, T cells are sensitised to MP antigens and the activated effector T cells, both CD4+ and CD8+, produce the cytokine interferon-gamma when stimulated by these antigens. The test that we use—"

I can hear the faint trickle of water just outside—a gutter overflowing perhaps. God, I'd do anything to be out there.

"Aurelia?" Alister holds my gaze, his green eyes wary. A hint of concern flickers between them.

"I need some air." I clutch my hands to my mouth, trying to sooth the panic rising in my chest. "Sir," I quickly wheeze.

"Here." He hands me a glass of water from a neighbouring bench, and I almost snatch it from his serpent-like fingers, emptying the contents in one desperate gulp. The cold water touches every inch of my throat before it lands with a splash in my stomach.

My face warms as his gaze sweeps over me, assessing, no doubt noticing the now-slow rise and fall of my chest, the calm now beginning to trickle through my eyes. The air seems more fluid now, easing back into my lungs.

"Are you okay?"

"What do you care?" I take one look at the almost genuine concern riddled in his eyes and grind my teeth. "Besides, of course, keeping me alive so that you can practise whatever experiment you are cooking up in here, sir."

His eyebrows furrow. "I do not need you for practice. I have mice for that. And you would do well not to test my patience, or would you have preferred that I left you in that bunker to die?"

"Why don't you just kill me now and get it over with?"

He raises a brow. "You really wish to die?" A flash of intrigue mars his expression.

"It would be better than being a prisoner, sir." *Your prisoner* is what sits on the tip of my tongue, but I close my mouth.

He takes an even stride towards me and I lurch backwards, stumbling into another workbench. It happens so quickly, there's barely time to react, to think. With the bench to my back and the solid wall to my right, I've nowhere to go, except for under—but he'd surely catch me before I so much as duck. His mouth is a hard line, eyes narrow and dark. It's enough to root me to the spot.

The edge of the bench digs deeper into my spine. We're only a whisper apart, and his warm breath licks my face as he growls, "You are never going to say that again, to yourself, to me, or to anyone else for the rest of your life, do you understand me? You are not a prisoner."

My hands tremble, and all I can muster is a quick, "Yes, sir," in response.

He studies my face carefully, clocking the terror in my eyes. It feels like an eternity before he finally steps away, releasing me. I release a long breath into the air between us, one I didn't even know I'd been holding.

***

Hours pass, every moment a test of mental and physical endurance. Physical because of the quiver in my bones each time Alister takes a step into my personal space to insert another slide into the microscope. The food is digesting and all I can feel is a rumbling ache as if my insides might explode at any moment. And mental because it's hard to concentrate on the reason I'm stuck in here, when all I want in the world is to be out there.

I try to pay attention as Alister explains how he has utilised the enzyme-linked immunospot methodology to enumerate *pneuculosis*-sensitised T cells by capturing interferon-gamma in the vicinity of T cells from which it was secreted.

"A blood sample is collected using phlebotomy and a blood collection tube. From that, we isolate the white blood cells," he says, taking a tray of blood samples from the fridge.

He's been explaining four years of trial and mostly error over the past two, maybe three hours now.

"The cells are cleaned, adjusted and counted to create a standard cell mixture," he says, placing the tubes on the bench in front of me. "Then, basically, a set number of cells is put into special plates. These cells are then exposed to specific substances that make them release interferon-gamma."

"To measure this interferon-gamma, antibodies that can capture it are used. After that, another labelled antibody is added, which attaches to the captured interferon-gamma, helping in its detection."

I nod, remembering the T-Spot test model from a textbook that Alister had given me once after class. God, how did I not see this coming?

"After adding a special substance that reacts with the labelled antibody, spots are formed where the interferon-gamma was released by the cells. By counting these spots, we can figure out if there's *pneuculosis* in our samples."

He looks at me expectantly.

"Streptomycin," I answer. "Sir."

"You remember it from our first class." My soul blisters under the heat of his stare. I nod slowly.

"Explain it to me," he says, taking a sample of clear unmarked liquid and placing a drop into one of the blood samples. He pulls the lens over the sample so that the cells are magnified and inspects it carefully. He's not watching me anymore, but he's listening eagerly, waiting for my answer.

Reluctantly, the words start to form sentences in my mind's eye, the page manifesting itself like an old movie.

"Streptomycin is a type of antibiotic. It works by latching on to specific parts of the bacterial ribosome, which is like a cell's protein-making machinery. Once attached, it messes up the teamwork between the ribosome and the messenger

RNA, making it harder for the bacteria to start making proteins. This interference slows down the bacteria's ability to grow and reproduce."

"And?"

"And it causes cell death, sir," I recite.

"Good," he says. "Here, put this on."

He hands me a pair of opaque rubber gloves and a white medical-grade double-elastic face mask. "Just to be safe." He shrugs, pulling the straps over his head. His green eyes intensify.

I lever the gloves onto my hands with a *thwap* and tug the face mask over my head. Images of my father flash into my mind, the memories far too painful to embrace for even a moment longer. I grind my teeth against the lump forming in my throat.

It matters little what Alister thinks of me. In the end, it won't make a difference to whether I live or die—and maybe it's the stubbornness in me, the part that still thinks I might get out of here one day—but for now, at least, I refuse to let him see me cry, to give him the satisfaction.

He motions for me to step in front of the lens. I'm careful not to take my eyes off him for any longer than absolutely necessary. He won't catch me off guard again. Alister seems to sense this because he takes a generous step backwards, giving me a much-needed reprieve.

Manoeuvring my bound hands, I lean over the lens. The cable digs into my wrists, red welts forming where my skin has been rubbed raw.

"Do you remember when I said that the—?"

I cut him off, "Pneuculosis-positive patients will have positive interferon-gamma. I know, sir."

I study the sample through the lens and immediately notice signalling proteins, the kind released in the presence of viruses. After studying the cells a bit longer, I find the interferon-gamma—IFNγ—and then the virus. A cold shiver climbs my spine.

"Sir, is it safe?" I ask, stepping back from the sample.

"Yes," he reassures me, and for some reason, I believe him.

"Now, look at this." He slides another sample across the bench, and I gently exchange them, careful not to damage the glass case, the only thing standing between us and death.

I slide it into place under the lens and adjust the focus. I peer down the neck to find that this sample is—

"Normal," he says.

"I don't understand," I say.

"This sample is half of the infected sample."

No. It couldn't be half of the infected sample because that would mean—

"Impossible, sir."

"Streptomycin." He sighs, slumping into one of the swivel chairs against the wall. He pulls his mask down, exposing his chiselled jawline. I curse myself for even noticing. He leans forward, elbows resting on his knees, his hands rubbing the stubble of his beard.

"The cure?" I demand. I feel the anger lingering at the edge of my patience. If this is what I think it is, then why am I still here? Why are any of us still here?

"*A* cure, not *the* cure," he clarifies, "and not one that works long term, anyway. Resistance is rapid and the condition returns, over and over with a vengeance. The reinfection death rate is one hundred per cent."

He lifts a grey sheet, exposing a line of cages on the far wall, each containing the lifeless bodies of white mice, thirty or forty in number.

"We have to be patient," he says, clocking my startled expression. His mouth tightens into a thin line.

My heart plummets. *Patient*. Patient meant more time in that confined room. More time underground. More earthy darkness. More silence broken only by the sound of my own breath. That gut-wrenching little cage that he shoves over my head. Suddenly, I'm grateful for the windows, the citric clean air as the ground rattles underfoot. I don't want to be patient. The only thing I want to be right now is home!

I slump onto a stool, my knees shaking so fiercely I can hardly stand. Alister studies me, his eyes etched with concern. Does he regret bringing me here? Does he regret not killing me when he had the chance?

"I want to show you something."

I trail him back into the empty hall. A warm light flickers overhead as if the laboratory is absorbing most of the power, leaving very little for the rest of the house. A generator would explain the strobe effect of the lights. How else would he have inhabited an abandoned prison for so long undetected? The more I learn about this place, the more I want to run from it.

We take a left at the other end of the hall, through a closed wooden door. The decor evolves as we step into the room. What was once cold laminate is now light oak floorboards, white walls and a fancy trim, and it's almost twice the size of any room I've seen so far. Immediately, I recognise the homely melange of aged paper and ink.

The scent of polished mahogany and weathered oak shelves blend together seamlessly. I can almost hear the click of typewriter keys, the scratch of pen to parchment. It's one of my favourite places. Maybe the only kind of place that's ever truly felt like home.

A library.

Hundreds—no, thousands—of books are organised in alphabetical order, by date and author, on towering shelves that reach up towards the heavens. As we walk into the room, the husky smell of fresh ink and parchment, new and old, fills my nostrils. I've never seen anything so grand before in my life. The space seems to breathe with the weight of centuries' worth of written treasures.

"What do you think?" He grins.

***

"It's incredible," I say in earnest.

In this room, time seems to stand still. A sanctuary of history and knowledge. Shelves, row upon row, house an endless tapestry of books, their spines lined up in perfect order, creating a rainbow of colours and titles. I'd once dreamed of having my own library, with reading nooks and windows to watch the sunset. Angus had been part of that dream once, lazing in an armchair beside me, stroking my hair while I lost myself in the pages.

The covers are firm and smooth as I run my fingers along them, walking the full length of the room. I catch some of the authors' names: AJ Peterson, SM Larkin. And some I don't even recognise.

"Can I?"

"Take as many as you like." His eyes are bright and warm. "Like I said, if you follow my rules, you can have the run of the place. I'm not here to torture you, Aurelia." He approaches, each step unnervingly smooth and graceful. He plucks a title from the shelf. "Start with Selman and make your way to Hopwood. They are my favourites."

The book is thick and heavy in my hands.

He shrugs. "Or don't—the library is yours to explore at your leisure."

Before I can even muster a response, the doors close with a familiar click as Alister vanishes, leaving me completely alone.

***

I spend the better part of an hour lost in the titles, though every creak and crack in the wood around me sends my heart into a flurry. *You're okay,* I remind myself, taking a deep, full breath. I glance at the doorway, the high ceiling, the spacious room. *You're okay.*

By the time Alister returns, there's a stack of books about six high on the wooden table. Titles I know aren't available in the local library, and not for lack of trying on my part to have them ordered in.

"Here," Alister says, placing a tender hand on my shoulder. It's the first human contact I've had in months, and my first instinct is to recoil. This doesn't seem to faze him as he takes the rest of the books from my bound hands and adds two additional ones to the pile for good measure.

"These should keep you busy for a few hours." His eyes gleam, and for a moment, I'm back in the classroom, with chamomile tea, mindlessly flicking through the pages of my textbook, and Alister sitting across from me, offering another biscuit.

If only I could return to that day, when the floral liquid warmed my soul with every sip and my entire future was laid out before me like a blank canvas, marked by endless opportunities, with Alister's watchful eye and guiding hand. I'd have run as fast as I could and never looked back.

Chapter Fourteen

I thrash and flail at the darkness, recoiling from invisible hands reaching out to throttle me. Sweat clings to my drenched nightgown, my heaving breath carrying like smoke across the cold air. The night-light next to the bed hums to life, casting long shadows around the room. None as chilling as those that haunt my dreams. None quite as dark as those in Alister's eyes.

My feet drag along the wooden floor as I stagger into the bathroom. Panting, I lean over the steel sink, steadying, grounding myself. But remnants of the night terror loom in fragments both vivid and cruel. The sound of running water echoes through the empty space.

Its icy tendrils sooth my sweaty face. I swipe at the steam; I'll be damned if I let the darkness creep up on me. A chill weaves its way through the room, but it does nothing to dry the sweat pooling in the small of my back. It's okay. *You're okay*, I remind myself.

I retch into the basin next to me, heaving into the silver bowl. Cutting my hands on both sides of the sword is something I've become accustomed to in the three months since he's been taking me up to the house. Before, I'd barely had a scrap of food to hurl.

Now, each morning before dawn, I find myself lunging for the rim of the toilet bowl, pouring the chunks of last night's dinner down the drain. At least my limbs remain unbound, and for that, I am grateful. I've earned it with every 'yes, sir' that I've muttered, endless days spent in the lab trying to decipher the works of those scientists who have long gone before me, and by following the rules.

I've also discovered the necessity of silence concerning the others. Just the other day, I asked Alister to ensure that Rose and Patrice steered clear of the two chemical compounds I was working on. His eyes rounded and his furrowed brows were etched with frustration. Maybe I'm not supposed to know about them yet. Maybe we're not supposed to speak at all.

"Not all echoes are the arbiter of truth," he uttered cryptically. A lesson, I suppose. Even so, I waited with bated breath later that night to see if dinner would come. And as I shovelled forkfuls of poutine into my mouth, I made a silent vow never to breathe a word about them again.

***

In a few hours, he will come for me. The dark hood will be draped over my head, hands bound by cable ties.

Fleeting memories of loose gravel, makeshift headstones, my name carved into the chalky surface flash through my mind like a spectre.

It unfolds like an eerie tableau, frozen in time. Even though it's been months since I've had that torturous wooden box on my head and felt those invisible hands tightening around my throat, every now and then, the air thins in my dreams, threatening to choke me anyway.

And I can only pray that dawn is enough to banish the demons of the night.

***

The days pass by in a blur, most of them spent in the lab with a full belly and fractured hope. Sometimes, Alister peers over my shoulder, and sometimes, the subtle creak of the floorboards is the only sign that he's ever existed at all.

Other days were spent poring over the pages of various books in the library, reading every single word, letting them carry me far away from this place. Questions still burn like smouldering embers in the back of my mind—why are we here? What is the purpose of all this? But I've long given up my pursuit of answers.

"I'll tell you when the time is right," is all he has said.

I daren't press him for more, not when it might cost me the only thing that matters now—my freedom. Three hours a day of sunlight and windows. Three hours of staring at something other than the encroaching four walls. I wouldn't sacrifice the light for anything in the world.

Not when I'd already spent so many months in the dark. Some days I don't speak, not to Rose or Patrice, or even myself. They don't seem to mind; without any progress to report, we've long run out of things to say.

My nights are filled with terrors. I often dream of being outside the wall, of large forests and fields and mountains and space. Wide, open space. But I wake to the crushing hands of darkness, grappling for my nightstand, only to realise that even the warm, illuminating light can't save me from the encroaching walls.

The blind trek from the bunker to the house is my only opportunity to breathe the fresh air, to smell the bark and dirt and pine. To smell anything but the damp dark of my room. Outside is the only place where I don't feel the fingers of claustrophobia winding their way around my neck–even if it is still a prison.

The fabric draped over my head leaves me stumbling, fumbling across the uneven forest floor, even when he slows our pace to a gentle shuffle. I can't know for sure, but we seem to take a different route every day. Whether that is for my benefit or his, I don't care. I'm just grateful to take more than four paces and not run into a stone wall.

***

I spear another blueberry with my fork. It's been twenty minutes and I'm sick of waiting, so I rinse the empty plate in the kitchen sink and make my way down the eerily silent corridor and into the lab, alone.

For the next few hours, I rummage through the cell samples in the cabinets, pulling out test tubes and micro lenses. There's no point wasting time, and I've got nothing better to do.

The scribblings of a madwoman, that's what the blue ink on the page in front of me represents. I'm that madwoman. The failings of all our hard work. None of the cells have shown even the slightest improvement. None of the mice have survived more than one night.

I flick impatiently through the notebook, through earlier pages where the handwriting turns bubbly and expressive, the language flamboyant, and at times, explicit. I hazard a guess that this writing belongs to Rose, and after reading a couple of pages, I'm almost certain. I'd have to agree with some of her chosen profanities; today has not been a successful one.

There's another style of hand script, old and faded, much tighter and smaller than the others. The words are meticulously placed, the spelling perfect. This must be Patrice's calligraphy.

It's strange, after all this time, to be able to see them, having only heard their voices for so long. It's no photograph, and nothing compared to meeting someone in person, but at least it's something, and something is enough to keep my mind from wandering to the dark places for now.

Outside, the light has greyed and faded, the clouds of the night sky starting to creep in. It can't be that time already—where has the day gone?

I jolt, nearly dropping the tray of test tubes as Alister saunters up behind me. "Jesus Christ."

"No, just me," he says, taking the tray from my hands and sliding it onto the bench. "But I've been called worse, trust me."

"You know if you took these cable ties off, I might actually be able to work, sir." I scowl.

"It's late."

"Yes," I say tersely as I adjust the lens of the microscope. "I lost track of time."

"I can see that," he muses.

I swap the glass slide with another, almost identical one. Only the two could not be more different. One, capable of killing you in hours, and the other, completely harmless. The tall chair beside me groans as I slump into it, arms twisted awkwardly in my lap.

He lifts a brow. "Having fun?"

Even if it were true, I wouldn't admit it. "I'm tired and hungry," I say coldly. And no wonder, if it is indeed nearly dusk.

"Come on, I'll escort you back to your room."

"Escort," I snort, "you almost make it sound chivalrous, sir."

His mouth tightens. "Do you still think so little of me, Aurelia? Even after all this time." The gentle tone in his words halts me, sparing him from my pointed retort. The silence draws out between us like a bowstring.

"What else would you have me think?" I say carefully. "I feel like a prisoner. Sir."

Alister's eyes darken. "Have I done nothing to earn your trust since you've been here? I provide you with three meals a day, fresh clothes, access to more books than your heart could possibly desire. I spared you when you tried to run, I have forgiven every insult, every transgression. I don't ask for thanks. I barely demand your respect. The least you could do is show me some semblance of trust."

Trust. But I *had* trusted him, hadn't I. And look where that got me. What does that feeble little word even mean now?

"Please," he says too quietly. His eyes are steady, gentler than I've seen them before. Something deep inside me softens at it, at the pleading in his eyes. At the words spoken, and the ones that aren't.

I shift uncomfortably, reaching for the test tubes, for a way out of this conversation.

"Tell me what I can do." He might as well be on his knees. "Tell me how I can convince you to trust me."

Immediately, I know my answer. "I want to know why we're doing all this," I say. "No one will tell me, and I've been too frightened to press the matter in case I wind up starving to death with a wooden box on my head."

This time, unease, not concern flickers in his green eyes, and I wonder if he ever thought I'd ask.

"To serve a greater purpose," he says.

"I want the truth," I push, knowing full well that this might be my only opportunity for answers.

"I wish there didn't have to be secrets between us, Aurelia, but I don't know if you can handle the truth."

"Tell me, please, sir."

A long pause. "I can't."

"But," I protest.

"I'll have to show you."

***

I trail with feather-light steps behind Alister. We enter the hall and turn left, towards the library—my sanctuary. I don't dare ask where we're going, and he doesn't offer any explanation as he leads us silently down the hall. There's one door to our right that has always been locked, despite my best attempts to rattle it when I thought no one was looking. Unsurprisingly, we come to a stop right in front of it.

There's nothing arrogant in his darting eyes, only cold, pressed fear. The fact that he won't meet my gaze tells me enough about what might lie behind this door. Tiny beads of sweat cluster across his forehead and my heart thrums against my chest, throat, and veins.

"Ready?" He asks, but before I can answer, he's pushing us through the open door.

***

Death. Worse than I could have imagined. The room reeks of it. Of flesh and bones and preserved corpses.

There's a king-size bed, one of the old kind with four wooden pillars at each corner and a sheer canopy stretched out over it. The decor is timeworn too, frills and lace that date back to the eighties. But something else bates my labouring breath.

On the mattress, tucked neatly under the sheets, lies a woman, as still as stone. Every cell in my body screams at me to run. To hell with freedom. I want to scream and fight and kick and beat my way out of this wretched place. But there's something about the way she's lying there that roots me to my spot.

"Is she—?" I've no room left for manners.

"Dead?" Alister breathes. "No."

"Who is she?" And if she's not dead, then why does it smell like a morgue in here?

He gently ambles to the bedside, kneeling next to the woman. He brushes a strand of hair from her forehead, and then, to my surprise, he leans over and places a kiss between her brows.

He looks up at me, eyes rounded, features soft as silk. "I would like to introduce you to my wife," he says, "Lucinda."

***

"I didn't lie to you," Alister says, hands raised in defence.

I fight the urge to run as fast as my legs will take me, away from this place. It doesn't matter that I have nowhere to go, or that this time my running would be a death sentence.

My stomach bottoms out. "You told me she was dead." I remember that conversation in the cemetery like it was yesterday, not ten months ago.

"Let me explain." Back on his feet, he takes a step towards me.

"Don't." Tears threaten to betray my courage as I back up towards the door.

"I didn't lie, Aurelia," he says again, his eyes pleading. "Her cells are infected, she's dying."

"You said at the cemetery, I saw her grave." My voice cracks. And I don't care that he can see the terror in my eyes. The fragile ground on which I walk starts to fracture and falter beneath me. If only it would open up and swallow me whole.

"My dog, Maggie," he says gently, "is buried in that cemetery."

She deteriorated very quickly. The doctors couldn't do anything for her, so I took her home. That's all he said about his wife. He'd muttered nothing about her death. A curated omission in a carefully crafted narrative, and I, the casualty of deceit, watching the pieces of the puzzle rearrange. A much more sinister picture now unfolding before my eyes.

I take one more step onto unstable ground, lifting my chin as I ask, "How long has she been—?"

His eyes slide away, face paling. A chill creeps through my hollow veins. I pull at my sweater, trying to cover my bare shoulders.

I force myself to meet Alister's stare, if only to judge whether what he says next is the truth, or another carefully carved-out lie. Though despite my gated stance, despite holding my breath to steady my voice, nothing quite prepares me for the answer.

"Four years," he says, nervously shifting his weight from right to left.

I look past Alister to the woman lying still behind him. For the first time, I notice the ever so subtle rise and fall of her chest. What must it be like, to be trapped in that grey space between living and dying? To be a soul so well and truly lost. Memories of the wooden box return like a tsunami, with pelting force.

"This is wrong." I rasp for air.

The ECG machine beeps, almost in agreement, but I barely hear it. There's a certain beauty to her appearance that transcends even the lifelessness of her. Had she been a kind person before all this? Had he?

"What happened to her?" I ask, not taking my eyes off the light brown bands of her long straight hair, still and dead as African mahogany. If it wasn't for the almost inaudible wheezing sound, it would be impossible to believe she was alive.

Alister glances towards his wife as if she might hear him.

"During her first line of treatment," he whispers, "she developed resistance. Her treatment was interrupted," he says carefully.

He turns back to her, crouching slowly at her bedside. He takes her hand in his, stroking the pale surface in gentle circles with his thumb. Her skin looks like paper, and why wouldn't it, after all these years?

"If I ever got my hands on those doctors," he seethes through clenched teeth.

I think of my father, the pleas I cried to the heavens, the bargains whispered into my tear-stained pillow. There's nothing I wouldn't have done in that moment, in the weeks and months that followed, just to see him again. To hear his voice one last time. My heart aches with the memory.

It is true that hospitals can keep anyone alive if they want to, letting the machines take their breath, keeping their hearts beating for as long as necessary.

It's a capacity and resource issue that forces family members to say goodbye. If they could put the decision on ice until someone found a cure for the illness, wouldn't they? Would I?

There are disturbing happenings here that I may never truly fathom, and yet perhaps, even more terrifying, are the things that I am already beginning to understand.

***

It's a relief to be back in my room, to feel the soft heaviness of my duvet as I sink into my pillow, exhausted and ready for sleep. Even the soft hiss of the air vent has a homely quality about it tonight. I've already showered, brushed my teeth and slid into my pyjamas, ready to drift off to sleep when Rose and Patrice pepper me with questions about my day.

"I hope you didn't waste the entire day in the library," Rose spits with a wink in her voice. The library is a liberty that Alister seems to have only extended to me. For this reason, I try not to speak about it too often. Not unless they ask.

I make a point of slipping a novel or two into the pass-through compartment in the wall for them. Books I've already read a thousand times over. Rose has never thanked me, but if I listen hard enough on particularly quiet days, I can hear the rustling of pages.

"What did you discover today?" Patrice asks.

So, I tell them. I tell them what Alister apparently hasn't. I tell them about his wife, every detail I can remember, the ECG machine, the life-giving drip planted in her arm. Of the number of years she has been chained to that bed. I speak for nearly an hour, barely stopping to take a breath. They listen in silence. Aghast, probably, as I describe everything I've seen.

Patrice falls back against her pillow with a thud. "Why did her treatment stop?" She asks. "I don't know," I whisper. I hadn't thought to ask.

As I close my eyes, the sound of my father's deep, soulful voice becomes so vivid, it's as if he's sitting on the edge of my bed. *See you in the sunrise*, he whispers. The words dance around the room like a gazelle, and I let them play, hovering there like smoke, until the world around me finally fades to black.

***

The next three months, I spend alternating between the library, the lab and the greenhouse. One hour every odd-numbered day—that's all I'm afforded under the open sky—watching the sunflowers evolve from seedlings to full bloom.

Watching clouds drift overhead, thicker and thicker every day, like papier mâché across the sky, preparing for a blistering cold winter. My time in the wooden box is finally fading from my memory, giving me some relief during the day. The nights are still filled with terrors, the worst being the feeling of long fingers wrapping around my neck.

I still end up with my face in the toilet bowl, retching until I hear the pitter-patter of Alister's feet, followed by the grind of the breakfast tray. By that point, my stomach aches so much that I can barely eat, so I flush most of it down the toilet. It upsets him when there's leftovers, and I can't risk my outdoor privileges being taken away from me. I'd rather end it all.

My hair has grown, hovering just above my tailbone now. Most of the time, it's tucked neatly in a braid—much easier to manage that way. If only someone could braid away the occasional ache of homesickness still gnawing at me. But at least the fresh air and open space are a good distraction, even if it feels as fleeting as the rays of sunshine piercing through the clouds.

Time doesn't really matter anymore now that I'm in here. The only measurements I concern myself with these days are the number of blood cells that manage to endure my rigorous testing, and the volume of books I can carry back to my room after each session.

The lack of cells that survived the night explains my tempered mood and my reluctance to water Rose's corpse flower, a plant so outrageously hideous that I doubt anyone but Rose would grieve if it suddenly died. The thought crosses my mind as I spy a bottle of weed killer on the bench to my right.

And just like that, it triggers a darker thought; how much would a person need to ingest to end their own suffering? Surely more than a sip, but the whole bottle; that would almost guarantee it. I'd be free. Dead, very dead. But at least my soul would be free to soar high above these retched walls.

Thoughts like these do no one any good, especially not me. So, I push them from my mind.

Despite my subdued mood, I'm happy with the haul from the greenhouse today—a handful of strawberries, two peaches, and some apples from a tree that Patrice must have planted when she first arrived. It might be the first fruit it's borne; I'll have to ask her when I get back.

Patrice is something of a whiz with gardening, planting all kinds of seeds so they sprout in the right seasons, collecting compost from her food scraps, sticking to a strict watering regime. As I walk along the narrow aisle through the centre of the greenhouse, carelessly spraying the plants on either side of me, I'll never quite replicate her eye for horticulture, the gifts passed to her from her late parents.

They passed away in a car accident when she was young, just like my grandparents. If only I could hug her; the idea of her being in that cell alone with a lifetime of grief bothers me more than I care to admit. Maybe I'll ask Alister tomorrow, if he's in one of his more generous moods.

By the time the entrance to our bunker appears through the trees ahead, the sun is well and truly on its way down. I press four fingers against the sky, measuring the distance between the sun and the tops of the pines. I can't tell for sure, because the technique only works when you marry your fingers with the horizon, and I haven't seen the horizon or anything remotely close to it for months.

I sit on a protruding tree root and bite into one of the soft peaches. The sweet juice runs down my chin, lacing its way through my fingers, dripping onto the dirt below. The forest around me is eerily quiet, save for the hushed rustle of leaves as the breeze bounces from tree to tree.

I'll never quite get used to the lingering feeling that I'm being watched. The shiver that crawls up my spine whenever I'm alone, in the library or the surrounding woodland. That someone might be lurking in the dense underbrush, waiting.

And maybe I've completely lost my mind. Either way, no one has reprimanded me for eating more fruit than I collected today, not yet anyway.

***

A soft bell chime demands my attention—Alister's way of reminding us he's still in control. The rubber soles of my shoes scuff the gravel as I hustle down the marked path from the greenhouse to the bunker. I don't dare stray from it, not when I might stumble across another pit of death, or worse.

Discoveries like that are enough to fuel ruthless nightmares for months on end. Only in the recent weeks have they finally subdued. I haul open the heavy wooden door and saunter down the stairs into the darkness, closing the door behind me with a thud and a cloud of dust. I meander down the dark stone hallway, kicking the odd leaf as I pass.

Straight ahead, is a semicircle court shape with three doors that mark a dead end. It's dark and difficult to see, but the silhouettes are still there if I squint hard enough.

The entrance to Rose's room is to the left. I run my hand over the splintery surface of the oak as I pass. It's the closest I might ever be to her, physically, at least. Next to it is the entrance to Patrice's room. Sometimes, I swear their rooms vanish in the darkness, and I've even had nightmares about such kinds of things.

I have to say, it terrifies me more than the wooden box. The only thing worse than being trapped in this place would be being trapped here alone. I'd go completely mad.

Resting my head against the cool surface, I tug at the bolts that lock the communication window. I so desperately want to see her, put a face to the kind voice that has kept me sane all these months. There's a deep, innate thirst for human contact growing inside me every day, having been denied it for so, so long. Angus's embrace is a memory so distant I can barely recall how it feels to be held, or even touched at all.

Sensing that my time is up, I push open the door to my room and close it with a heavy thud. Alister's footsteps trail close behind. Without a word, he pulls the door shut the rest of the way, the chains jingling as he bolts them, locking me inside. Suddenly, there's an explosion next door.

"Rose?" I call in panic.

"Wowee," she croons, "this sound system is next level."

It must be sarcasm, because through the loud explosions is the most irritating static sound.

I bang on my door. "Yuck, Rose, can you turn it down?"

Rose groans but does as I ask. "It's *Lethal Weapon Two*—don't tell me you don't recognise the soundtrack?"

I vaguely recall hearing my dad watching it on our downstairs television box, but I can't be bothered explaining this to her, so I lie, "Mmhm, I'm watching it now."

Instead, I grab one of the books from the pile on my desk, climb onto my bed and sit with my back against the wall. But the sweet juice of the peach still coats my lips, and it's hard to pay attention to the words. The pillow absorbs me as I fall back against it in defeat, staring at the blank ceiling.

"Patrice?" I call quietly in case she's sleeping.

"Yes, baby?" Her soothing voice grows more and more tired every day.

Bang! The sound makes me jump.

"Damn, Gibson, you are one sexy man!" Rose cheers, drumming on her bed frame.

"Tell me more about Arna," I say quickly, trying to tune out the noise.

Sheets ruffle next door, and I imagine Patrice rolling over to face me.

"It's her birthday today," she says soberly. "She will be seven."

I swallow hard, wishing I'd not asked the question. "What was she like?"

Patrice clears her throat. "The last time I saw her, she was wearing a pink Rapunzel dress I couldn't get her out of, no matter how many bargains I tried to make with her." She laughs. "Her shoes were clomping on the floorboards, you know, those tacky plastic princess heels they make now? Or at least, they did back then."

"Was she well behaved?" I ask, rolling over to face the wall.

"Arna? No, she had a mind of her own, that kid, and could throw a tantrum better than anyone I've ever met. She'd make a fine lawyer."

"Even Rose?" I tease.

"Heard that," Rose shouts over the noise of the television.

Patrice laughs. It's been a long time since I've heard her laugh.

"I can't wait to meet her," I whisper, placing a flat palm against the stone wall. If only I could look into her eyes when I say, "I'm sure she's beautiful."

We fill the rest of the afternoon with small talk until eventually, we are interrupted by the sound of footsteps and my growling stomach. Dinner time. The smell of thick, sweet gravy and warm roast pork with caramelised pumpkin fills the room. It must be Sunday. Alister is nothing if not traditional, with his choice of meals at least.

"Let's pray," Patrice says quietly.

I stop chewing and put down my cutlery. I've never prayed, except for chapel services at school. But it can't hurt, and honestly, we need all the help we can get these past few days.

"We used to pray a lot as a family when I was growing up. My mother would take us to church every Sunday," Patrice says. "I stopped after they died. I didn't want to believe in someone who could watch a child's parents be taken from them and choose to do nothing about it."

"I'm more of the Buddhist type," Rose says.

"Rose!"

"Relax, newbie, I'm joking."

We have been living with each other for almost ten months, and still Rose insists on calling me *newbie, new girl, fresh meat, boiled potato* and any other variation she can think of at the time. So common is it that I barely notice anymore.

Rose claps her hands together dramatically. "Ready when you are, ladies."

"Dear Lord, thank you for—" Patrice pauses, and I get it; it's hard to practise gratitude in a place like this. "Thank you for the food we have been given today, the everlasting love that you have for us, for being alive, for the fresh air outside, for Rae's library, for the life that we had."

Had. I flinch at the word. At the weight of it. Of everything it means we've lost.

"Please watch over my daughter, Arna, Aurelia's mother, Angus and Jade."

"Don't forget Andy," Rose yells.

"And Rose's guinea pig, Andy," Patrice adds. "We pray that we will see them again one day, and in the meantime, we thank you for each other. Amen."

"Amen," I say.

Chapter Fifteen

My joints ache and my left arm has been asleep for so long, it takes several minutes of rubbing to bring it back to life. I've been in the laboratory two hours, but there's been no progress, so there's nothing to show for it.

The sky outside is a clear, pale blue for the first time in the twelve months that I've been here. Rays of sunshine blast through the wall of windows in front of me. They may be double-glazed, but I can feel the warmth on my skin. The leaves have changed now too.

The first hint of fall sits in glorious shades of red and gold and yellow and orange as if someone has dragged a paintbrush across the trees. Days like these are a rarity in the Shire, even in the warmest months.

Based on the notes—scribble—that one can only describe as the scratchings of a lunatic, it's clear Rose has all but given up. The most recent is a drawing of a man hanging from the gallows, three women looking on with grins on their faces.

Maybe it's the sunshine, but I find myself smiling at the thought of Rose digging her pencil deep into the paper, furrowed brow as she imagines Alister's timely demise.

But there's little time to dwell; Patrice's daughter will be depending on today's progress and I can't, won't let her down. Patrice isn't rostered on until this afternoon; Rose has developed a fever and I've got nothing else to do with my day, so I've acquired the extra shift.

I study last week's cell sample carefully. Rose's formula includes streptomycin and levofloxacin. Levofloxacin is the antibiotic highest in anti-mycobacterial activity, or so I read. So far, the studies have only been completed on animals, and they certainly weren't attempting to cure mycobacterial pneuculosis. It's risky and uncharted territory, but these days, ideas are as rare as company. Anything is worth a shot.

But what started as a glimmer of hope has now been replaced by this—a sample so consumed by the black cellular mould that is MP that it's barely recognisable. Dark, bitter frustration consumes me.

Pages tear free from their binding as I thrust the notebook across the room, floating towards the ground like snowflakes. The stool behind me groans under my weight. Useless, hopeless. How can I tell the others that we've failed again? That we're no closer to going home than the day we arrived.

I groan begrudgingly when an alarm shakes me from my stupor. My shoes scuff against the squeaky laminate floor as my feet drag me towards the cupboard at the far end of the lab. I shove the necessary items into a tote—a new cannula, fluids and a fresh colostomy bag—so distracted, I almost forget the observation sheet.

Silently, I slip into the hall. Her bedroom is a mere fifteen steps from the lab, but it feels like the Iditarod. I move swiftly, careful not to waste any time. It's mid-morning, but only a few candles light the dark hallway, probably to preserve the generators humming away outside.

Switch, hitch and ditch.
Switch, hitch and ditch.
Switch, hitch and ditch.

Simple. The instructions repeat in my head as the door to Lucinda's bedroom swings open. I'll never get used to the smell, no matter how many times I've been forced to tend to her these past two months, a chore that I've somehow earned enough trust to undertake. It's a fair trade for an additional hour in the fresh air each week.

I suck in a breath and lean over her, gently unwinding the lure lock tacked onto the needle in her arm connecting the IV drip. There's no way this could work, no way that she could stay on life support for this long and not be permanently incapacitated. If it weren't for the numbers on the ECG, I'd have sworn she was—

Jesus Christ.

I stagger back in surprise, my thundering heart beating like a drum in both ears as she sucks in a deep breath of air.

My hands tremble. "Lucinda? Can you hear me?"

Silence.

Of course she can't. When the blood finally stills in my veins, with trembling hands, I gingerly finish replacing the drip. Just as I reach for the needle on the bedside table, something else catches my eye.

The electricity port. Its rectangular frame is adorned with outlets. Small indicator lights glow softly, the gentle hum of power flowing through the wires and into the very machines giving her breath, a heartbeat, life.

With the flick of a switch, she would be dead. It would all be over; we could go home. She wouldn't even feel a thing, I'd make sure of it. Her soul would drift off to wherever souls go—heaven, earth, afterlife, I don't care; we would go home.

Alister is pottering about in the kitchen; I can hear the clang of pots and the almost inaudible beeping of the microwave. He wouldn't get to me in time. He wouldn't even notice until it was too late; her body would begin decomposing within the hour. And maybe he'd kill me for it. Maybe he'd kill all of us. But no one else would come to harm at his hands, no more of us plucked from our lives like sitting ducks.

I trace the cord that runs from the ventilator to the electricity port in the wall. One firm tug, that's all it would take, and it would be over. Her soft eyelids flutter gently, her lashes resting on the crown of her cheekbones. Her violet face is so pale. And no wonder—she wouldn't have seen the sun for years.

Her mouth is at ease, but her brow is tense. Too alive to be dead, but too dead to be alive. I can't shake the sinking feeling that to do this would be nothing short of murder. I'd be no different to Alister, maybe even worse.

Releasing the cord with a sigh, I let my one chance at freedom slip through my fingertips and back into its hanging position beside the bed. Tomorrow, I'd think about it again tomorrow. But even in quasi-death, this woman carries kindness in her features, from her dimples to her rounded cheeks. If the only thing I get to keep after all this is my humanity, then so be it. He won't take that from me as well.

Cold leeches through my body. "Everything okay?"

No, no, no. I whirl in the direction of Alister's voice; he's standing behind me. My stomach plummets as his eyes flicker back and forth between the ventilator and my hand, now pinned tightly to my side. *Christ.*

"Fine, thank you, sir," I murmur. My attempt at a reassuring smile is nothing but a pained grimace. I make a point of checking the readings on the machine, writing the numbers on her chart, preparing the next dose. "Everything looks fine."

He grabs my wrist, mere inches from her arm. "I'll take it from here," he mutters, snatching the needle swiftly from my hand. He knows, he knows!

I stumble back two paces, watching as the needle gently disappears into her arm.

I pray that this stunt has not cost me my garden privileges. The thought of not looking up to anything but the artificial fluorescent light bulb above my bed makes my skin crawl. How could I have been so rash! I'll be lucky if this doesn't cost me my life.

The reality is, we're not getting out of here until Lucinda is waving goodbye to us from the front porch, wherever that might be.

He doesn't turn to look at me when he says, "It's a nice day out, you should spend the rest of the afternoon in the garden."

I know better than to argue with generosity, even if I'm chomping at the bit to try a new antibiotic combination in the lab. Besides, the sunlight always helps me to think, and it's much better than the vitamin D supplements we're given— the ones that leave a chalky aftertaste in your throat no matter how many gulps of water you try to drown them with.

"What about you?" I ask.

"Go, enjoy the day, you've earned it." He continues to brush the strands of hair around Lucinda's forehead as she lies there still, moving only when the machine fills her lungs with air.

I shudder to think how weak her bones must be after all this time. Even if we do find the cure, would she even be able to walk? To talk? I must weave some calcium supplements into her treatment on my next rotation. If there is one.

He doesn't make any move to escort me, and it takes me a long moment to realise he's not going to. So, I turn on my heel and march down the hall before he can change his mind, my feet quickening with every step.

***

My eyes sting as they first meet the light. It's painful, but I'm grateful for the feeling. I step out onto a wooden landing with a set of three steps that lead down to a gravel path. The crisp cool air fills my lungs deeply. The subtle scent of fallen leaves, morning dew and melting snow coats the inside of my nose.

Behind me, the building is made of old grey stone. Some of the larger stones are chipped and cracked, which is unsurprising given the number of winter storms they must have endured over the years. I can't even begin to imagine how long it must have taken Alister to renovate the inside into such a modern dwelling.

The greenhouse is about five hundred yards to my left. I can just make out the glass through the foliage. Pine trees line the pathway, their trunks as wide as wine barrels, their branches like sieves filtering the fall sunlight through the shade. Dark pink creeping phlox grows in wild patches like a carpet across the ground.

If I look out ahead of me, the trees are thick and lush, even though most of their leaves and needles coat the snow-melted ground beneath them. So much colour, so much peace and quiet. It's beautiful, a beautiful fall day; it's almost enough for me to forget that we're in a cage, that there are four stone walls not more than three hundred yards or so beyond us.

To think, it was around this time last year, I was in a car heading to Whistler to watch Angus play in a golf tournament. This time last year, he handed me that gold pendant and told me he loved me. Something thick lodges in my throat at the memory, but I choke it down quickly.

Pessimism will not serve me well, so I turn my attention to the marigold-lined path in front of me. With the weather taking a pleasant turn today, the vibrant flowers atop sturdy stems flourish outside the greenhouse. It's amazing how much better everything thrives in the light, but I don't think about that for too long.

I trudge further down the path until some of the landscape starts to look familiar. The bigger trees with their gnarled branches stretched out like welcoming arms. Scattered wildflowers intermingle with pine needles along the ground, fallen trunks and crackling twigs underfoot.

The subtle sound of the bubbling brook reaches my ears, and I know now that I'm only twenty or so yards from our bunker. Instead of taking a left towards it, I carry on walking, until I'm standing at the foot of a rusty black iron frame, grudgingly hoisting up four walls and a glass ceiling.

It's as elegant and timeless as it is filthy. I'm careful not to brush up against the grime as I slip through the door. The warm sunlight is nothing compared to the torrent of heat inside. One of the sturdier tomato plants steadies me as I take a moment to adjust.

When the dark spots over my vision subside, something trickles over my fingers. I look down to see the broken, wrinkled skin of a red tomato. The juices are equal parts tart and sweet against my lips and my stomach howls as the flesh tears between my teeth. I take another, and another, and another. By the time my stomach is full, only three are left dangling on the vine.

Why does it take so much longer to create something than it does to destroy it? Unless you're Lucinda, of course. At the rate we're going, by the time we find a cure, she'll have been dead much longer than she's ever been alive.

***

The sun clears its peak faster than I hope it will. Hours pass like minutes, pure bliss and quiet, save for the subtle hooting sound of the pigeons that dare to dart over the wall. If only my arms could sprout wings that dance on the breeze as easily as they do, letting it carry me like a tune, up, up, up and away from this place forever.

But if my attempts at launching pitiful scraps of paper in an array of artistic contortions over the formidable wall are anything to go by, flying over it is an endeavour more daunting than I initially perceived.

Yet, in doing so, I can only envision the countless hours of amusement I've afforded Alister, the laughter that must have echoed through those hollow hallways as he watched my desperate efforts. I might not be able to conquer the wall, but at the very least, I will have conquered his solemn mood for the day.

The ground beneath me yields, cradling my body as though folding me into a long overdue embrace. Immersed in the pages between my hands, every word a thread weaving me deeper into the threads of another world.

A treasure I found, squeezed between textbooks in the library, buried beneath thick layers of dust—a marker of time.

After diligent scrubbing and repeated sneezing, the title finally emerged. A refuge from the weight of academic tomes that cast shadows of doubt like confetti, this work of fiction is a haven, offering answers, where heavy textbooks offer only mysteries. My senses dance with the words of its sixth chapter, stealing me from the burdens of reality.

And then, a long shadow stretches over me, shattering the sanctuary like glass. Dread churns in the pit of my stomach. After this morning's antics, the concept of letting bygones be bygones seems as fragile as a wisp of smoke. If he is to kill me here, at least I would have the company of Atticus Finch.

"Fiction?" Alister's voice breaks the silence as he settles onto the grass beside me.

"Yes," I say, my tone edged with a hint of brusqueness, my gaze steadfast ahead. Despite his best attempt at conversation, the last thing I'm in the mood for is trivial chitchat. Fiction, on the other hand, offers an escape—a portal beyond these confining walls. Even if it means journeying to lands teeming with faeries, wolves, and all manner of weird creatures, I'd choose that over the desolation of this place any day.

"Are you happy here?" His question catches me off guard, igniting a trail of heat that courses upwards from my chest to the crown of my head. He can't be serious.

In an instant, I weigh the odds of honesty against the burden I've carried since the day I arrived here. The darkness, the never-ending tunnel. But then, there's today, an unexpected reprieve. The garden, the freedom. Maybe a glint of something good. Maybe.

"Yes, sir," I say, though my eyes must give me away, like windows, revealing both truths and lies alike. Or so my father would tell me.

Alister's brow furrows, fingers idly plucking at the grass.

"I understand." His voice wavers as he searches for the right words, his contemplation lending a vulnerability to his features. "This isn't where you want to be right now, and your heart aches for your friends and your mother. I'd be blind not to see it in your eyes. I acknowledge that what we are doing here is far from conventional."

One way to put it, I suppose.

"But I'm not wicked." His voice holds a plea. "Just desperate. I can only hope that someday, you'll come to see it that way too. Maybe they all will if we can find a cure."

Alister stands, brushing grass fragments from his jeans as he regains his feet. "Regardless," he offers, his tone sincere, "if there's a way to make your stay here more comfortable, please let me know."

"Wait," I call out, just as he begins retreating towards the main house. Summoning a surge of courage that overrides my better judgement, I say, "I would really love some coffee."

***

My steps are lighter as they tread towards my room, the remnants of my earlier mood fading like shadows into the dark walls of the bunker. It's mostly because of the secret I keep close to my chest. Their elation already echoes in my ears. With the first light of dawn will come the sweet aroma of freshly brewed coffee, the small taste of freedom that we have been yearning for so long.

I only wish I could see their faces when they find a large coffee from Henriette's Bakery on their breakfast trays tomorrow morning. Across my cheeks spreads a smile that pulls at the corners of my mouth so tight, it might rival the spans of the sunset itself.

"Watered the basil," I call out into the shadows, my voice dancing through the muted corridor.

As I glide past the dark end of the bunker, I lash my knuckles against the wood, a secret code between friends. Two knocks: *I'm back* and *Alister's coming.*

I leave the door slightly ajar so that Alister can lock it from the outside. He should be here any moment now. The second I'm alone in my room, I carefully unfurl a sunflower from under my sweater and place it in a cup of water. I'm careful not to damage the petals, though some have already browned on the short journey here.

There's no shame in grasping at happiness wherever you can find it, or in this case, smuggling it in like contraband. I put the flower on my bedside table so that it will be the first thing I see in the morning. But for the gentle hiss of the air vent, the room is quiet, just how I like it.

"Aurelia," Alister says quietly. He appears in the doorway, shifting his weight nervously from right to left. "There's something that I need to tell you. Will you sit?"

I remain perfectly still. The air shifts in the room and a heaviness settles over Alister's eyes. A knot tightens in my stomach. "What is it?"

"It's Patrice." He stumbles on her name. "She's—"

The world shudders around me, the walls pressing in. "What?" I ask. "What happened?"

My heart cinches, a pain shooting down into my toes when he says, "Aurelia, she's gone."

"Where did she go?" I ask with fettered hope, but the tears are already pooling in my eyes. I wipe a loose one from the crown of my cheek. "Is she with her daughter?"

Alister's head angles to the side, a quizzical tilt that reeks of concern and sympathy. A silent conversation between us. The depth of his expression absorbs any hope that I'd held moments ago.

"When?" I sob. The words lodged in my tight throat.

"Last night," he says carefully, his narrow eyes lingering, studying the thoughts that must be splayed across my face.

There's a tacit sense of something more, a secret hidden in the depths of his eyes.

He opens his mouth as if to speak, but closes it again. "I'm sorry for your loss," he says carefully.

I imagine Alister crouched on all fours like a dog, face burdened with a morbid expression. I imagine his trembling form leaning over her silhouette. A life extinguished.

I recoil from the truth, even as it presses in on me. I try to banish the thought, to crawl desperately out of this pit of despair, but as I claw and pull desperately at the edges of this dark well, I'm met only with loose gravel and dirt. There's no way out.

"Thank you, for letting me know." The words leak from me in a broken sob with a sadness that echoes against the walls. My voice is fractured, as if shards of glass have wedged themselves into my chest, scraping their talons against my heart.

"Aurelia? What's wrong?" Rose whispers, her voice as faint as a gentle breeze in this chaotic storm. She has no idea what horrors lie in answer. Alister ignores her completely as if she'd never even said a word. He can be so cruel, so careless.

Tears cascade unchecked, a torrential downpour that blurs my sight and chokes my voice into inaudible sobs. From the vent above, an ethereal white mist falls, shrouding the room in a ghostly cloud.

Stumbling as if wading through molasses, I wage a war against the seductive haze, my determination warring against the enchantment now beckoning my eyes to close, for the world to quiet again.

I stumble as the earth's contours blur into amorphous shades of existence. Oblivion. My final memory is of the soft embrace of my pillow and Alister's smooth tones weaving promises of comfort, of a utopia.

"Everything is going to be alright," he murmurs as the room fades to black.

Chapter Sixteen

I pat the soft, brown dirt that now lines the ground. Buried. Before I can even finish processing that she's dead. Patrice was my only friend—well, the only one that didn't scare me. There's Rose, of course, with her quick wit and sharp edges. She can be harsh, and at times, cruel. It took a trowel and a very steady hand to chip away at her, so careful I was not to damage the raw feelings that lay beneath.

Patrice was tenacious, motherly, and infinitely more compassionate than any of us. Of all the mountains we've climbed together, this one ahead will surely be the hardest, even more so without her by our side. Blood laces my tongue as I bite my lip hard to keep from letting out a cry.

"She meant a lot to you," Alister says. Grey eyes and curved shoulders, dressed impeccably in all black from his suit pants to his black tie and shirt.

He kicks at something invisible on the ground. It's been four years, after all; had they shared something of a connection too? Would he miss her, mourn her like the rest of us?

"More than you can imagine, sir." My bottom lip trembles, my voice breaking on the words. It's the first I've spoken since it happened.

When the endless night broke, and the morning finally came, my eyes were crusty and dry, red and raw. My throat burned like hot coals, my body heavy as lead. I was plagued by ruminations. Had the end come quietly? Had she fallen into darkness as gently as one falls to sleep? Had she heard her daughter's laughter? Remembered to pack that school bag one last time? Where had her mind wandered in those final moments?

My heart aches like a swollen drum, the only peace in knowing that as she drew her last breath, the memory of her little girl, right there beside her, would walk her into the afterlife. I never even saw her face.

Everything inside me wants to collapse at the sight of this pitiful ceremony. At Alister. At the injustice of it all. Here we stand, side by side in the northernmost part of the forest, a place that I vowed never to return to. The only solace is that she won't be alone here.

The orange leaves overhead rustle against the falling snow. The breeze bites at my skin. I should be cold, but I don't feel a damn thing. No one is congregating around the headstone; there are no bouquets or pleated grey skirts, no misty-eyed handkerchief-wielding family members in black.

They aren't late, they're simply not coming to say goodbye, to drop petals or tears. No one will even know she's gone. As far as everyone else is concerned, Patrice died years ago.

I guess this is the moment that a rubber-soled minister of the church dressed in a long black robe would read a passage from the bible. My father's funeral was the last I'd attended. But unlike my father's funeral, there's no sermon, no prayer and no afterlife. Just a burial and a bitter goodbye.

"Goodbye." I weep, casting my last sunflower onto the loose dirt. The rest had perished overnight in preparation for a cold winter, ending their vibrant display in a swift and silent demise. I could grow more, with the greenhouse and the seeds that I've saved, but I won't. It doesn't seem right anymore.

There's something so false about standing here, made so much worse by the sheer lack of company—living company. The other three bodies lie dormant beneath us, their souls destined to haunt the grounds here for eternity.

Never to be found.

Maybe Patrice is with them.

My blood thickens, freezing as a hand grazes the crown of my shoulder. I haven't felt the lingering heat of human touch in such a long time that it's completely foreign.

We lock eyes, tears in mine.

"I'm sorry," he says, brushing a fallen leaf from my collar. He hesitates, his hand hovering near the side of my face before it drops back to his side. "I know you two were close."

You don't know anything about us.

When I turn back to face the freshly carved headstone, Alister's arm lingers against the small of my back. I lose a breath, goose bumps rising on my skin, completely uncertain if they're welcome or not, and too emotionally exhausted to care.

In the corner of my eye, his dark hair, slicked back with gel, shows more of his face than usual. The look softens his features; his eyes are a little rounder, the piercing green of them dimmed by worry. A few tears escape their hold and roll down my cheek. I can barely find the will to breathe anymore, let alone face another day here.

Alister inches a little closer, and I find myself fighting the urge to fold myself into his arms, to press my head against his strong, broad chest, feel the beating heart of another person. What if, only for a moment, I let him take the weight of my grief, just until I can steady myself again?

What if I just gave in? A loud *bang* startles us both. I clutch at my chest, at ease the moment I recognise the sound—fireworks. They had them at my school fair almost every year since I was six.

Sure enough, through a small gap in the trees, I make out the fiery orange glow, popping against the pink sunset sky.

This one's for you, Patrice, I whisper.

***

I wonder if the next time I'm allowed in the garden, I might be eaten by a wolf or a mountain lion. I'm not that lucky. Those animals would have just as hard a time getting in here as I'm having getting out. Unless, of course, they grew wings.

I wonder for a moment whether something like that could have happened in the time I've been cooped up in this place. How long does evolution actually take? But I'm being dramatic; it's only been just over fourteen months.

A groan startles me until I realise that I'm the culprit. I clutch a hand to my hollow stomach. The wolves wouldn't take much notice of me in this state. I haven't eaten more than a few spoonsful in weeks. Food won't stay down; my own grief won't let it. With skin like rice paper, if I had the energy to try, I could probably count my ribs.

Every cell in my body wants me to close my eyes and never open them again. But Alister's voice coaxes me, albeit reluctantly, into consciousness. I try to shut him out, but the gentle, coaxing tones of his voice lull me into a trance.

"You won't feel like this forever." He's standing casually at the foot of my bed, hovering like a vulture over a dead carcass.

"How would you know? Sir," I spit. "You had the chance to let go and you didn't." I roll over to face the wall, hopeful that he'll receive the message and leave me alone.

Alister pauses thoughtfully, his gaze like a heat against my back. "I suppose you're right," he says too quietly. "Move over."

"Just leave me alone," I shoot, but the bullet shimmies past him as my voice cracks, deceives me. It's exhausting, constantly fighting. Battles that can't be won. I'm tired of being the lamb.

Alister sits on the bed beside me with a dark, graceful ease that burns a quiet fire in the pit of my stomach. Wanting or warning, I don't know.

"Aurelia." His tone is soft, feather-light. "I know how it feels to lose someone you love."

"It doesn't count when you put them on pause while you try. Most of us aren't that lucky."

"I'm not talking about Lucinda," he growls, his face adorned by a look of displeasure.

"Who was she then?" I ask, teetering on the edge of his tolerance.

He grins, all trace of that darkness slipping away. "You assume it was a woman?"

He glances over his shoulder, clocking me as I roll onto my side. "Who, then?"

"Fine, it was a woman." His mouth morphs into that easy, wry smile.

Something triumphant fills my chest, but I try to keep my facial expressions plain, bored. He'll never know how uneasy his dark, rigid beauty makes me.

He runs a steady hand through his raven-black hair. "My mother." Pain manifests in his eyes. "The sheriff hauled me out of a dumpster when I was four years old." He raises an eyebrow. "There was always something different about her. I have snippets of memories that for a long time I thought were nightmares. Frantically shoving clothes into overnight bags, hiding in closets to be safe from 'the others', constantly moving around. Always on the run."

"I guess that explains why you're so adept at hiding. Sir." I'd do well to keep my mouth shut, but for some reason lately, around Alister, I find it an increasingly difficult task.

He laughs. "I've never thought about it, but I guess you're right."

"What happened when they found you?"

"How could you possibly remember that? You were so young."

His eyes are vacant, as if the memories are so vivid, he's watching them play out like a film. "'They're coming, they're coming, they're coming.' That's the last thing I remember her saying before the metal lid closed on top of me. And then she was gone."

He shrugs. "I guess some memories are so traumatic that they transcend age. The sheriff picked me up the next morning after a homeless man came across me while rifling through the trash. I spent a night at the station and was dropped off at a foster home the next day. They called me Dumpster Baby for years. I was in every newspaper from here to New York."

"What happened to your mother?" I ask.

"I tried to find her as soon as I was old enough to know where to look. But she was committed to a psychiatric facility in Oregon. She took her life after the first few months. I would have been six years old when they buried her. For as long as I can remember, I dreamed of the day that I'd see her again. So that we could be a family again. Turns out, I'd been dreaming about a ghost."

My hand finds his shoulder. I know—better than most—how it feels to lose a parent. At least, I'd had the benefit of knowing mine. "I'm so sorry, Alister." And I mean it.

He turns to me, his green eyes bright and alive to the furious thumping of my heart.

"It's not all bad." He shrugs, and my stomach stirs at the gesture. "The universe took my mother from me, but it gave me Lucinda."

"How?" I ask.

"It was my fifth foster home in three years. She came in not long after I arrived, in a pink fairy dress—wings and all. I fell in love with her instantly. She's the closest thing to family I've ever had. When she got sick, I—"

"Felt like the world had fallen out from beneath you?"

His green eyes gleam. "Yes."

He gazes towards my bathroom, or beyond it, to where Lucinda lies dormant in her bedroom. Trapped in a broken human body. Trapped by their memories, their connection. By the love of a man who has been abandoned by every person who has ever cared for him. Cursed to roam this world alone. My heart aches.

In the recess of my memory are the initial moments between Alister and I. The ones right before he noticed my lingering gaze. I'd been lost in the beauty of his dark features, the endless depths of his emerald eyes. The face of my dreams and nightmares. Back then, I'd wanted to run for my life and never look back. When had the darkness left his eyes?

"You never told me why she stopped responding to treatment."

"Who, Lucinda?" Her name is like a melody on his soft lips.

I nod, as the shadows creep back into his eyes.

"At first, she wouldn't tell me, she just cried unstoppably for days. It took four months for her to finally say something. I couldn't work out why after six months of treatment, after showing clinical improvements, her symptoms started to return one by one. Regardless of her diet, she couldn't put on any weight."

"Resistance." I'd recognise those symptoms any day.

He nods, but his eyes won't meet mine. "It happened during one of her overnight stays." His deep voice wavers. "He came in during the night while she slept. I'm not so sure that this was the first time that he—"

"Who?" I demand.

"Doctor Geoffrey McDonald."

More lies. It has to be. Geoffrey McDonald is a name I've read about countless times in various medical journals. Likely the most renowned doctor in America—maybe even the world. Responsible for curing over half the world's diseases. Retired, watching his work heal patients at their bedsides.

"She said that she woke up to a weight on top of her, and then a pressure between her legs. He covered her face with a pillow so that she couldn't scream. When he was finished, he told her that if she breathed a word about it, he would kill her."

My stomach clinches so tight it throbs. Surely not.

"That's when he—" He looks away as if tearing his eyes from a gruesome scene in a horror film. His hands clench into fists and his chiselled jaw tightens. "If I ever got my hands on him, I would—" He steadies himself.

"She didn't tell anyone, but he reduced her treatment anyway. She developed a resistance to both rifampicin and isoniazid after receiving the first line of treatment. She was receiving nothing more than a painkiller and some fluids. He was killing her anyway, just in case."

Ice seeps into my veins. Apparently, there's a part of me that genuinely believes what he's saying. "That's why he let you take her home," I say.

A nod is his only reply.

"What did you do?" But I already know the answer. Denial has a funny way of keeping people blind to the things they don't want to see. No one would ever believe that such a deeply admired man would do something so heinous to one of his patients, even if he already had—maybe more than once. Maybe many times.

I shudder at the thought.

"She couldn't bear a trial while she was still so unwell. No matter how many times I begged her to talk to the police, she swore me to secrecy. I didn't want to. I should have done something."

In spite of my own inner turmoil, the pain that courses through my weary bones and the fragments of my shattered heart, I stifle any lingering traces of scorn I once harboured for him.

"I can't imagine how hard that must have been," I say.

"You're the first person I've ever told," he says, almost bashfully. And then whatever shame had crossed his enigmatic eyes vanishes, replaced by fear. "Promise me you won't tell her."

I can't help but wonder, had our paths crossed under any other circumstance, maybe in a different life, could that initial spark between us have become something more? "I promise."

Alister coughs, and his eyes clear. "Anyway, you have enough grief to keep you occupied. With the passing of—" Alister's brows furrow.

"Patrice," I growl.

Of course he would forget her name; she was nothing but another rat in his cage. All traces of empathy seep out of me like secrets whispered in the dead of night, leaving behind a wrath far bigger than my frail body can contain. Every attempt I make to hold it in fails.

Suddenly, I do not care that he is the controller of my every breath. I do not care that my life sits stark in the palm of his hand. I do not care that there is a cemetery full of bodies as careless and rash as I'm bound to be. I can only think of her voice, her orphaned daughter, my shattered heart.

"Why should I help you?" I demand. "Why should I believe anything you say to me? Why should I care about Lucinda? You might as well taxidermy her and have her sit at the dining table. At least that way you would have some damn company!"

Alister's eyes widen, and then furrow. He grimaces in a way that suggests at least some insight into the gaping hole he has dug for himself. If I didn't know any better, I'd almost say he looks worried.

He winces as he stands to leave. "You're grieving," he says in a moment of vulnerability. "You don't mean that."

The anger roars through me. "Did you ever consider that she might be better off dead?"

Alister moves for the door, but before he turns away, I catch a glimpse of my beastly features in the reflection of his gaze. His face is a mask of calm, but his eyes prickle with tears.

"You have every right to be angry with me, Aurelia." He doesn't look at me as he says, "But I have never known you to be so cruel."

He does not glance back at me as he leaves the room, the wooden door closing gently behind him. I wonder—with panic rising in my chest—if it will ever open again.

The wall is cold against my back as I slump against it, sliding to the floor. I wrap my arms around my knees, curling myself into a ball. If I squeeze tight enough, maybe I'll disappear.

Thoughts of Patrice flood my mind, and I ponder the myriad paths a soul might tread to lead them to the bitter end. Hope is a dim light at the edge of a very long and very dark tunnel. Perhaps, when you find yourself at the precipice, you've already fallen right in.

***

After a long, sleepless night riddled with ruminations, the morning finally arrives. Just as I'm about to pull the lever, Alister knocks on the door, breakfast tray in hand. His idea of a personal touch, I suppose.

He's wearing all black, his hair falling in perfect loose waves around his face. A look of worry morphs his dark, sensuous features. A mix of relief and guilt washes over me as our eyes lock. His are sunken and tired, their usual unearthly emerald glow reduced to a dull, muted meadow colour. My stomach stirs—I did that to him.

My voice quivers as I offer my white flag, the apology I've been dreading since last night, "I'm sorry for what I said. I didn't mean it, sir."

He sighs, his gaze softened by weariness. Had he slept a wink since we spoke?

"I should have been more sensitive," he concedes, his voice carrying a tone of regret. He gazes up at me with gentle, piercing eyes. "I'm sorry too."

And with that, the light starts to filter through the dark and lonely tunnel. Understanding hovers between us like a delicate, hopeful promise. His eyes meet mine as he chuckles softly, and I find myself doing the same.

It's only a few seconds before he breaks the silence between us. "Would you like to spend some time in the garden today?" He says, his voice softer than I've heard it before. It's a tentative olive branch between—dare I say it—*friends.*

The prospect of feeling the sun on my skin fills me with a renewed sense of hope, so I nod, strengthening our fragile truce.

In the garden, time takes on a different rhythm. The sound of rustling leaves carries in the crisp morning air. Sunlight filters through the lush canopy overhead, dousing the path before us in a mosaic of warm, golden hues. It's the best fall day we've had in a long time. I shudder to think I might have missed it.

Side by side, we walk the garden's winding trails, our footsteps falling into rhythm. Distracted by the songs of birds and idle chitchat, the idea of a world beyond these towering walls seems to fade away into the warm air.

Chapter Seventeen

Angus

I wake up in a pool of my own sweat, strands of my hair plastered like wax to my forehead. I dreamed of her again—dressed in gold sashes of fabric, hovering high above the ocean. The cliff, a sheer drop between us. I called out to her, but her hands were bound by thick rope, her mouth blanketed in tape.
She fell to her knees, her eyes round and wild. I backed up a couple of paces, launched myself into the abyss. I always take the leap, over and over, clawing through space and time and impossibility, just to get to her. Just like each time before, I start to fall, plummeting towards the jagged rocks below.

Bathed in cold sweat, I wake with a gasp, my heart thundering. Aurelia, always just out of reach.

I peel myself from the damp sheets and skulk over to the window. Throwing open the curtains reveals a sky both bleak and grey. Four hundred and twenty-seven sunrises, and each one has grown more dull and depressing than the last. But that sort of thinking isn't helpful, not when so many others have already given up on her.

My sweat-soaked shirt slumps into the laundry basket with a thud. The cold bites at every inch of my bare skin. My shower is cut short today because it's 7 am and I'm already late.

Once I'm dressed—dark denim jeans and a white long-sleeve to match the dribble of snow that fell overnight—I grab my laptop. Just as I'm leaving my room, a glimmer of light catches the surface of a picture frame sitting on my bedside table.

It was taken only a week before Rae disappeared. The first tolerable day of a long winter, not dissimilar to today. We spent it sitting in the park eating Cheetos until our hands were orange and our tongues were swollen. She didn't know I was taking the photo; it was one of those old-fashioned film cameras.

When I finally had them developed, after she had disappeared, most of the pictures had a finger across the lens or had been washed out by the light. But amongst the chaos and carbon, there was this absolute diamond of a photograph, perfect, just like her.

You can see her darling mouth covered in a ring of orange dust. She was looking past the camera at me, with a smile that still fills me with light and longing. What I wouldn't give to pull her into my arms like I had that day, to kiss those lips, Cheetos dust and all, just one more time.

Heartache in tow, I head downstairs before I lose it completely. There are much more productive things to do with my time than sit in my room and fawn over an old photo. It's what she would have wanted.

The house is quiet and empty; it's been that way for months now. My parents stayed home for a while after it was clear Rae wasn't coming back. Eventually, they had to move on, we all did. I forgot how lonely it could be in this house.

I grab the basket of vegetables and ready-made meals from the kitchen bench. Carrot and ginger soup splashes against the clear container—her mother's favourite. She would have wanted me to take care of her like she used to.

It's not that I mind doing it, but there's something about the hollowness of her eyes—a deep grey that seems to swallow up all the light in the world. It bleeds into her every word. She winces at every movement as if the part of her that's missing is the oil that made everything work. Somehow, even in her company, I feel lonelier. Maybe even a tad bitter.

I grab a banana from the refrigerator, a protein bar from the pantry, and head for the door. I take a deep, steadying breath, watching it dance against the windscreen. I don't look back; my car tyres screech forward, just like yesterday and the day before that.

And the day before that.

***

The double doors of the waiting room open up like a giant mouth, swallowing me as I walk inside. Am I imagining it, or does the whole station seem to sigh deeply the moment I arrive?

My rubber soles squeak underfoot as I tread gingerly. A pickled-looking officer greets me at the front counter. She's short in stature and round in shape, her face stony and harsh as if maybe she's never laughed about anything, ever.

The thin coat of red lipstick only enhances her greying mop, relentlessly heaved back into a tight bun. A smile certainly couldn't worsen her appearance.

She doesn't even have to ask me my—

"Name?" She grunts.

But I guess she's going to anyway. As if we haven't been doing this every day for almost a year and a half now.

"You again," she huffs.

I bite my tongue and slide a copy of my driver's licence under the thick plastic screen. "Me again."

You know she probably ran off with another man. She'd said it to me within a month of Rae's disappearance. I'd been attending the police station daily to help with searches, check for updates. Alister had accompanied me that day. He didn't say anything though; he was probably just as shocked as I was.

"Did you bring any coffee with you?"

"Not today, I was running late."

"Overslept?"

"Something like that."

She rolls her beady round eyes and grunts. "Here." She slides the licence back under the screen. "You know where to go?"

I nod, because the next thing I say might have me locked up in one of these cells for the night.

Officers glance up from their screens as I pass. It's mostly security footage. There's almost one camera for every inch of the town, from the park closest to the university to the grocery store down the main drag. How someone could disappear with so many eyes on them has been the source of my nightmares for months now.

Next, I'm led past the cells. It seems like every day, there's someone new being shackled and shoved into the fishbowl for an interview. Every morning, I glance at them, only for the briefest of moments, wondering—hoping—that this time they might tell us something, anything, that we didn't already know about Aurelia.

I find Detective Annabelle Lawson in the smokers' area of the police station, a courtyard in the centre of the complex with a few plastic chairs and an ashtray on a skinny-legged table. She prefers to be called Anna. Anna takes one last drag from the small butt between her fingers and taps the end into the tray.

"Angus," she breathes through a cloud of smoke, "you're here."

"I didn't know you smoked," I say.

"I don't," she says, turning to face the wall behind her.

But her clothes reek of tobacco, and I can't know for sure, but I'm almost certain that her skin would smell of it too.

"What happened?" I ask. My voice betrays my lack of courage, "Is she—? Did you find—?"

"No," Anna says, turning to face me. Her eyes are sunken and dog-tired, not a wink of rest between them.

"What is it then?"

"They're closing the file, Angus, it's over."

She reaches into her pocket, pulls out a packet of Marlboros and offers the half-opened box towards me, nodding. "Here."

I don't smoke, I never have. But I take one of the cigarettes and hold it against the flame. "Thanks," I say, watching the tip spark to light.

A group of officers walk past the glass window, throwing glances like stones. I quickly turn my back to them, judgemental bastards.

"Ugh," Anna groans, "don't worry about them. The highlight of their day is watching the vending machine being restocked. Fucking state troopers."

We stand there in silence as I draw back on the butt, trying to concentrate on the warm, burning sensation of the smoke filing down the back of my throat. I choke quietly, a dry hoarse cough as the chemicals fill my lungs. I lean the cigarette against the ashtray. It continues to smoulder, drawing in all the oxygen, taking on a life of its own. It doesn't need me; it never really did.

When I first walked into the police station to report Aurelia missing, I was told what everyone is told when they try to file a missing person report—*she is a young adult, she has probably gone away for the weekend, she will turn up eventually, were there any problems in the relationship?* There was no point arguing with them; you don't need to be a bricklayer to recognise a stone wall.

I tried her cell phone every hour for three days. I spoke to every person that she knew and even those she didn't. Nothing. It only confirmed what I already feared. After days of driving around town with her photograph in hand, asking strangers if they had seen her, I walked back into the police station with a little more force than I had in the days prior.

"I need to report a missing person," I said to my pickled-looking friend at the front desk.

She asked me to take a number from the machine and pick a seat. I looked around the empty waiting room and frowned. "It's urgent."

"Take a seat," she ordered. "Someone will be with you shortly."

I felt the anger rising in my throat. I slammed my folder on the bench. "There are two women missing from the same university in a town with a population of thirty-thousand people. My girlfriend makes the third. I want to see someone—now."

Before the officer could protest, a tall, dark-haired woman with a thin frame, pencil skirt and black-rimmed glasses that covered half her face—but still managed to make her look fashionable—stuck her head through the doorway. "What's going on?" She asked, her eyes darting between me and the officer who was clearly drowning in the weight of her uniform.

"My girlfriend is missing—no one has heard from her in three days. She goes to the local university here," I said breathlessly.

She studied me for a moment before saying, "Show him to meeting room five."

Reluctantly, the uniformed officer led me down the hall and into an interview room with nothing more than a table bolted to the floor and three chairs. We did not exchange more than a 'thank you' and a grunt as we arrived at the door. I took a seat on the chair closest to me and she closed the door behind her as she left.

After fifteen agonising minutes, the door opened again and the stylish woman with black hair appeared, carrying a clipboard and two thin manila folders.

"My name is Detective Annabelle Lawson," she'd said, holding her hand out to me, "but you can call me Anna. Do you know what a cold case is?"

"I've seen the TV show," I said. "I know enough."

She slid the two folders across the table towards me. "These two women disappeared within twelve months of each other. Both students from the university. We have no leads, no suspects, and no one looking for them. Not anymore."

My heart had sunk so deep into my chest that I thought it might spill out my back.

"This is different," I said, climbing to my feet.

She looked at me with a feigned half-smile and a world of sympathy. "How?" She'd asked.

"Because I'm going to find her."

***

"Cold case," I mutter under my breath, my thoughts drifting to a time before when Anna had muttered those very words.

"Indeed." She sighs through a thick cloud of smoke. "I'm sorry, Angus."

Her words are like a physical blow, and the room seems to grow colder. A grim juncture—fifteen months of relentless searching, interviews, countless sleepless nights, and unwavering hope have led us to nothing but this. The end.

"What can I do?" I ask in a shaky voice.

Anna pushes her butt into the ashtray and looks me straight in the eye. Her perfect face is drawn, tired. Dark circles sit beneath her light brown eyes. "We keep our chin up and our friends close, Angus. That's all we can do now."

Ice grows rapidly in my chest, enough to freeze hell and earth.

"I can't just—" my voice catches again, the corner of my eyes burning. "She's still out there somewhere."

"Listen," Anna says, placing a perfectly manicured hand on my shoulder; it provides little comfort. "I'm not giving up on her. I will allocate resources to her case whenever I'm allowed them. You need to start living your life again, Angus. You've put everything on hold now for so long."

"You've done everything you possibly can for her. Maybe even more. You don't need to stop loving her, but you need to give yourself permission to move on. We all do."

"She is my life," I say, at risk of sounding as useless as I feel. Finally, the last fifteen months' worth of cracks are starting to show.

Finally, the jagged pieces might rip me apart.

Chapter Eighteen

I'm sitting on my neatly made bed reading my book, wiggling my toes between the softest linen sheets I've ever slept in. The peach and pastels glow in the warm, bright light trickling through the open door. It's so hard to remember the fraying edges of my own quilt cover back home, what it smelt like, how it felt against my skin.

I don't dare to think how much these would have cost Alister, and then he barges through the doorway for the second time this morning. "I come bearing gifts."

He's barely visible through the stacks of satin boxes being hauled into the room. All this, for me. As if I've ever cared for such luxuries. As if I've ever deserved them.

It's been like this for weeks now. I look over towards the empty space where my television used to sit. Now, there's a pile of clothes with the tags still on, spare sheets and essential oils. The gifts ooze with the scent of first-hand fabrics and fresh pine, a smell I could imagine getting used to, but know I never will.

My favourite of the new additions is a giant Cyperus plant with long winding vines now coiling their way along my desk. It's silly, but it reminds me of Patrice.

"Why?" I ask, studying the varying shapes and sizes of the new boxes.

The joy in his eyes falters as he considers his answer carefully. "I—" He trails off as I crawl to the end of my bed and reach for the box closest to me. "This one first," he says.

He stares at me, the words still lost on his lips. His fingers brush mine as I take the weight of a small black box. I can still smell the thick, royal scent of the store on its perfectly smooth surface, and I imagine the woman who sold it to him dressed in a crisp black suit with a large golden hoop dangling from each ear. A harsh stare, and a feline smile for a mysteriously handsome man.

I unfurl a satin cloth and unveil a silver heart, a small diamond at its centre. Light gleams off its perfectly mirrored surface. My hand reaches up to my mouth, and then to my chest, where my heart is racing with a kind of shock, joy and woe. As if it can't seem to make up its mind at all.

What I do know is that there's not a single store in this town, or any town within one hundred miles that would sell such a delicate piece. How far had he travelled to find it?

He reaches out to me and for a moment, I wonder if he might strangle me. More heat as his fingers graze my neck, straightening the bevelled gold heart that still hangs there.

He doesn't look me in the eye as he says, "I hope that maybe one day, you might forgive me. That you might even—"

My heart catches in my throat and I splutter before I can form so much as a vowel. He offers me a smile riddled with sympathy.

"Why does it matter to you what I think?" I ask flatly.

He places his hand over mine. Answer or gesture, I don't know. "Have dinner with me tonight," he says, his voice a caressing murmur. He brushes a rogue tear from my cheek with his thumb. I hadn't even noticed it fall.

"Where?" I ask.

"At the house, where else?" He laughs.

My cheeks burn. Where else would it be—at Romano's?

Idiot.

"You're laughing at me." I scowl.

He grins, his eyes shimmering. "I would never."

"Well, what should I bring?" I demand. "A cheese platter?"

Alister's lips twist into a broad smile and my heart quickens. Devil or not, there's no denying his dark beauty. My eyes trace the landscape of his face, from his harsh jawline to the soft roundness of his lips. Alluring, captivating, his very own siren song. If I were to listen to the melody, even for a moment, I would lose myself completely.

"Aurelia?"

"Mmhm?"

He smiles lazily at me. "Italian, I know it's your favourite."

My cheeks burn again; when had I become so visible? All I can manage is a quick nod as our eyes struggle not to meet. My feeble attempts only seem to entertain him.

"Well, if you'll excuse me, I am going to start preparing for dinner."

When I can no longer hear his footsteps down the hall, I saunter into the bathroom to study the two hearts dangling side by side across my own. Night and day; light and dark; summer and winter. They hang heavy around my neck.

Even with my eyes closed, I can barely feel the tingle of Angus' lips on mine anymore; I press myself against him, into the memory, but it's no use. His name has barely been more than a whisper in my mind for months now. I haven't wanted to wander to those dark places, the ones where the shadows and filth taunt me with his voice, our memories, the future we could have had.

Because now I know that there isn't one, not for us. I pull the golden heart from my chest in one motion, feeling the clasp break silently against the back of my neck. The small shape sits delicately in the palm of my hand. What had Alister seen when he looked at it only moments before? The gesture of love between Angus and me? Or did he see a chain? A shackle to my old life. Above all else, a reminder that this will never truly be my home.

I pull the heart to my lips and whisper, *I love you.* Memories of Angus consume me for the last time. With trembling fingers, I clutch the delicate necklace, its pendant glinting in the soft bathroom light. I slowly move it over the open drain, the metallic surface cool against my skin.

It feels like a pivotal choice, a symbol of letting go of the past. The pendant dangles precariously over the dark void, mirroring the uncertainty that fills my heart. And with a deep breath, I release my grip, watching as it tumbles into the abyss, disappearing with a faint echo of farewell.

Gone, forever.

***

As it turns out, the other locked door to the right is a second dining room, which leaves me wondering exactly where Alister sleeps at night.

This room appears even more affluent than the grand hallway, the library and Lucinda's bedroom all put together. Dark, opulent floorboards stretch out beneath my feet. Floral Art Nouveau patterns cover the walls in varying shades of light and dark greens. A long oak table takes up most of the space in the room, flanked by chairs of dark green velvet—enough to seat ten people, or more.

The sweet waft of tomato permeates the room. The table is laden with bowls of steaming pasta, salads, lasagne and bottles of wine. It's a feast fit for a mayor. I look down at my ripped blue jeans and grimace. Distinctly underdressed.

Alister pulls out one of the velvet chairs and motions for me to sit. I don't protest; I don't mutter so much as a vowel. The white napkin unfolds delicately across my lap.

He falls gracefully into a chair at the head of the table, leaving a spare seat between us. Thankfully, the lack of a third place setting tells me that there will be no unexpected guests tonight. Not even Rose. I try not to think about that for too long, ignore the guilt churning in my stomach as Alister smiles brightly in my direction.

"Please, eat," he says, pouring himself a glass of wine.

He looks younger tonight, more relaxed—neat and stylishly dressed in an open collar, white button-up shirt with his sleeves rolled to his elbows. His black trousers look freshly pressed, and his shoes newly buffed.

His thick black hair is combed back in a wave that sits with a flick at the nape of his neck. Had we met at a restaurant in town for a first, second or even third date, I might have even thought him handsome. Maybe part of me still does, despite everything.

***

Sometime during the course of the evening, maybe between cackles and sips of wine, a lightness befalls me, and for the first time in a long time, I feel free. As if I've shed a layer of skin. As if all the worries I carried with me each day in the real world have just turned to ash on the floor. Ready to be swept away forever.

No responsibility, no burdens, just free. Funny, isn't it, how it can take being locked up to finally find release. I shove the last bite of cherry pie into my mouth. My stomach groans, not from hunger, but from belly-busting, jean-ripping fullness. It's the most I've eaten in months.

"Are you happy?" Alister asks between mouthfuls.

The question catches me off guard. Freedom and happiness are two entirely different things, aren't they?

"I don't know," I manage to say. Not a lie.

It's been so long since I've thought about myself—in fact, since I've thought about anything except the lab. I wouldn't know happiness if I tripped and landed in a pile of it.

"Well," I say, clawing for the truth. "I've never had so many nice things before."

Alister fiddles with his fork, pushing pieces of pie mindlessly around his plate.

"You're wearing the necklace," he says, his mouth stretching into a handsome grin.

I nod, my cheeks bursting into flames.

"You look beautiful," he says carefully.

More heat. I keep my eyes low, reaching to pour a glass of water to clear my lumpy throat. A couple of lonely droplets fall from the pitcher. *Great.* I sigh.

"Oh, let me." Alister stands, rounding the table until he's hovering just behind me and his breath catches on the back of my bare shoulders. Everything in my being tells me to move, to pull away and run for my life, but I've never been so perfectly still. As if my bones have turned to marble, and my heart to stone.

He leans over me, filling my glass with water from an extravagant crystal pitcher. He catches my brooding stare.

"Aren't birthdays supposed to make people happy?" He asks, the warmth of his voice sending shivers from the top of my spine to the ends of my toes.

"Birthdays?" I mutter. "What?"

He pauses, pitcher in hand.

And then it hits me. "Wait, what day is it?" I demand.

Alister laughs. "You really don't know?"

I shake my head slowly.

"September thirteenth."

"I had no clue," I mumble, feeling a warmth bloom in my cheeks. This isn't just an impromptu dinner gathering, and those presents were not just random gifts; it's a birthday celebration. For me.

"Well, happy birthday," Alister says, reaching for my hand. He pulls it to his mouth and presses his lips softly against my fingers.

The feeling is startling enough that as I turn, I can do nothing but think about the light bouncing from his emerald eyes and the suppleness of his lips. When he releases my hand, I take a winded breath, not realising that I've been holding it since the moment he stood from his seat.

I cough, but the lump in my throat won't clear.

Alister laughs. "I'm sorry, I didn't mean to make you uncomfortable."

"No," I mutter awkwardly. "It's okay."

And again, I find myself straddling the line between truth and lies, not really sure where I've landed.

Chapter Nineteen

It's about 7 pm and there's an hour of daylight left. The end of my first week as a twenty-six-year-old. I spend it amongst the tulips and peonies, my back to the daunting thick trunks of the forest, reading my book. Every now and then, a waft of rich red rose fills my nostrils, the sweet scent caressing my consciousness like a lullaby.

The remnants of the spring afternoon sun keep me warm and I need not the sweater lying tangled in my lap. I fold the corner of my page, close my book and shuffle down until I'm lying in the grass, staring at the smoky clouds gliding high above me.

They grow and clash as they cross pockets of heat and light. The transformation is a marvel—two forces destined to meet, join and create something bigger.

"I've been looking for you everywhere."

I sit bolt upright at the sound. In the shadow of the sun is the silhouette of a man. Alister.

I clutch my chest. "Oh, it's just you."

"Who else would it be?" Alister grins, stepping out of the shadows. His dark features take shape bit by bit. He looks even more relaxed today than he ever has in his white flowing linen shirt and black denim jeans.

I turn my attention back to my book, blissfully unperturbed by his approach. He pulls up beside me, close enough that our elbows brush and I'm left with a sear of tingles up my arm. Hiding them is a waste of time; we're too far down that rabbit hole for me to care.

I shrug. "I don't know—the pizza guy."

His brows furrow. Surely he can't think I'm serious? Just as I am about to speak, his mouth cracks into a sensuous half grin. Only half, but I'll take it.

"For you," he says, holding out a pink rose.

I set the open book down beside me. Our fingers brush, and again, I'm met with a rush of heat.

"Thank you." I smile broadly, putting the flower to my nose. An incandescent sweet smell, rich and warm.

"You are welcome," Alister says, folding an arm behind his head and lying back to stare up at the sky. "You know something?" He says, closing his eyes. "I like it when you smile."

"Don't get used to it," I snap.

His mouth is firm, but a satisfied grin dances across his lips and comes to rest on the lids of his eyes.

His shirt, casually unbuttoned at his chest, cuts close to his body. It's a new look for him, almost naked compared to his usual floor-length coat and collared shirt, never without a dark jacket and thick boots, but now, the curves of his chest peek through, surprisingly tanned and much broader than I've ever allowed myself to imagine. I try not to focus on that area, but I fail—spectacularly.

"What's the occasion?"

"Do I need one?" He props himself on an elbow and leans towards me. It's incredible how unrelenting his gaze can be, and yet, how totally at home it feels now, like a warm bath in a bitter winter.

"I guess not." I shrug and turn back to my book.

"Fine," he groans, and I can almost see the last fragments of his resolve float away with the passing clouds. "It seems your birthday has provided us both with some luck. I was going to wait until we were in the lab so that I could show you, but I can't wait any longer."

"What is it?" I ask, sitting up.

"You remember when you asked what would happen if we took streptocylin out of the treatment because it seemed to have the highest rate of resistance of all the drugs?"

"Yes?"

"And you asked what if there were substitute drugs that cells hadn't yet become resistant to?"

I nod.

Alister smirks. "Well, I tried it."

"And?" I demand.

"We found the other drugs. Or at least one of them."

My neck nearly snaps as I whirl to face him. "You're saying—"

"I'm saying," he says, taking my hand, "I took your sample of levofloxacin and kanamycin, and I added linezolid and clofazimine."

"And?" I demand again.

"And it's negative—so far." A wry smile spreads across his lips as he returns to lying on the grass.

But for the spark in his eyes, and the cheeky Cheshire cat grin on his lips, I might have wondered if he even cared.

I lean towards Alister. I can't see myself, but I can feel the look of desperation on my face.

"How long has it been?" I ask with my heart on my sleeve.

"Seven days." His eyes sparkle and dance in the light.

I just stare, unable to find the words—any words. A million thoughts course through my mind in no manageable order. And then silence. "Progress."

"Progress." He laughs.

"Progress!" I cry. "It's working!" I leap to my feet, spreading my arms wide like wings, twirling in the sunlight like a child, so incredibly elated that the clouds could whisk me away on the breeze.

As I turn to Alister, my ankle falters on uneven ground, sending me hurtling towards the earth. I cry out, shielding my face as I plummet forward into a wild cranberry bush.

Alister stifles a laugh as I emerge from the bush, shrugging off leaves and sticks, relieved to find no broken bones. I wipe my face, and when I look at my fingers, they are ruby-red. Not blood, but berries.

Alister takes one look at my face and bursts into a fit of howling laughter. "You look like you did that day in the cemetery."

"I could have broken something." I glare.

My once white t-shirt is now covered in splattered dollops of fading pink. My jaw tightens, and before good sense can prevail, I take a bunch of the ruby-red fruit and aim it straight for Alister's head.

He tries to duck out of the way, but not before the crimson bush slams him smack bang in the chest. "Oh for fu—" he curses.

Laughter spews out of me, a full-bodied, deep-bellied laugh. The sound startles me at first. I can't remember the last time I laughed. Alister studies the splatter of red paint sitting over his heart.

"It looks like you've been shot," I say, wiping a tear from my eye.

"It's lucky you have such a beautiful brain," he snaps, brushing a leaf from his shoulder, "or I'd have to over-salt your dinner."

"You've been doing that since the moment I got here," I tease, and we both laugh.

I clear away a few sticks and plop myself on the ground next to him. "So, what now?"

"I guess we wait." He grins.

***

I wake to the sound of crackling wood, and when I peer through the slits of my tired eyes, I find a small pile of sticks and pine cones glowering amongst orange embers.

"Are you going to burn me at the stake?" I ask, rubbing the smoke from my eyes.

Silence ripples through the night, while the stars gleam overhead. Stars—in the almost year and a half that I've been living here, I've never caught a glimpse of them. Tonight, they paint the sky, almost by design.

It's daunting how small they can make the world feel, and yet, no one has been able to find me in it. Is anyone still looking for me? Did anyone ever look up at the stars and remember how much I had loved them?

From the bottle of champagne, picnic blanket and s'mores, it seems either Alister knows me better than my closest friends ever did, or perhaps—even more confronting—maybe we are more alike than either of us will care to admit.

Alister still hasn't appeared from the tree line when I pop the cork on one of the champagne bottles. The bubbly liquid pours like a fountain from the neck and spills out into two waiting glasses. It pains me to admit that a surge of overwhelming relief threads through me the moment he appears from the woods, carrying another pile of sticks. I wouldn't dare tell him that it was fear and not hope that sat waning in the pit of my stomach when I woke up alone.

"You're awake," Alister calls as he dumps the pile of kindling next to the fire. "I thought I'd have to drink all this myself."

I'm too busy staring at the spitting firelight cracking against the dark sky to pay him any attention until he comes to sit beside me on the picnic blanket.

"You looked so peaceful, I didn't want to wake you," he murmurs, and something about the way his eyes glisten against the starlight has me heating from the inside.

"I haven't seen them for so long, I almost forgot how beautiful they were," I say without looking at him. I'm aware of every inch between us, of where his shoulder brushes mine, of the heat that radiates between us, in stark contrast to the chill of the night. He leans across me to reach for a glass of fizzing champagne. The scent of the earth and all its seasons carry with him, stirring something in my chest.

"They're almost as beautiful as you are, Aurelia."

If he notices the roses that bloom on my cheeks, or the racing of my heartbeat, he doesn't say anything, and for that, I'm grateful.

We sit in silence for what feels like an eternity, but neither of us seems to mind it. Not when the sky is putting on such an exquisite performance. I wonder for a moment what is happening in the Shire, and whether anyone else is celebrating such a clear autumn night. For the briefest of moments, I swear I can hear the sound of beating drums and trumpets playing in the distance. A festival, perhaps.

We polish off the first bottle in a matter of minutes, the champagne travelling like silk down my throat. With every sip, another muscle relaxes, and the chains that wind so tight around me start to fall loose. Just for one night, I'd let caution carry on the late-night breeze.

Besides, this is a celebration.

***

"Dance with me, on this spectacular night, at least until the stars disappear into the dawn."

"You're kidding." I laugh, but his face is firm. He's completely serious. "Fine," I groan, letting him take my hand.

In a swift, gentle motion, he pulls me to my feet and sweeps me into a waltz-like dance, one arm wrapped around my waist, and the other extended alongside mine, our fingers entwined. We spin and twirl and whirl our way around the campfire until the world around us blurs into an artist's colour palette, dancing to the tune of our own laughter and the far-off beating of drums, as if we're the only two people on earth.

Our footsteps slow as the moon reaches its apex in the sky, dousing us in stardust and light. "You're beautiful," he says, tucking a loose strand of hair behind my ear.

I drink it in, the places where our bodies' touch, the spark at every point of contact, the moon dust dancing across his perfectly crafted features. His eyes lock with mine, glistening like polished gemstones with the luminance of a thousand stars. It's no wonder I was drawn to him at first glance. It's no wonder I could barely tear my eyes away.

I lean into his chest, my head coming to rest over the gentle thrumming of his heart. My breath catches as his hands roam the small of my back in soothing circles that leave a trail of fireworks in their wake. I lean my head back even further as he twirls me under his arm, again and again until the sky becomes a ripple.

"Again," I cheer. "Twirl me again."

"You'll fall, Aurelia."

"Then catch me!" I laugh, pushing off his chest and gliding into another spin. This time, just as he had predicted, my bare foot lands on uneven ground, causing me to fall backwards, my limbs flailing helplessly in the air.

Strong arms encircle my waist, wrapping around my back like a net, until I'm suspended above the ground, panting furiously. When I open my eyes, I find a pair of familiar green ones staring straight back at me. Eyes that I have come to recognise as home.

"You caught me," I say, our faces so close that I can taste the sweetness of his breath on my lips. It reminds me of summer storms and salty air—not the kind we get here in the Shire, but in the warmer states where you can smell the clippings of cut grass more than once a year.

"I'll always catch you," he says through panting breaths.

"I know," I whisper, holding perfectly still as Alister leans in towards me until there's barely a breath's width between our lips. He pulls back slightly, his eyes searching my own for an answer to his silent question.

My hands find the nape of his neck, fingers running through his hair, gently coaxing him closer. I meet his stare, our lips mere moments from each other. His eyes sparkle like the stars as he leans in and kisses me. What begins as a gentle brushing of lips becomes faster and harder as I pull him into me.

His mouth is like velvet, and the taste is sweeter than anything I could have imagined. Starving, that's what I've been, and by the way his lips are dancing with my own, I'd hazard a guess that he might be too. Alister lets out a low groan as I drag my fingers through his black hair, tugging him closer again until our bodies are jammed together.

He pulls back slowly while his hands roam my face, my neck, and my sides. Before I know it, every inch of my body is electrified by his touch. There's an insatiable hunger in those crystal eyes, rivalled only by my own pent-up lust. When my panting breath finally settles, he again presses his lips against mine, this time slower, more intimate. It caresses something deep inside me, setting me alight.

Tears seep from the corner of my closed eyes as our souls dance together, opening the valve of grief and loneliness I've tried so desperately to keep closed.

***

The morning light seeps into the room at a steady rate, and in between the rhythmic throbbing of drumbeats and champagne bubbles, I begin to recognise the markers of my bedroom. The lack of windows and fresh air remind me of the creature comforts I still yearn for. When was the last time I saw the sunrise?

Had my head not been thrumming by the time Alister carried me to my room, I might have even asked him to leave the doors to the bunker unlocked. But there's always tomorrow, and the day after that, and the day after that.

"Rose?" I whisper, my voice hoarse from the festivities.

Quiet.

"Rose?" I call, louder this time.

Minutes pass, and nothing. Nothing but sullen silence. She hasn't spoken more than a few words to me in almost three weeks, not that I'm counting. When I asked Alister about it, he simply shrugged and told me that I shouldn't worry. But it's hard not to feel the threads beginning to unravel.

Had I noticed Patrice doing the same, I might have been able to do something to help her. But they're two very different people, and it wouldn't be the first time that Rose chose to keep her silence. It seems that Patrice's death caused more than a rift between us.

"Rose?" This time with more clout. "We did it."

Not even a whisper for reply. It would be years still before we would be able to trial the treatment on Lucinda, but it's the nearest we've ever been to freedom.

If only she would talk to me long enough to share it with her—that and the other secrets that I now harbour deep in my heart.

Last night with Alister, amidst the swirl of intoxication, he peppered me with kisses that were soft and moist and hot and breathy. Until our mouths were chaffed and our lips swollen.

The taste of alcohol still lingers on my lips, among the confusion that now consumes my every thought. An unguarded moment, the boundaries between captor and captive, lion and lamb blurred into oblivion, leaving my soul naked and confused. Was it the pull of the full moon, or the haze of champagne that entwined us?

The protective cloak of darkness, the twenty-foot walls around us, separating us from the world, and everything that might hold us back. Hidden desire churns in my stomach as my fingers brush the places where his lips lit fires across my skin. A deep hunger thrums within me, aching for more contact. That momentary enchantment, designed to dissipate with the morning light, has loitered long past dawn.

But what about Lucinda, Angus? Perhaps the kiss had been between two people whose soulmates were always just out of reach. Has he told her yet? Has he sat by her side whispering the soft melody of hope into her ear?

The thought of his lips grazing her skin unsettles me more than I care to admit, so in an effort to divert my thoughts, I fixate on the wardrobe before me, filled with an assortment of vividly coloured dresses, each with the tags still swaying gently from their strings.

The door creaks and it startles me. Relief, and more of that aching sensation deep between my thighs.

"You," I say as his rough hair and dishevelled clothes stir life into the dormant wings in my stomach. Not even the cool silk of my white pyjamas can stop the heat seeping from my body, craving the feel of his hands roaming over my skin, breasts, and back.

"Me," he says with a shy smile that barely meets his too-tired eyes.

"Have you heard of knocking?" I tease, a playful grin tugging at my lips.

"Not that I can recall." He sighs, the taunt sparking something in his eyes. "But then again, my memory is a little hazy today." There's that wry smile, cunning and untamed. Gone is the impeccably dressed, rigid man that I have come to expect. Last night, I cracked the shell, hard enough that it may not repair. It's with a light heart, and fistfuls of prayer, that I hope it never will.

Remnants of wine and champagne cloud his eyes, greying them. At that moment, I realise there's nothing I wouldn't do to see the light again, to draw the stars from them. To dance around the bonfire like wild children and untamed spirits, free from the burdens of the world, much like the flames that flicker and leap in the night. To feel the sparks fill my heart and stir my soul.

Thick silence between us stretches out like a black void—or maybe it's just the champagne still whirling in my stomach. And maybe it's my groggy heart, or the looming threat of yet another rug being torn out from under me. Maybe it's all the long nights spent longing for the touch of another.

Maybe I know that it's wrong to feel something, anything for this person beyond gratitude for letting me live. And for the first time ever, maybe I just don't give a damn. After all, it was only after Beauty was free to leave that she longed to return to the Beast.

"You know, your persistent effort not to talk about it is actually making it more awkward." I snort, surprised by my own self-confidence.

"Here I was thinking it was you who was avoiding the subject." He raises an eyebrow. "I guess we're both wrong."

"That's such a male thing to say." I groan, falling in a heap on my bed and sending a pile of clothes scattering across the floor.

"You think men are so complex?" He says, sitting himself on the edge of the bed next to me. "I could travel through space and time for all eternity, and still never catch a glimpse of the galaxy of secrets held in a woman's heart. In yours."

I prop myself up on my elbows. "Am I that hard to read?"

"No," he says, keeping his eyes low, looking anywhere but at me. "You're impossible."

"Really?" I purr in a voice that doesn't even sound like my own. I edge closer until I'm hovering over his shoulder, until my lips are a hot breath away from his ear. "I could show you."

He turns slightly, enough that our faces brush, and a shot of electricity glides through my body like a tempered bolt of lightning. If he turns another half inch, our lips will meet.

The scent of him is an intoxicating blend of autumn leaves and sandalwood, as if the fresh air has followed him into the room. The pull to him has grown exponentially overnight, and what was once a gentle tug, is now the force of a thousand tides, and growing with every thundering beat of my heart.

Something about the distance in his eyes lends me to believe that there's an inner war still raging. The way he bites the inside of his cheek tells me it might have only just begun. A warm hand reaches up to touch the side of my face, and before I lose myself completely, another wraps effortlessly around my waist, pulling me onto him in one swift movement.

I'm straddling his hips as he pulls at my satin shirt, exposing me fully while his lips trace a line over my skin, from my chest to my neck, and along my jaw. A starved groan escapes me as I lean back, giving in to his wandering mouth. I grab at the thickness of his raven-black hair as his lips find the peaked part of my breast, tracing circles at an agonising pace. I let my fingers thread through the soft locks as he hardens fully between my legs.

"We should stop," he whispers in panting breaths against my skin.

An ache blooms between my thighs as he gently presses his lips to my chest, and it's so light and slow this time that I'm sure I'm imagining it. The heat coursing through my body is the only remnant of the passion that consumed us both moments ago.

I want his hands roaming my body, I want his mouth lighting sparks across every inch of my skin. I want to feel the ravaged tug of his teeth on my bottom lip, grazing my breasts, my neck. I want him to shred the clothes from our bodies like tissue paper until we are nothing but a tangle of limbs and sweat and ardour.

"We shouldn't do this," he says again, this time leaning back to see my face. Beads of sweat line his forehead, and weariness dances slowly in his eyes. It's as if the conflict is written in bold typescript across his soul.

"You are so beautiful, and I'm—"

"Married?" I sigh, rolling my eyes. "I know." I guess it still counts as marriage, doesn't it?

I mean, they never formally divorced, and she's not exactly dead.

"I should go," he whispers, pulling the back of my hand to his mouth, and then setting it down between us.

Silence falls as he gets to his feet, straightening his black jeans and light shirt. I sink into the bed, burying my head into the pillows. I look up just in time to see him hesitate as he reaches the door, his eyes steadfast ahead.

I should say something. I should tell him to come back. Should tell him that none of it matters to me that I want to forget about the rest of the world and anything outside this room, just for a few moments of pure, impulsive bliss. But instead, I say nothing, and watch him walk out the door.

Chapter Twenty

Angus

I slam my fist against the steering wheel like a child throwing a tantrum. A sharp sword of anger winds into my chest and I want to scream, or fight—or both. Losing her all over again, that's what it's like. And now more than ever, the grief is leeching through my carefully curated shields, and I realise that the barriers I've built are no stronger than threads of cotton against a flood.

The tyres skid and the engine hums as I plant my foot hard against the accelerator, heading east. When the pedal meets the floor, the buildings pass me in a blur. But I don't slow down as I head for the highway. I have not a clue where I'm going; I just know that it's away from here, and fast.

The momentum builds and builds until the revs level out at seventy miles per hour. The Beamer glides around the bends with the ease of a snake, boneless and smooth, freed from the slow-paced streets of Brunswick Shire where the maximum speed limit is rarely more than thirty miles.

I'm teetering on the edge of danger, and the rush of adrenaline gives me a moment of weightlessness, freedom. Like it might all be over soon.

Cold case.

The words troll my mind relentlessly over and over until they're like a roaring in my ears.

No more funding.

Apparently, there was a double homicide in Whistler overnight and the entire Brunswick Shire police force was required to respond.

Could I pay another private investigator? What's the point? Thousands of dollars thrown against the wall, and for what—a quick Google search, a scroll through her mobile phone, and a few telephone enquires that told us all the things we already knew; she disappeared without a trace.

My phone buzzes and Alister's name flashes like a warning, probably to let me know that he's arrived safely in Port Stevens. His father owns a holiday house out there that they often use in the winter. I'm to head there in the fall. Here I was hoping I wouldn't be going alone. Perhaps this is a reminder from the universe that I should slow down. Or maybe I just don't care anymore.

Alister is the only one who seems to remember that Rae is missing. For everyone else, after the first few months, it was business as usual. I envied them; I still do. I can't remember the last time I allowed myself to be that ignorant.

Jade was no better than the rest of them. Grief kept her locked in her room relentlessly for months. It still does. When was the last time I saw her, I mean really looked at her? It must be months ago now. Darkness had crept into her brown eyes, now almost black in the shade of her midday-drawn blinds. Plates of half-eaten heat-and-eat meals overflowed in the sink. Bread with patches of blue-grey festered in the cupboard.

Jade, who loved Rae with such ferocity, who never went more than a few hours without her best friend, now spent all her time alone, a frosty, broken rage brewing quietly behind her eyes. A bitterness behind each word, giving her permission to push everyone away. Including me.

She didn't help with the searches; she didn't check in to see if we had made any progress. Sometimes, I would pass her in the hallways at college, her lips pulling into a half-smile that didn't even come close to reaching her eyes. When was the last time we spoke more than a few words to each other? Maybe we remind each other a little too much of what we've both lost.

It was Alister who checked in every day when we dredged the lake in the south of the forest for the second time. When Anna and I ran a trace on Rae's cell. He's even offered to search the eastern woods near the old gaol on foot, while Anna and I searched the north.

Between us and some local volunteers, we searched every inch of that damn forest, three or four times over, to find nothing more than a few gum wrappers and some used condoms. Nothing that would lead us to Aurelia, not even a hint. I don't have the heart to tell him that it's over. It might break him too.

He'll hear it in my voice, in the roar of my tyres. He'll tell me to slow down, maybe even bore me with some lecture on physics. Maybe he's right, but I'm not in any state to slow down now, not when I have so little to lose.

"Where are you?" I shout, my anger turning to fog on the windscreen, so much so that I barely see the deer as it leaps out of the tree line and onto the road in front of me.

***

My eyes are so heavy, it takes four attempts to open them. It isn't until I do that, I realise down is up. Or maybe up is down, I don't know. Blood fills my mouth, and I reach a stiff arm to my face to check that my teeth are still in place. Smooth, no gaps. The blood must be coming from somewhere else.

I feel for the seatbelt buckle to my right and it takes all my effort to unclip myself. I hit the floor—or the roof—with a thud before I realise how stupid that was. The bone in my left arm has cracked and torn through my skin like paper.

The pain strikes like a sledgehammer and I cry out, clutching my elbow. My head spins and throbs and suddenly, I'd give anything to be unconscious again. I'm almost there, nearly blacking out when, through the metallic smell of clotted blood, there's the subtle scent of smoke. If I don't get out now, maybe I never will.

I feel for anything I can use to break the sharp shards of glass protruding from the window. Blood runs down my face and into my eyes, so thick and fast that I don't even bother to wipe it away. Finally, my hand grips the branch of a tree jutting through the passenger window.

I'm grateful for my blurry vision. I'd hate to think how close I came to being impaled by it. Every movement is endless agony, but I finally clear the window, just wide enough for me to crawl out without shredding my skin—or what's left of it.

The smell of smoke is thick and it's billowing now, like the breath of some beastly creature. A quick stocktake tells me I've got one good arm. I mean, there's a two-inch gash along it, but no broken bones—that's a win. My legs seem to be working, which means I might not have damaged my spinal cord.

There's a dull ache coming from the left one, though, and when I look down, there's a piece of sharp, jagged metal sticking out of it. But despite the searing pain, it's good enough to get me out of here, for now.

Using my good arm and my right leg to push, I pull myself through the small window and out into the thick, snow-capped underbrush of the forest. Despite my best efforts with the tree branch, my skin rips and tears on jagged shards of glass, tiny pieces edging into the already gaping wounds. I dread what it will take to pick them out again.

I crawl as far from the wreckage as I can, wincing with every movement. My good arm gives way at the foot of a thick pine tree and I collapse, exhausted and drained of blood. Just before I close my eyes, I watch the flames engulf the rubble in a lethal blaze. And then everything is dark.

***

I wake to the sound of crackling flames and a mouth full of dirt. The charred smell of metal and pine coats the air, and my lungs burn with it. The car is mostly a skeleton of ash now, and only a few tree branches are alight. It's late afternoon, but still light enough to see the mess that I've found myself in. I shiver, but not from the cold, although there's that too.

I try to manoeuvre myself into a sitting position, but a fresh wave of pain rocks me, and my body buckles once again. I could just let it crush me. I'm exhausted, in every way a person can be. My heart aches, and I was broken long before my car plummeted into that tree.

Maybe she's already dead. Maybe she has been the entire time. And maybe this is the closest I'll ever be to finding her.

"I'll see you soon, Rae darling," I whisper as the darkness consumes me once again.

***

After I wake for the second, or maybe third time, I decide it's not my time yet. I use whatever scraps of will left in me to clamber to my feet and start hobbling in the direction of the road—or at least where I think it is. I must be a long way into the forest, and a fair distance from any known road, because it's late afternoon and there's nothing but the sound of a breeze echoing through the trees.

If I were anywhere within half a mile of the road, there would be the hum and crackle of tyres passing, or at the very least, the roar of logging trucks. Retracing the path my car took through the forest proves impossible through bloodstained eyes, a foggy head and the fresh coat of snow that now covers the ground. There's no sign of tyre tracks—it's almost as if I'd teleported in.

Determined to reach the road before nightfall, I stumble through the thick underbrush. Exhausted, my arm throbbing like a heavy metal band, I stop every few steps to catch my breath, trying to count to five before I need to stop again.

Just when I'm about to give up, I stagger out of the tree line and into an opening, where the brush and undergrowth subside, making way for a gravel road, just wide enough for a vehicle.

Some deep-rooted animalistic desire to live keeps me thrashing along the path, but after an hour of nothing but dirt and another layer of snow, it appears I'm only heading deeper into the bowels of the forest.

***

I fumble through the silent forest for another three hundred feet or so, pausing to listen for the hum of tyres, only to be disappointed by the still landscape before me.

Darkness steadily creeps through the trees, shrouding the road ahead in darkness until it starts to resemble a tunnel with no end, a cave. My legs sting with cuts and lashings from the weeds and sticks. My broken bones throb relentlessly, and I'm exposed out here in the open.

Bears haven't roamed these forests in years—the hunters made sure of that decades ago. But Vancouver is famous for them. It wouldn't be surprising to learn that one had wandered back into these parts. Even so, it's the wolves I'm more concerned about; they tend to stick to the caves down by the lake, but it's been a warm year, and a few have been spotted as close as the bakery in the main street.

I hobble back into the tree line and off the open gravel road. The sticks and stinging vines start biting at my ankles again, and it's enough to bring me to my knees. The air is colder, far colder than when I stumbled from the burning vehicle.

The parts of me that aren't fractured and splintering tremble as it dawns on me that I'm going to die out here, alone. I'm just about to curl up beside a thick log to let death take me willingly when my eyes fall upon a stone wall. Great, now I've lost any semblance of sanity I had left.

But when I hobble towards it, reaching a hand through the shrubbery to touch the cold surface of the stone, it doesn't buckle or ripple like a mirage would. It remains perfectly still and intact—real.

There's an old gaol towards the east end of the forest, but it's miles into the forest, a place no one would ever go, least of all at this time of night. There will be no help for me here.

When the screeching of car tyres sounds in the distance, I know I've finally lost my mind. For lack of anything better to do in my final moments, I stumble towards the sound.

An orange hue douses the trees in bright, warm light. Sounds burst through the silence like a symphony—first the click of a car door, the patter of footsteps on gravel, the shovelling of dirt and branches, and then the creak of metal hinges.

Easing myself onto higher ground atop a fallen tree to get a better vantage point, I rub my swollen eyes, certain now that I'm hallucinating, that death is lurking closer than I'd thought. Sure as day—the long trench coat and tailor-made black boots that mark his approach, the thick blanket of shiny black hair I've envied for years, chiselled jawline and long limbs. But it couldn't be, because he'd told me that he was in Port Stevens this weekend at his family's holiday home.

I slip on the slimy trunk, putting my foot on the ground to steady myself. The sound of snapping twigs carries through the forest like a bolt of lightning. I hold my breath as Alister whirls in my direction. Thick, dense bushes shield me from view, but something primal tells me to stay quiet, hidden.

I risk a glance around the curve of a pine tree, but he's already turned away, disappearing into the earth through a wooden trapdoor. When it closes, it's as if it never existed at all, totally invisible unless you knew where it was.

A chill crawls up my spine and lingers there. I half expect to wake up in the comfort of my bedroom, the nightmare coming to an end, with the fire still crackling. My mind struggles to make sense of what is unfolding before me, of the fact that Alister is manoeuvring that trapdoor as if he'd done so one hundred times over. Of the fact that he's lied, maybe more than once—maybe about more than just this.

But the throbbing in what feels like every inch of my body reminds me that this is no dream. A cold, dark thought settles into my mind, churning fear in my stomach. Of all that's just unfolded before me, only one thing I know for certain—I have to make it back, I have to tell someone what I've seen here. Even if it costs me my life.

Chapter Twenty-One

The next day, dawn wakes me from a groggy sleep, and not from Alister's lips, booze and Bailey's this time. Thick golden streaks of unfiltered light flood my room as if the heavens themselves have opened up. Am I dead? I rub my crusty eyes, sure that my imagination has taken some creative licence because no matter how many times I blink, the door to my room remains wide open.

***

A breeze lifts the strands of my loose hair as I meander through the snow-limned forest. Flakes of ice land on my cheeks like frosty kisses and I'm glad for the thick woolly coat keeping me warm. The waft of smoke fills the air from somewhere deeper in the forest, beyond the stone walls. Already I miss the warmer days, though they were a gift to add an air of surrealism to the past week. We'll likely never have another autumn like it. Nothing good ever lasts, that's one thing I've learnt the hard way over the past fifteen months or so.

A bubbling brook leads me through the dense canopy of trees, the branches winding into a silent cathedral above me the deeper I go. The ground beneath my boots is a cushion of untouched powder, muffling every step in a hushed symphony of winter.

The bubbling brook, veiled by a blanket of snow, continues to guide me along the masked path, its gentle murmur the only sound. As I approach the edge of the forest the rocks and markings start to look familiar, the main building taking shape in the distance, nestled between trees, adorned with frost. An inexplicable warmth falls over me as I walk towards it. Home, that's what it is.

Wooden floorboards creak underfoot, despite my best efforts to tread softly. The door to the left takes me into the lab, and the one to the right leads to Lucinda's bedroom. My hand hovers over the left door handle as my eyes dart to the other. Switch, hitch and ditch—it's like a choreographed dance burnt into my subconscious.

But not today. Today, I'd happily let her drip run dry—an act of pure bitterness and scorn. Petty, is that what I've become?

"Fine," I groan out loud, trudging reluctantly across the hall.

When I push through the door, I'm met with a waft of lavender and citrus. A candle at the end of its wick flickers in the corner of the room. I know exactly how that feels, to be boiled down to the core, where not even a spark or a bolt of lightning could enliven me.

A fan oscillates gently, blowing the floral scent around the room, but it does nothing to mask the smell of rotting flesh that still permeates. How can she still be among the living, when every atom of my being is alive to the presence of death in this room?

I'd once thought hospital room flowers were a gift to uplift the spirits of the sick and injured. Now, I know it's to mask the smell of grief and loss.

The room is otherwise free from clutter, insipid with clean lines, stylish and graceful. Her hair wafts slowly with the breeze, her brow soft and worn and furrowing ever so slightly, as if my presence here is causing her concern. Has he told her about me? About what we've done?

Ridiculous. I'm being ridiculous. Her discomfort is more likely because she's trapped in a flesh casket. If I was reckless, I might even risk it all to set her free. Maybe I'll be content with it being the last good thing I ever did. But pessimism is like salt to a pastry dish; the right amount adds flavour, too much will ruin it completely.

I approach her bedside, reaching behind her to fluff the soft white pillow. A quiet jealousy seeps into my heart and my stomach churns until it's as thick as butter. It will be her he smiles at each morning. It will be her ear his lips brush as he whispers quiet words of affection.

I have a sudden urge to throttle her right now while she sleeps. It would be quick and painless. She wouldn't feel a thing. But he would never forgive me for it, and then where would we be?

As if she can hear my thoughts, she takes a deep, artificial breath. Almost a sigh. This train of thought is a landing with many doors, each one more grim than the next. I try to shut them as quickly as they open before I get trapped inside.

***

I barely notice Alister leaning against the threshold as I turn to grab another test tube from the laboratory supply closet.

And maybe it's the nylon glasses covering half my face, and the soft coat of my breath against the plastic, but his dark hair looks ruffled and worn; he's casually dressed in a navy jumper and light auburn pants, the kind of handsome that gets into your bones and rattles them, that sings a ballad before he's even spoken a word. As if he invented the feeling tapping on the cavity in my chest.

I lower my gaze to hide the internal furnace blooming in my cheeks, lest I be caught naked with my thoughts on full display. He smiles lazily and I know that my feeble efforts to conceal my lust are in vain. But he does not utter so much as a word as he shoves his hands into his pockets and pushes off the doorframe to meander my way.

A stool scrapes against the laminate floor as he pulls up beside me. I can barely keep my hands steady under his gaze.

Lucinda, Lucinda, Lucinda.

The echo of last night's rejection rings loud in my ears.

"What are you doing?" He asks, barely a foot between us.

"Tinkering." I huff, taking a few drops of saline solution to add to the test tube. I am a means to an end; my purpose is to find a cure to save his true love. Fine, I can accept that, but I might as well do it with my chin held high and my dignity intact.

"Tinkering, hmm?" He says playfully. "Tinkering with what, exactly?"

His stare holds an intense heat that seems to carry with it. I won't let it in, not this time.

"None of your business," I snap, pulling the microscope towards me and away from him.

"Okay." Alister laughs, raising a defensive hand. "I deserved that."

His palm comes to rest on the stool behind me, his fingers grazing my bare arm as they pass.

Not mine, not mine, not mine.

But I commit the feeling to memory anyway, for later.

He smiles lazily, his green eyes gleaming in the artificial light. "Come for a walk with me," he says. "I want to show you something."

"It's raining." I point towards the windows where the soggy, grey-lit afternoon sky is now slipping through the trees. Even the leaves are cold and miserable.

"What's not to like about the rain?" Alister asks, a grin playing across his face. His eyes glimmer and I'm lost in their labyrinth.

My eyes ache, but I manage to tear them away. "Fine." I shrug. "I was just finishing up anyway."

"You should freshen up," he insists.

I glance down at the stained lab coat draped over my black turtleneck and tight jeans, cross my arms, and frown.

"I just mean, this," he points to the coat, "is not suitable attire for a dinner party."

"A dinner party?"

"Yes, now hurry before it gets dark."

***

Fortunately, Alister needs to run back to the main house to get his jacket, and I'm given an extra couple of minutes to ready myself—for what, I have no idea.

I'm stuck in a labyrinth of tangled sentiments, where every turn seems to lead me to an uncertain end. We started the day at opposite corners of the maze, and yet as I prepare for the evening ahead, this invitation beckons with the promise of pulling us back onto the same path.

I'd be silly to start caring now, and utterly stupid to get my hopes up, and yet, from the collection of possible clothing options hanging in my wardrobe, I choose the loveliest dress.

Its bodice, crafted from a rich, textured knit, provides a comforting warmth like a soft hug. The sleeves, long and snug, will shield me from icy winds while showing off intricate flakes of winter. The high neckline offers a touch of sophistication, and perhaps a hint of an older time.

The skirt, gracefully falling to my mid-calf, sways with every step. The colour palette mirrors the winter forest landscape—deep green emeralds, icy blues and gold flecks.

I've never been one for dresses, but this gown is something else entirely. The dress hugs my figure intimately at every curve; I've never felt so exposed and yet so incredibly warm. When I first saw it hanging there, I was sure I'd never wear it.

Certain that even if by some miracle I were invited to an event that would require such glamour, I'd never care enough to wear it. And yet, here I am, tugging my hair into a neat bun at the nape of my neck, letting loose strands purposely frame the edges of my face. If I was so vain, I'd say I looked a little bit like a princess.

I sigh at the heaviness in my grey-brown eyes, and I know immediately that it's come from my heart. I can't even remember what I looked like before I got here. I'm glad for that fact because I don't intend to go back. That girl was weak, brittle and frail. Responsibility and guilt weighed so heavily on her bones that they chipped and cracked. Had I ever really been happy? Or was that part of the mask too?

Alister knocks on my door, just as I finish with the mirror.

"You look beautiful," he breathes, rubbing the back of his neck. "The dress barely does you justice, Aurelia."

"Thank you," I tease, taking the edges of the gown in my hands and giving him a dramatic curtsy.

"Ready to go?" He asks, offering an elbow.

"Ready."

***

Flashes of light dance against the blindfold as Alister guides me gently through the dense and clammy forest, my arm entwined through his. I stumble every tenth or so step, but he catches my weight each time, steadying me with a gentle hand on my back.

These parts of the forest are familiar enough that I know we're heading towards the east, somewhere I haven't been, or bothered to explore since my first few weeks here. Even then, I'd been so busy trying to find a chink in the armour of the prison walls, I'd barely paid attention to the way the trees evolved and changed through this part of the woods.

My blindfold shifts slightly as I stumble over a fallen tree branch, just enough that I can see, ahead and above us, the tall trees folding over each other, entwined like fingers, sheltering us from the spitting rain. The rest is something of a fairy-tale, as if I've tripped and fallen down the rabbit hole, only to be spat out in the Mad Hatter's woods.

Beneath us, a long wooden deck replaces the dirt and pine needles, flanked by wooden railings covered in winding green vines. Golden lights dangle from the low-lying branches above us, twinkling like falling stars.

"Oh my." I slowly lift the blindfold.

In the centre of a clearing, surrounded by towering trees, sits a long oak dining table. My breath catches. The twin chairs at opposite ends of the table answer the question I've been too nervous to ask. All of this, just for me?

I glance at Alister who is behind me, staring. His weight shifts between his left and right feet—nervous, maybe? His face gives none of his feelings away, but his eyes paint a picture his words never will. I've seen that look before so many times in my own reflection.

Guilt.

I don't pretend not to know why, but it's hard to see the sadness in his sunken eyes. Countless years of hope and heartbreak. I want to reach for him, to fold myself into his arms, into his life. It wouldn't—couldn't ever be the same. I'm not Lucinda, with her perfectly soft features, rosy cheeks and gentle eyes. But I might be just enough to fill the void in him.

Alister catches my gaze. "Come," he says, holding out a hand. "I have more to show you."

I smile and take his hand without a second thought.

***

My palm rests on the small curve of my stomach, full and warm. Scraps of chargrilled baby carrots, roast potato, green beans and pork are splayed out across the table. The waft of sweet, earthy gravy with sprigs of rosemary weaved throughout tempts my already bulging belly.

"Dessert?" He offers.

I wave him off as another sip of deep red wine trickles down the back of my throat like velvet. "God, no, I'm so full."

As we sit across from each other in the dimly lit ambience of the fairy-light dinner, I can't help but be aware of the air of mystery that surrounds this place, and the many, many questions that have kept my brain thrumming in the night. It seems as good a time as any to find some answers.

The flickering flames of candlelight cast shadows over his face, magnifying the emerald glint in his eyes. "So," I begin, swirling the remnants of wine in my glass, "how does a person come into possession of an old prison in the middle of a forest?" And why is it that no one has bothered to search inside of it.

His eyes meet mine, holding a depth that hints at untold stories. A half-smile plays on his lips as he leans back. "Ah, that. I wondered when you'd ask."

"So, you'll tell me?" Hope catches like a lump in my throat.

Alister hesitates, fingering the stem of his wine glass. "The prison was purchased five years ago by Winchester McGuire Limited."

"Who are they?"

"Me." His lips curl into a wry grin.

"A fake company then?"

He nods. "It was a rather complicated process, actually, and it took longer than I anticipated. Creating the shadow company allowed me to purchase the property from behind the corporate veil. If anyone looked into it, they'd find it quite difficult to locate the director of that company, considering they don't exist."

"You're a puppet master," I say, taking a large gulp from my glass. "How do you just invent another person?" I've lost count of the number of times I wanted to reinvent myself.

"It's amazing what you can purchase on the dark web. I only needed to open a bank account and apply for a social security number. That's how Mr Roy Coulton was born. No one needed to know that I existed, and despite this state's flimsy privacy laws, hopefully, they never will."

"No wonder they've never searched this place."

"Even if they tried, they'd never find a way in."

His words leave a subtle shiver in the air, a chill that creeps up my spine. The charm that envelops him like a cloak woven with mystery, begins to fray, leaving me with the unsettling realisation that some secrets might be better left buried.

I move on to simpler topics of conversation.

I lean forward, pushing my glass to the side. "When did you build the bunker?"

"Renovated," he clarifies. "The bunker was there long before I discovered it."

"What was it used for, before you renovated it?"

"It was a communication hub, I think. There was some old gear down there when I came across it for the first time. It was as good as dust. None of it was preservable."

"How old is this place?" I glance at the trees towering over us, with trunks four feet thick.

"As far as I know, it was a penitentiary built in the early nineteen hundreds."

"Old then."

"Very."

I pick at the scraps of pumpkin and pork on the plate. We sit in silence, and I run every inch of the prison over and over in my mind. Suddenly, the walls press in on us. As I look up, his gaze meets mine.

"Are you feeling alright?" He asks, worry flickering in his emerald eyes. "You look pale."

"It's winter," I lie. "What do you expect?"

Alister laughs softly, and then the smile fades from his face. "Do you think what I've done here is wrong?"

"I think that if you had asked for my help, instead of forcing me, I might have said yes."

"Ah, but you might have also thought me a monster and gone straight to the police."

I can't disagree with him when I remember seeing Lucinda's lifeless body for the first time, how much I'd wanted to run away screaming.

"Even if it what you're saying is true, I couldn't risk the years of progress for anyone, not even you, Aurelia."

The air turns stale between us and he avoids eye contact.

"I never meant to judge you," I say, my voice measured. "I just didn't understand."

A flicker of something unreadable passes through his eyes—a mix of defiance and a hint of vulnerability. "And now?"

"Now?" I shrug. "I don't know. I guess I have more reasons to stay than I do to leave."

"The rest of the world would drag me to the gallows and hang me for what I've done." He pushes.

I meet his gaze with a gentle nod. The urge to ask him about Rose and Patrice rises to the top of my throat, to know their histories, the details they'd never share with me. The things I never dared to ask them myself. But something dark and deep within warns me against it, lodging the questions thick in my throat.

"Fortunately for you, they don't hang people for kidnapping," I say instead. "At least, not anymore."

Alister slouches back in his chair. "Lucky me."

Instinctively, I reach for the pendant at my neck. I seem to have found myself in that space between light and dark, day and night. In the grey somewhere, my own limbo, reaching for a hand—his hand—to pull me out.

I don't mention the warm flutter; the gentle beating of wings in my chest; the dull ache that still looms there. It's too difficult to explain, that although the dark man with starlit green eyes sitting opposite me has taken me from everything I've ever known, now I'd be willing to tear the world apart just to stay.

I squeeze my fingers into a fist around the silver heart.

"You think this is goodbye," he says, not a question. His lips—as smooth as silk, the rest of his features just as soft—pull into a half smile.

I take my time answering him, casting my eyes over the dark pine floor beneath us, the brown trunks surrounding us, the dark green trees above us, and my favourite—the bobbles of warm bulbs of light swaying gently in the breeze. Like stars. Winter birds chirp in soft lullabies somewhere beyond the forest, over the wall maybe.

It could be midday or midnight; I can't tell under the shadows of the trees. Even the stunning dress glimmering against the pins of light is barely comparable to the dainty fairy-tale landscaped forest around us. Fit for a princess, not a handmaid like me.

My eyes ache as I force myself to meet his eyes. "I hope not," I say. I don't feel like telling him that even the idea has me feeling like I might tear apart. Even if Lucinda is the Cinderella of this story, not me.

I push against the wall of frustration, fear and sorrow, and swallow hard. I clamber for a semblance of conversation, anything but this wretched silence, and pity riddled in his eyes.

"Well," I say, smoothing a wrinkle in my skirt. "Since you seem to know so much about what I'm thinking, and since you're about as easy to read as a Shakespeare script, it seems only fair that you share some of your thoughts with me."

Alister clicks his tongue. "I'm thinking," he says carefully, "that I would have liked to have met your father."

"My father?"

"At the very least to thank him," his eyes gleam, "for bringing such an incredible light into this very dark, and very cold world."

My cheeks flush.

"You helped me—hell, for a moment, I even thought you wanted to."

"I do want to help you."

"And I know that you were distrusting of me at first, and maybe I scared you just a little, but right when I was sure I was destined to be alone, there you were with your kind eyes and warm smile." He pauses, and my eyes brim with tears. "You reminded this hollow man that he still has a heart."

**

As the sun dips below the horizon somewhere beyond the wall, casting a warm glow that gradually surrenders to the cool embrace of twilight, the trees undergo a mesmerising transformation, each passing minute a brushstroke of time. The rain seems to ease with the comfortable silence between us.

Alister glances above us as if he can see something I can't. "It's getting late."

"How can you tell?" I squint into the trees. Branches and leaves, nothing else.

He shrugs. "Years of practice, I guess."

"Do you bring people here often?" I tease.

Alister frowns. He faces me now, his eyes dark and pleading. "Who else would I have brought here?"

Our eyes hold across the table, the silence felled only by the whistles of the birds humming through the trees.

I'd spent the past two weeks playing my role perfectly. I'd tended to Lucinda despite the creeping rage I now felt every time I opened her door. I'd watched patiently as he tucked her in every night, felt the ache of jealousy burrow into my chest like a seed planted and watered.

I'd feigned more excuses than I could count to remove myself from the room where I had to endure the sight of Alister fawning over her. I'd manufactured gratitude when he offered me pain relief, only to spit it into the nearest bin when he wasn't looking. Each time the ache grew until finally it bloomed. Blossomed. Flourished.

I'd risked my life to flee from his claws, had nearly starved myself to death just to try. Yet, for every foul word I'd thrown his way, I'd said more kind ones.

For every fist thrown at the wooden door between us, I'd extended my hand to him more.

"What?" He asks, matching my stare.

"Nothing."

"Tell me."

"No."

"Tell me!" He growls.

"Fine," I groan. "Do you think the cure will work?"

"Why do you ask?"

"Why wouldn't I?" Words stagger out of me, wet and thick and cruel. I straighten, tempering my frustration. "I just, I would have thought you would be desperate to see if it works, that's all."

Alister swirls the remnants of red liquid around his glass and moves to sit beside me as a breeze rustles the leaves above, sending shivers up my spine.

"It's been five years," he says carefully. "I think part of me might be too afraid that it won't work. That it will all have been for nothing."

"It won't have been for nothing." I reach for his hand. He looks at me, and I look at him. A long silence falls between us. Even the birds have stopped singing.

He pulls my hand to his mouth. Lighter and softer and warmer than I remember, his lips leave small fireworks in their wake. I lift my head to scan his face for an answer, for a hint, for something—anything that might tell me whether he feels the same flicker of hunger burning inside him.

"Aurelia, I—"

Just before he can finish, an alarm sounds from his pocket.

"Excuse me," he says casually, pulling out the device. "Sometimes the surveillance cameras pick up animals walking past."

He frowns, squinting at the screen. "It's not possible," he curses.

"What's wrong?"

Alister's eyes become round, the colour draining from his face like waves from the shoreline.

"Alister?"

"We need to leave. Now."

He stands abruptly, reaching again for my hand, but there's no trace of the softness I'd felt before, just cold, clammy fear. There's barely a moment to process what's happening before he pulls me close to him, barely a breath between our bodies, our eyes locked like chains, his mirroring the tumult of a storm-ridden sea. Pure terror.

"What—?"

He presses his lips to mine in a swift, desperate movement. Fire ignites through my body, from deep in my chest to the ache between my legs. It is this—these soft, sensuous lips I'd craved for countless nights since I first tasted their sweet nectar.

I push against them with equal hunger, pulling at the collar of his shirt, wishing I could tear it from his body until there's nothing left between us. Our lips move in sync, his teeth tugging at my bottom lip. I let out a low groan as he grabs my hands, pushing me away.

"Aurelia, run."

***

Before I know it, I'm putting one foot in front of the other faster than I can think. He's tugging my arm as he runs ahead of me. I fumble, fighting to find steady footing amongst the gravel and pine cones. There's no counting how many times I've nearly plummeted towards the ground, my legs stinging with lashings from low-lying branches, my dress dragging like a parachute to slow us down.

Through the blurry mess of trees and wood, the entrance to the bunker takes shape. I've run through every possible scenario I could think of, every threat. None of it seems plausible, none of it makes sense. This place is impenetrable, untraceable. It couldn't be. But then I hear it. Silent at first, almost inaudible. Footsteps, hushed voices.

"In," Alister pants, ushering me underground.

He slams the door behind us as the voices grow louder.

"You need to go to your room, close the door and stay quiet," he whispers, pulling me in for a kiss. Terror sets in like a sudden chill.

"Go." He pulls away before I can protest, pushing me gently down the hall.

"Who are they?" I ask. He pulls a silent finger to his lips. The terror in his wide eyes rolls my stomach like waves. The door closes behind me, locking me inside.

The bolts grind into place and the keys jingle quietly. I'd hoped the locks and chains were long behind us.

"I don't know," he whispers through panted breaths. "Everything's going to be fine." The lie is as plain as day.

"Alister?" I whimper.

He presses a hand against the window, with a half-smile that doesn't reach his eyes. "I'll be back soon, I promise," he whispers, and before I can protest, he slams it shut, his hurried footsteps fading into the silence.

Clutching my pillow to my chest, I bury myself under the covers and close my eyes.

"Rose?" I whisper through tears.

Silence. I clutch my pillow a little tighter in the darkness as one hour passes, then two, with no word from Alister or Rose. Where are they? Suddenly, the silence is interrupted by the sound of footsteps echoing in the corridor. Rubber boots and the rustling of uniforms.

As the heavy door creaks open, flooding the dim room with blinding light, I recoil into the corner between my bed and the wardrobe, desperate to cling to the shadows. My eyes, now accustomed to the gloom, squint at the figures emerging from the brightness. Fear tightens its grip, and I instinctively shrink back.

"We've got her," a man says into his radio as more dark shadows fill the narrow hall. My head swims as darkness swarms around me.

"She's alive."

***

Angus

The line between hell and earth is blurred by the flashing lights of ambulances, five of them, because no one knows how many bodies are going to be wheeled out of this place. Cars—windshields, tyres, car doors—for as far as the eye can see, dotted amongst the forest like Morse code.

I would be out there shooing them away if my leg was not wrapped in gauze and bandages, and if their lights were not helping to illuminate the forest. It wasn't hard for Anna to retrace my steps once they located the burnt-out car. I'd managed to stumble along the road for about a mile before I came across some campers.

By the time I called the station, I could barely hold the phone to my mouth, let alone speak. I must have told them enough, though, because when I woke an hour later, I was lying on a gurney in the back of this ambulance with a drip stuck in my arm and Anna crouched beside me, barking orders at the officers outside.

When I was lucid enough to listen, Anna explained that sirens were blaring through the main street by late afternoon, and by that time everyone knew, or at least suspected that we'd found something. With unease haunting her eyes, she admitted that she still wasn't quite sure what we'd found.

Helicopters roar above us. I shiver against the foil blanket, my left arm tucked tight into a sling. My body throbs like a pulse, but I assume it's Anna I have to thank for the fact that I'm not stuck in some over-sanitised hospital room. She knew I would have been ropeable if they'd taken me anywhere else but here.

It's completely dark now; they have been here for hours, just waiting. Anna's officers are doing their best to create a private space between the ambulances and the onlookers, but the silver screens say more than they could ever hide.

From the back of the ambulance, watching the chaos unfold, I can vaguely make out two bodies lying motionless on the gurneys as they pass, their faces covered by silver sheets. They're not Rae though. Anna would have told me if it was.

Officers, ambulance drivers and firemen channel around me in a blur. The hum of the excavator rings in my ears, digging under cover of flashlight; the paramedics thrash across the road with another stretcher; police hurry to contain the crowd that has now massed; and I am wrestling with the truth—no one is coming out of there alive.

We were too late.

Chapter Twenty-Two

Aurelia stirs beneath the papery hospital sheets. They seem to smother her like a straitjacket, or maybe I'm just imagining it.

It's been a decent six hours since the nurses wheeled her from the ambulance and into the recovery room, and she's still unconscious. She'd fainted when they found her, that's what they told us anyway. They want to hold her overnight for observations. It's a good idea considering they haven't worked out what cocktail of drugs caused her to fall unconscious in the first place.

"Angus?" It's one of the nurses, the nicer one with soft eyes and wrinkles that mark the corners of her mouth. She leans against the doorframe, her hands tucked into the front of her gown, stethoscope draped loosely around her neck.

"You can't still be here, honey, you need to go home."

I look out the window to my right. It's only small, but the golden hue pours through. I can't believe it's dawn already.

"But," I protest. My stomach churns at the thought of leaving her again. "I only just got her back."

One look from the nurse, and I close my mouth.

"I can stall them for ten minutes, but that's the best I can do. You can come back during visiting hours." She gives me a quick wink and takes off down the hall. I wait until the squeak of her rubber shoes fades to a whisper, and turn my attention back to Aurelia.

I sigh at the monitor beeping gently in tune with nothing. I want to say she looks peaceful, but there's something restless about her.

Her hair drapes in curtains over her shoulders, ragged and wild. It's a good deal longer than the last time I saw her. Still perfect though, just like the rest of her. Her eyelashes rest gently against the crown of her cheeks. Rosy pink, and a tad flushed.

Tears sting my eyes as I brush a strand of hair from her face and tuck it behind her ear. I lean over, pressing my lips lightly against hers. They're soft and warm, exactly how I remember them. What I wouldn't give for her to just open her eyes, even for a second so I can show her that I'm right here with her. So I can tell her that I'll never leave her again.

She shifts a little before slipping away. If it weren't for the gentle rise and fall of her chest, she could be dead. I can't help but wonder, with everything that she's been through, would she prefer to be?

There are a few things I know for sure; the story will be breaking news, plastered like graffiti across every television screen in the state, maybe even the country. They will drag her out of her life before she has even had an opportunity to start living it again, forcing her to relive the horrific details of her capture. Did he hurt her? Christ, did he touch her?

Droplets of blood pool in my palms as I loosen my clenched fists. If I ever got my hands on him, I swear to God. Millions of people would know his name by now, his life ripped open like an infected wound. People will look at him with disdain, utter repulsion. I couldn't give a damn. The disgust that I feel. The truth only crawls under my skin.

Every day he called me, texted me. And while I spoke to that monster, he had her trapped in that prison. Like a slave. I dig my nails back into my palms, anger threatening to spew out of me. Deep breaths, and Aurelia. That's what will get me through this. I can be strong, for her.

If you didn't know her, didn't love her, you wouldn't notice the slight furrow in her brow as she sleeps. Where are your dreams taking you? I wonder.

I lean over the bed rail and find her hand amongst the ocean of sheets. I squeeze it gently, grateful to be close to her again. Maybe she wouldn't forgive me for what I'd done, presenting her to that wolf like a lamb to the slaughter. Maybe this is the mistake that will capsize the boat and drown us both. Maybe it already has.

Either way, I pray her dreams are better than the nightmare she is about to wake up to.

Suffering, I've learnt, is waking up every morning wondering whether today will be the day they find a body. Its warrants for arrest, invasive home searches, pushing slices of birthday cake through the bars of a cell wall, begging inmates for information, a lead, anything.

Suffering is waking up every morning, wondering the same thing that everyone else who is watching the 9 am news is wondering—how the hell had we missed this?

***

Aurelia

I am dragged from groggy slumber slowly, like a bleeding carcass being pulled along the ground. Thankfully, my huntress is nowhere to be seen. Pain—in my back and sides and a throbbing in my forehead—is the only sign that I'm again back in my body, and alive.

The room pulses with every thrum, and it takes minutes—a good ten of them—before the watercolour smear around me starts to take shape. Slowly, so slowly my mind starts to reclaim my flesh and bone.

An invisible weight hovers over me, my leaden legs too heavy to move. Rolling nausea churns in my stomach. The insipid smell of the red roses on the chair to my right only makes it worse.

I take in the pale blue laminate floor, the artificial light seeping through the slits in the blinds. The only similarity this place bears to my home in the bunker is the lack of exterior windows and light. Only, it seems darker in here, somehow.

Figures move quickly in the darkness behind the blinds, casting drawn shadows into the room. Almost silent, save for the hideous squeak of rubber on vinyl, the rustle of paper and the scratching of pens.

Hospital.

Suddenly, I'm standing on the edge of a precipice and a long dark depth stretches out before me. And I'm falling, falling, falling. Every aching muscle and bone tenses as pockets of memory burst wide open, the puzzle pieces finding each other in the wreckage of the present.

Alister.

Panic ripples through me. I can see it as if it's happening right in front of me. The final scene of a movie on repeat. Over and over again. His lips caressing the back of my hand, my heart fluttering like moth wings. And then the terror in his eyes, our hands separated by nothing but the clear window between us. He'd known it was a goodbye, he must have. But he'd reassured me anyway. Promised it was all going to be fine.

He'd lied.

Suddenly, my stomach is a nine-foot swell and I lurch, clambering for the bucket on the table next to me. An empty barrel, it groans and roils, cramping with every heave.

Hot beads of sweat slide down my forehead, my trembling hands clutching the bucket like a life raft. A quivering sob, a small broken sound escapes my lips as I cry out his name, "Alister."

When the nausea subsides, when my stomach finally settles into a mild whitewash, I lean back into my pillow. Sleep beckons me, coaxes me like a lullaby, and I don't have the strength to resist its pull, not anymore.

As I drift away, far, far away, I swear—as faint as a whisper and as light as a breeze—I hear Alister call my name.

Chapter Twenty-Three

My head pounds so hard, the room starts to bounce with it. As I cling to the scraps of consciousness like a life raft, beneath me scratchy, papery sheets line the padded bench they call a gurney. There's a dull ache and a sharp pinch in my left hand where clear liquid flows from masses of tubes and bags of fluids.

If I were in a movie, I'd probably pull the needle from my hand and try to make a run for it, sneak past the unsuspecting nurses and out into the open air. Maybe even scrounge enough strength to make a rescue attempt at the local police station.

But since I have no idea what exactly they are giving me, or how much they know, I release the tension from my arms, and ease back into the pillow, content to wait for a nurse or a doctor to give me some answers.

***

The next time I wake, it's to the sound of angry, beeping machines. Am I dead or just dying? No, neither, apparently. I strain my eyes to study the squiggly lines on the screen. A nurse meanders silently into the room with the elegance of a swan. Just an empty drip then, or else they'd be running.

When it starts to feel like the consciousness is going to stick for once, I go to ask the nurse for the time. But where the thought is clear, my words are a thick mass that can't seem to take any audible shape. Interesting, maybe I've got some sort of brain damage, trapped like a prisoner in my own bones. But I don't remember hitting my head, or breaking my spine, though I don't suppose I would.

As the darkness creeps back into the edges of my mind, the quiet footsteps of the nurse echo like a lullaby, until before I know it, I'm out again.

***

When I open my eyes again, they don't feel as hefty. Groggy and tired, but not heavy like lead this time. And I can't explain it, but I'm certain a great deal of time has passed.

My toes and fingers wiggle at my command under the sheets, but the rest of my limbs succumb to exhaustion, unable to move more than an inch. I roll my head from right to left until the room starts to focus.

I'm alone, save for the hunched figure tucked tightly in the corner chair, eyes shut tight. How long has she been here? Judging by the scent of lavender wafting from her, and the obvious absence of hard liquor, I'd say no longer than an hour. The overnight bag and wrinkled sweater, though, tell a different story. Maybe even a sobering one.

The possibility of it cracks something deep in my chest, but I can't think about that now; they will learn the atrocities I've committed. The part I chose to play. How much do they already know?

"Mum," I whisper, but the word is like sandpaper in my throat and barely audible enough to draw a stir. The effort of it saps the remnants of my energy, and I close my eyes to rest for just a little bit longer—rest I might very well need for the treacherous road ahead.

***

I spend the next three days drifting between the darkness and the light. At some point, I've been promoted to a larger room with two chairs and a red stain-glass window.

Sometimes, when I peer through the slits in my eyes, my mother is sitting in the chair, and sometimes, she's not. Occasionally, I'll feel a gentle tug on my hand, the warmth of skin-on-skin contact. The brush of familiar fingers that traced comforting circles on my back as a child. I haven't the courage or the will to speak to her. What could I possibly say that wouldn't terrify her beyond repair?

But this time, I open my eyes to find a familiar face. One that I'd almost forgotten, or maybe I'd tried to bury so deep in the recesses of my mind that somehow, without even knowing it, I'd managed to succeed. Only now, bathing in the warmth of those icy blue eyes, the ocean of memories swamp me like a tidal wave. Like a key to a lock, I'd thought was lost forever.

"Angus," I whisper, my voice croaky and hoarse.

In one swift step, he's at my side, wrapping a giant paw around my hands, dwarfing them. "Hello, beautiful," he says, bringing the back of my hand to his lips.

His arm is hanging in a sling, bandages flash beneath his white shirt, and his perfect face is marred by purple bruises and stitched-up gashes, one of them as long as my little finger. What happened to him?

His blond hair is a good inch shorter than I remember, barely touching his shoulders. But the rest of him is exactly how I left him—every bit the ruggedly handsome face I'd fallen so easily in love with—what feels like a lifetime ago.

So much has changed since then.

Maybe I'd never really felt good enough for his pure heart and clean soul; I'd suspected it all along. Every inch of my body aches with filthy lies, an endless stream of them, each as delicately crafted as the one before. The person they had once known died in that prison.

Don't ask me exactly when it happened, I'm not sure. Was it the first night, when I awoke in that bunker? Or was it when I crouched at Alister's feet in the cemetery and begged for my life?

Maybe a better person would have held on to hope, would have resisted the tug and pull and lure of Alister. Maybe a better person would have kept their feet and wouldn't have tripped, stumbled, fallen in love with the wolf like a stupid little lamb. Maybe a better person would have ended it all, like Patrice had.

My eyes well with tears, obscuring my view of Angus—a reprieve. He reaches over to brush the strands of loose hair from my forehead, swiping a tear from the crown of my cheek. I fight the urge to fold into those muscular arms, to bathe in the comfort of them, a safe place in this fraying world.

But I can't.

Rescued. That's what I am to them, even if the ivory walls of my bedroom seem more like prison bars than the bunker I've been living in for the past fifteen months. Even if the thought of going home makes me want to hurl my guts up. Even if every slanderous mention of Alister's name has me wanting to throw my fist through the television screen.

Angus keeps a tight grip on my hand as if I might turn to steam and slip out through the crack in the window. Oh, how much easier it would be for everyone if I could.

***

Not much has changed since I've been gone, not according to Angus, anyway. Though if he is to be believed, he spent every waking minute in the Brunswick Shire police station assisting the search. I don't doubt it—not for a moment.

My cohort graduated without me, but not without a disgustingly large tribute with ticker tape and flourishes and drapes of blooms, toasts of wine and champagne in my honour. Which is ironic, given that I never could stand the taste of either—that is, until recently.

Apparently, my mother was asked to give a speech to the newest members of the medical society. I hear she broke down halfway through, tears staining the trembling parchment in her hands. I don't blame her; she thought I was dead—they all did.

But what surprised me the most was news of Jade, trading her college degree for a one-way ticket to Alaska to study mating patterns in native wolves. I wonder if she has received word of my return, rescue.

In answer to my silent question, Angus says, "She's on a flight back home as we speak, and apparently, she's bringing company." Angus raises a brow, his mouth tugged into a smirk. "She would have been here days ago, but a snowstorm grounded the planes."

I wave him off. "I'm just glad she's okay and on her way back here." The truth flows out of me with the ease of a liberated breath. "I can't wait to see her."

"And what about you, did you? You know," I venture, tripping on the words. The churning in my stomach is a reminder of what I'd once felt for him. Of what fragments might still remain.

"Rae." Angus sighs, his eyes bashful and avoiding.

"It's okay, if you—I was gone for a long time."

"Aurelia," he breathes my name like he's been whispering it every night in his dreams.

I hold tight to my bated breath, not entirely sure what answer I'm hoping for.

"You could have been gone an entire lifetime and I would never have stopped looking for you."

My heart shifts in my chest. "I wouldn't have wanted that."

"No?" His brows furrow.

"No." I straddle the palisade between truth and lies. "I would have wanted you to move on with your life. Even if that meant being with someone else."

"Rae, sweetheart," Angus whispers, taking my chin in his hand. "You are my life."

Instinct has me leaning back, creating subtle space between myself and the former love of my life. Maybe we'd crawl back to it one day. Maybe the world would right itself again. But I can't think like that. Not when there's so much at stake.

"I'm sorry."

Angus simply nods, deep in thoughts of his own. His eyes scan my face, maybe looking for some trace of the person I used to be, the one he'd fallen in love with. Over time, it would only disappoint him—I would only disappoint him. Maybe even break what's left of his heart.

It's that thought alone that niggles at my stomach. *Guilt,* that's what it is.

***

That night, I manage to sleep in the brief moments between gut-wrenching panic and Alister-fuelled nightmares. Tendrils of guilt wind their way through my dreams like hands wrapped around my neck. Precipice after precipice, and a plummeting darkness stretched out below, beckoning me, coaxing me off the ledge.

By the time the sun slips over the horizon, my nightwear is soaked through. I am drenched in sweat, and in desperate need of a shower.

Footsteps echo in the hall long before the hushed voices. I strain my ears towards the sound, but the belligerent, doleful blabbering of the mid-morning news stifles it. It would seem that after three full days, nothing else has happened in this town, and Alister's arrest is still headlining the broadcasts.

Angus appears at the door first; the sight of his short waves of blond hair, denim jeans and a white t-shirt that clings to his muscled body draws a pink blush from my cheeks. A tall woman with dark features flanks him, their footsteps aligned as they move purposefully into the room.

"Rae, darling," he purrs, "this is Detective Annabelle Lawson." There's a hint of pride in Angus's voice. "She headed the investigation."

That explains it.

"I was fortunate to have a great deal of help." She smiles modestly, her eyes lingering on Angus.

He grins in response—an ear-to-ear display of perfectly white teeth—a smile once reserved for me. Her dark eyes gleam through the midnight rims of her glasses, which seem to add a certain poise to her features. I've already decided that I don't like her very much.

"Please, call me Anna."

"Am I being recorded?" I ask dryly, enough of my voice now returned to communicate my distaste.

"No," she says, "not unless you want to be."

I shake my head.

"I'm here to take your statement if you're feeling up to it." Her smile is genuine enough—she thinks I'm going to help her.

"I want to talk to Rose." What does she make of all of this? What has she already told them?

Angus stiffens at her name, busying himself rearranging this morning's half-eaten breakfast on its tray.

"What?" I demand as they exchange uneasy glances.

"When my team went into that bunker, they searched it—twice. When you mentioned that there was someone else in there with you, I had them search it again."

A new kind of horror begins to rise inside me as I picture them rifling through our bedrooms—our home.

"Where is she?" I ask, my voice catching. "Where is Rose?"

"Rae—" Angus starts, but he's cut off.

"When they didn't find anything, I searched the damned place myself."

Damned. Something in my chest tightens at that word.

"We didn't find anyone else inside."

"Look again," I say through clenched teeth. "She's in there."

"No, she's not."

"How do you know—?"

"Because we found her, Aurelia. We found her and two others."

The woman's dark eyes soften, the gleam of sympathy so thick and cruel, it could swallow me.

"Then where are they?" I ask, but the tears are already streaming down my cheeks, as if my soul already knows what my heart won't accept. "No," I whimper.

She reaches for my hand and squeezes it tightly. "We finished identifying their bodies—or what was left of them—yesterday." I barely feel it as the weight of the room grows bone-crushingly heavy, the air as thin as a blade. My heart burns until I'm sure collapse is inevitable.

"What are you saying?"

She breathes deeply, and when her gaze finally returns to mine, her eyes flicker with quiet rage. There's the same look in Angus' eyes and his good hand crunches into a fist.

"We received the results of our chemical analysis this morning. My team found traces of hallucinogens in the vent above where you were sleeping. And there were substances that we haven't seen before. That's why they've had to keep you in here longer, to make sure there has been no long-term damage to your brain."

"What are you saying?" I cry, but deep down, a part of me already knows the truth, has suspected it for some time now. The way their voices were so familiar. The way that they appeared when I felt most alone, most afraid.

"Lola Rose and Darcy are the names of the women whose bodies we excavated." She hesitates. "There was no one recovered with the name Patrice."

My head thrums so hard that flecks of light like stars start to appear over my vision. "I think I'm going to be sick," I announce, reaching for the bucket.

Angus is at my side in an instant, rubbing circles over my back.

"This is too much for her," he growls, with more authority than I'd ever heard from him. "She needs to rest."

"She has a right to know," Anna says plainly, brushing him off. It's clear they've been at this for a long time.

"Then who was in the room next to mine?" I ask, clutching at the pieces of shattered glass, desperately trying to hold myself together.

"Don't," Angus warns.

But Anna waves him off. "Aurelia, sweetheart, there was no room next to yours."

***

Angus

"You shouldn't have done that," I growl as the doors to the hospital close behind us and the pathway opens up to a small bitumen car park. "She wasn't ready."

"She needed to know, Angus, and sooner rather than later was my preference." Anna trudges off ahead towards her all-black Ford Torino.

It's a wonder the thing still shifts gears, it's so old. The hub cap is missing on both back tyres, and there's a dent in the side panel that's rusted and worn. Why she hasn't asked the Sheriff's Department to replace it, I'll never understand. Though I do know what it feels like to want to hold on to the past, even if it's literally falling apart at the seams right in front of you.

"She's fragile," I say, with more force this time. "You can't just dump this on her all at once. I know her, she won't cope."

Anna pauses at the boot of her car and turns to me. "Do you think that the defence is going to be gentle with her? Do you think that they care? They're going to rip open her life like an infected wound and pour peroxide on it just for show. If she walks into that courtroom and starts talking about her imaginary friends, the lawyers will have a field day and the jury will discard everything she says from that moment on."

"It's better I tell her now than if she finds out from a tabloid, or worse, on the stand. You should be grateful that someone else told her, and that you didn't have to."

I slowly rub my face with my hands. The car door creaks when I press my back against it. "I don't know how to help her."

"Just make sure that when the trial comes and it's time for her to choose a side, it's ours."

I groan into my palms. "I barely recognise her. She won't talk to me, not about Alister, not about any of it. I don't want to push her because I'm scared I might lose her again. Part of me wonders if she ever came back at all."

"She has been through a lot—you need to give her some space."

"But you just said—"

"I said you need to give her some space, not me. I'm a detective. It's in my nature to probe." Anna rounds the side of the car and slides effortlessly into the driver's seat.

"I thought once we got her back, it would all be over," I say, leaning in to the open window.

"Unfortunately for Rae," Anna says, "this is only the beginning."